Neighborly N

In the dim light of a distant street lamp, a man was lying on the cold, dark ground. He was motionless—except for one arm that jerked around convulsively.

I stared in shock. It was my nemesis, Pop Doyle. A gun lay on the ground beside him, and blood oozed out of a hole in his neck.

I fought off nausea and leaned down toward him to see what I could do. His arm flew up and hit me on the nose. I jumped back, startled.

Pop opened his eyes a little. His breathing was raspy, and when he opened his mouth, blood spilled out.

But then two words spilled out, too. "Shot me," he gasped.

I waited for more, but he just coughed weakly. So I asked, "Who? *Who* shot you?"

Pop started to answer. But then his eyes met mine, and he recognized me. He got a pained, disgusted look on his face, like he was thinking, "The last face I see before I die is *this* clown?"

And then Pop closed his eyes and died.

Praise for Matt Witten's Jacob Burns mysteries:

"Jacob Burns is a wise-cracking, write-at-home dad with a nose for trouble. While solving mysterious deaths in Saratoga Springs, he manages to see into the heart of his community with a great deal of humor and tenderness."

—Sujata Massey, Agatha-winning author of *The Salaryman's Wife*

GRAND DELUSION

A Jacob Burns Mystery

Matt Witten

SIGNET
Published by New American Library, a division of
Penguin Putnam Inc., 375 Hudson Street,
New York, New York 10014, U.S.A.
Penguin Books Ltd, 27 Wrights Lane,
London W8 5TZ, England
Penguin Books Australia Ltd, Ringwood,
Victoria, Australia
Penguin Books Canada Ltd, 10 Alcorn Avenue,
Toronto, Ontario, Canada M4V 3B2
Penguin Books (N.Z.) Ltd, 182–190 Wairau Road,
Auckland 10, New Zealand

Penguin Books Ltd, Registered Offices:
Harmondsworth, Middlesex, England

First published by Signet, an imprint of New American Library,
a division of Penguin Putnam Inc.

First Printing, January 2000
10 9 8 7 6 5 4 3 2 1

Printed in the United States of America

PUBLISHER'S NOTE
This is a work of fiction. Names, characters, places, and incidents either are the product of the author's imagination or are used fictitiously, and any resemblance to actual persons, living or dead, business establishments, events, or locales is entirely coincidental.

For Nancy

ACKNOWLEDGMENTS

I would like to thank my literary agent, Jimmy Vines; my editor, Joe Pittman; and the folks who helped me along the way: Carmen Beumer, Betsy Blaustein, Nancy Butcher, Gary Goldman, Navorn Johnson, Bonnie Resta-Flarer, Larry Shuman, Matt Solo, Justin Wilcox, Celia Witten, and everybody at Malice Domestic, Madeline's Espresso Bar, and the Creative Bloc.

Since this book is set in the West Side of Saratoga Springs, I also wish to express my appreciation to all the people at the West Side Neighborhood Association and Spaha who volunteer long hours to make the West Side a better place. Thanks to Rose Zacek and company, the West Side is coming back.

Finally, many thanks to Nancy Seid, who is not only my wife and girlfriend, but also a darn fierce editor.

AUTHOR'S NOTE

WARNING: This book is fiction! The people aren't real! Nothing in it ever happened!

In particular, I in no way mean to impugn the fine name of the Saratoga Springs police force, which protects its citizens with honesty and zeal.

1

I walked out my door into the silent one a.m. darkness. Had I dreamed those tortured screams, or were alley cats fighting in my neighbor's backyard?

Neither. I heard a desperate, low-pitched moan. And then I saw him.

In the dim light of a distant street lamp, a man was lying on the cold, dark ground. He was motionless—except for one arm that jerked around convulsively.

I moved closer, then stopped and stared in shock. It was my nemesis, Pop Doyle.

His eyes were shut. A gun lay on the ground beside him, and blood oozed out of a hole in his ripped-up neck.

I fought off nausea and leaned down toward him to see what I could do. His arm jerked and hit me on the nose. I jumped back, startled.

Pop opened his eyes a little. His breathing was raspy, and when he opened his mouth, blood spilled out.

But then two words spilled out, too. "Shot me," he gasped.

I waited for more, but he just coughed weakly. So I asked, "Who? *Who* shot you?"

Pop started to answer. But then his eyes met mine,

and he recognized me. He got a pained, disgusted look on his face, like he was thinking, "Jesus H. Christ, the last face I see before I die is *this* clown?"

And then Pop closed his eyes and died.

It took me about half a nanosecond to realize I was in deep trouble. Any cop with any brains would immediately suspect me of killing this foul fiend.

You see, Pop Doyle was the landlord for the house next door. For years we'd been sniping at each other about the endless parade of scuzzbag tenants he rented to. Then, during the past twenty-four hours, our skirmishes suddenly exploded into all-out open warfare.

The war was triggered last night at three a.m., when my wife and I were awakened from a deep sleep by Pop's latest drug-dealing tenants and their horn-honking customers. A carful of guys roared up in a black Trans Am, and the driver leaned on his horn for a solid two minutes. Finally one of Pop's tenants ambled lazily out of the house, stuck a small packet into the driver's hand, and took a couple of bills in exchange.

I couldn't understand it. Me, if I were buying drugs, I'd do it quietly. No fuss, no muss. But these folks were always honking, screaming, and pounding the living daylights out of each other. During the entire two months since the drug dealers had moved in next door, Andrea and I hadn't slept through the night once.

So we called the cops, like we'd done so many times before. "I'm reporting a disturbance at 107—"

"107 Elm Street, right," the dispatcher interrupted, sounding like she was stifling a yawn. "Okay, we'll send someone out."

The cops went through their usual, utterly useless

routine. By the time they arrived half an hour later, the Trans Am was long gone. The cops didn't even bother to get out of their patrol car, just hung around for a few minutes and then left.

Eventually Andrea and I were able to get back to sleep. But before dawn had a chance to break we were awakened all over again. This time the noisemakers were Pop's tenants themselves, a black guy named Zapper and a white guy named Dale who lived in the two adjoining front apartments.

Zapper was huge and sullen looking, with the biggest muscles I'd ever seen this side of WWF wrestling. No doubt he'd acquired them in prison. In contrast, the almost albino Dale was hollow chested, with arms and legs thinner than mine. But even so, he frightened me far more than Zapper did. The man *twitched* too much. He was always smoking cigarettes, and my guess is he smoked a lot of his own product as well.

Despite these unpleasant personal characteristics, the two men had no lack of girlfriends. One of them was sleeping over that night, and now, at 4:30 a.m., Dale was loudly threatening to do a variety of unspeakable things to her body. Meanwhile she was screeching, "I just took one little blast, that's all, I swear!"

So we called the cops for the second time in one night. They came by eventually, and as far as we could tell from looking out our window, did exactly what they always did. Which was nothing.

Why were the cops being so infuriatingly blasé? We lived on Saratoga's West Side, so we were used to the city treating us like second-class citizens. But still, this seemed extreme. Andrea and I were pretty sure we knew the real deal: The cops didn't want to mess with Pop's tenants because they didn't want to mess with *Pop*.

See, Pop was a cop, too. And lest you be misled by his nickname into thinking Pop was some kind of beloved Spencer Tracy–type father figure, worshiped by all the local prepubescent boys, let me set you straight. Pop Doyle was not exactly the fatherly sort. At least, not any sort of father you'd ever want.

Once when I was fixing lunch at the Saratoga soup kitchen, a homeless man with a face full of purple bruises gave me the lowdown on Pop. "Damn cop caught me sleeping in the park last night, said, 'I'm gonna pop you one.' Only he don't pop me *one,* more like *one hundred. Pop, pop, POP.* Wish I had it on video, I'd git me twice as much green as that fool Rodney King ever got."

But so far no one had ever gotten Pop on video, so he just threw his weight around and did whatever the hell he wanted. Though he was the worst absentee slumlord on the whole West Side, his decrepit firetraps never got cited. No one had the balls to take him on.

And as a result, Andrea and I were turning into basket cases with permanent large bags under our eyes.

After Dale, Zapper, and the girlfriend who "just took one little blast, I swear!" quieted down, Andrea and I did manage to fall asleep yet again that night as dawn started sneaking through our window. But then Babe Ruth and Wayne Gretzky, our two sons—their real names are Daniel and Nathan, but they prefer Ruth and Gretzky—came into our room to cuddle with us. We were so tired we yelled at them. Sleep-deprived parenting, I'm convinced, causes more misery than any neurosis Freud ever dreamed of.

Looking for a little sanity, I walked the boys downstairs and threw their favorite Teenage Mutant Ninja Turtles video into the VCR. I know the Ninja Turtles are hopelessly passé, but our kids somehow discovered their old videos and can't get enough of them. "Hurray for Daddy!" they called out ecstatically when I took the video out of the box. They'd only seen this one about two hundred times, so they weren't tired of it yet. I silently hoped the electronic babysitter would make sure they didn't light any matches or run outside, and stumbled back to bed.

But then Andrea and I overslept, so we yelled at the kids all over again to hurry through breakfast. Of course, yelling at our kids to hurry only puts them into molasses mode. They spent an hour or two just putting on their sneakers—and we're talking Velcro here, not big-boy shoestrings. After Andrea microwaved a bagel, picked up the screaming Gretzky, and hauled him off to preschool, and after the Babe and I dashed madly to his elementary school bus stop and made it, gasping, barely in time, I was so irate at the drug dealers who had caused all this aggravation that I wanted to string them up by their toes and make them watch endless *Teletubbies* episodes until they begged to be put out of their misery.

On a less satisfying but more realistic level, should I simply knock on their door so we could discuss this problem like regular, rational people? After all, it was in their best interest too, not just mine, for them to follow their criminal pursuits more quietly.

But I didn't exactly share a great rapport with these guys. When they first moved in, I went over to say hi and do the drop-by-if-you-ever-need-a-cup-of-sugar routine. But Zapper and Dale just stood there staring blankly over my head until I finished my Welcome Wagon *shpiel.* Then they went right back in the house without saying a word to me. Probably muttering "fucking yuppie scum" under their breath.

With two neighbors like these, I was grateful that the third rental unit at the back of the house was temporarily unoccupied. But if there weren't any tenants I could go to for help, and the landlord and cops just ignored me, then how in the sam hill was I supposed to stop these late-night horror shows?

To add insult to injury, right across the street from the dealers lived Dave—and Dave was a cop himself, for God's sake. Why didn't *he* put an end to their nefarious activities?

As I dragged my tired self back home from the bus stop, I heard the whine of weedwhacking coming from Dave's backyard. In the past, whenever I harangued Dave about Pop's tenants, he sloughed me off. But today, by gosh, I was mad as hell and I wasn't going to take it anymore. I decided to go back there and confront him.

Dave was an uptight type of guy, and even his lawn looked uptight that chilly October morning. There wasn't a single cedar chip or blade of grass out of place. In his defense, I suppose Dave had to be on the cautious side to survive as the only black cop in Saratoga.

After a brief obligatory compliment of his yard work, I got right down to brass tacks. But Dave responded with an incredibly irritating shrug. "What makes you so sure they're dealing?" he asked.

"Give me a break! Cars drive up in the middle of the night, people go in for one minute, then they come out again. What do you think they're doing in there—playing speed chess?"

"Look, what do you want from me? I can't just break into their place without a legal reason."

"How about the empty vials on the sidewalks?

What are you waiting for—a red neon 'Crack for Sale' sign on their front lawn?"

"My suggestion is, if they get noisy, start honking their horns or whatever—"

"They *do* honk their horns—at three in the morning. You must hear it!"

"No, my bedroom's at the back."

"Well, bully for you!"

"You know, no one's ever complained about them except you—"

"Because the old lady on the other side of them is stone deaf! And the elderly couple behind them are scared that if they open their mouths, these guys will come in their bedrooms with sharpened screwdrivers!"

He held up his hands. "Hey, as I was trying to say, if they get noisy, call the cops."

"That's what I'm doing! I'm calling *you*!"

He didn't speak for a moment, just rubbed a hand through his closely cropped hair as he gazed up at the autumn sky. Sometimes Dave's exaggerated carefulness made me want to shoot him. "Is it because Pop owns the place?" I challenged him. "Is that why you're not doing diddlysquat?"

His grip tightened on his weedwhacker, but he still didn't answer me. "Come on, Dave," I pleaded angrily, "do you *enjoy* having crack dealers across the street? We've got to *do* something."

Dave was my friend. He snow blowed my driveway in the winter, and I trimmed his hedges in the summer.

I even solved a murder for him once. Got his picture on the front page of the *Daily Saratogian*. If that's not friendship, what is?

But I guess friendship has its limits. Because Dave

just squared his jaw, turned on his machine, and got back to weedwhacking.

At the time I thought he was being a typical stonewalling cop, protecting a fellow man in blue against even the most righteous civilian.

It didn't hit me until later that actually, Dave might be scared of Pop.

Scared to death.

2

I walked away from Dave's backyard shaking my head. I mean, this wasn't the crime-ridden Brooklyn neighborhood where Andrea and I used to live; this was beautiful, small-town Saratoga Springs. And ours was not a block where you'd expect to find crack dealers. In addition to Dave the cop, we had a retired blacksmith, a bookkeeper, a social worker . . . "good people," as the old West Siders would say.

I should explain about the West Side. Here in Saratoga, tourist town supreme, all the blue-blooded heiresses, polo-playing princes, and high-tech zillionaires have their summer homes on the *East* Side of Broadway. During the August horse races or the July ballet season, the East Side is the Saratoga place to be.

And the *West* Side? Well, when the West Side gets mentioned in the *Daily Saratogian,* it's not usually in the society pages. It's in the police roundup.

But hey, so what? We West Siders think the West Side is the *best* side. We're a tad touchy about it.

If you live on the wrong side of the tracks in your city, you know exactly what I'm talking about. And if you live on the right side, it's like this: Except for the occasional pesky drug dealer, we're solid, middle-class folks. Maybe our places aren't as fancy as all of those East Side Victorians, but we mow our lawns, plant daffodils and tulips, and even paint our houses, when we get the money or the time.

The West Side got a bad reputation in the 70s and 80s, when absentee landlords began subdividing a lot of the old homes into shoebox-size apartments. When I say "absentee landlords," some of these creeps actually lived in Saratoga (on the East Side, of course), but they still didn't give a wet goose fart about keeping up their properties.

So economics being what they are, the old-timers—the Italians, Irish, and blacks who've lived on the West Side for over a century—watched their nice friendly neighborhood start rotting away.

But amazingly enough, this story has a happy ending. Five years ago, the old-timers decided to do more than just watch. Yes, these grizzled old men and feisty old ladies got organized. They formed the Save Our West Side Association (affectionately nicknamed Save Our Side, or S.O.S.) and held monthly meetings at the Orian Cillárnian Sons of Ireland hall. Soon a hundred West Siders would show up at an average meeting, and soon every politician in town started showing up, too.

Suddenly, abracadabra, the city began replacing our missing street signs, putting flower barrels on our corners, and smoothing out the rutted, bad-hop infields at the West Side Rec. Meanwhile the local Donald Trumps got hauled into court for violations that had been ignored forever, like broken beer bottles on the sidewalks and abandoned pickup trucks rusting away on front lawns. Best of all, we even got a beat cop to patrol Lower Beekman Street, the seedy neighborhood near the cemetery where most of our five or six drug dealers lurked.

Yes, the West Side was coming back. And as for

myself, I enjoyed being part of the neighborhood renaissance, even though I'm kind of an odd bird to be living on the West Side. The thing is—well, let's see, how do I put this . . . I'm rich.

Since I feel a little funny about it, let me hasten to add that I haven't *always* been rich. I used to be a perpetually struggling writer with two young children and a family income that consisted mainly of my wife's modest salary as a community college professor. When Andrea and I bought our house we had no trouble at all qualifying for a SONYMA, a cheap New York State mortgage for first-time home buyers who haven't got a pot to piss in.

But then about eleven months ago, I struck it rich (that word again). What happened was, after fifteen years of laboring away at avant-garde plays that got performed off-off-Broadway for audiences of about four people, I took it into my head to write a hack screenplay called *The Gas that Ate San Francisco.* It wasn't very good, it took five weeks to write, and it made me a million dollars.

Even after taxes, and after agents, managers, lawyers, producers, and other bloodsucking parasites ate their fill, I still ended up with 300K, free and clear.

We could have taken the dough and bought a new house on the East Side. But the thing is, we *liked* our house, an attractive old Colonial with a big backyard. We liked the local elementary school.

And we *loved* the idea of saving that 300K and socking it away in mutual funds. As long as the stock market held up, we could live a comfortable life off the interest whether I ever wrote another hit or not. It would be our "fuck you money," to use Hollywoodspeak. That means, if someone offers you big bucks to write a movie you don't want to write (like, say, an action-adventure about Uzi-toting Micronesian terrorists scheming to set loose a thousand cloned grizzly bears in New York City), you can just lean back, smile, and say fuck you.

That felt great because, truth to tell, I wasn't really into writing these days. At the age of forty, after years of agonizing over every syllable, I was taking a well-deserved sabbatical from fictional characters, plot twists, and other writerly cares. I played handball and chess, taught Creative Writing at the local state prison to satisfy my do-gooder urges, and fell asleep peacefully at night instead of lying awake wondering how the mortgage was going to get paid.

Andrea was enjoying these halcyon days, too. Liberated from the long-suffering-spouse-of-a-starving-artist role, she had actually gone months (instead of hours) without having to reassure me that I was a truly great writer who would one day be discovered.

Yes, even a cynic like myself had to admit: life on Elm Street was good.

Except for those dagnab neighbors.

It was absurd. It was outrageous. I'm an American, by God. "Life, liberty, and the pursuit of happiness—" doesn't that include the right to a good night's sleep?

So when I left Dave's backyard that morning, I didn't just go home and sulk. I did the Jimmy Stewart thing and marched off to fight City Hall.

Having lived in big cities most of my life, I expected to face thick layers of municipal bureaucracy. But as it turned out, all I had to face was one red-cheeked, gray-haired lady in the city clerk's office. As a West Sider herself (I recognized her from the S.O.S. meetings), she was more than happy to help me. She found the file for Elm Street in record time. Obviously she was the person who actually *ran* the city, while the East Side politicians shook hands and took each other out to lunch.

I quickly located the zoning status document for 107 Elm, the offending house. "Excellent," I said out loud as I read it. The house was supposed to be a one-family—not a three-family, the way Pop had been renting it out for years. I'd always suspected Pop was skating on thin legal ice, and now I had proof.

"Find something good?" the gray-haired lady asked.

"You bet," I said, and explained my plan. "I'll get Pop cited for zoning violations. Then he'll be forced to tear down the cardboard walls that split the place into three peanut-sized apartments. And once that house goes back to being a moderate-sized one-family, like it should be, we'll have good people"—jeez, I was talking like a native—"moving in, instead of crack dealers."

Grayhair got up and stepped over to a file cabinet. "This is 107 Elm you're talking about? Are you going to the hearing tonight?"

I stared at her. "What hearing?"

She handed me an official notice. "The zoning hearing. Pop is selling the house, and he applied to get it officially re-zoned as a three-family so he can get more money for it."

My jaw dropped. "Shit—excuse my language. If they re-zone it so it's permanently three-family, I'll be stuck with scumbag neighbors forever!"

"I'm surprised you didn't know. The Zoning Board is supposed to notify all neighbors in a hundred-yard radius."

"*I* didn't get notification, and neither did anyone else on the block. They'd have told me."

She gave a tight, ironic smile. "Maybe the post office lost it."

"Yeah, sure. I guess Pop has connections on the Zoning Board."

"How about you?" Grayhair asked. "Got any connections?"

Connections.

Well, all right, I'd *make* some darn connections.

Back in my teens, I was a political activist of sorts. We played hookey from high school to protest the Vietnam War, beat up any kids we caught eating non-union grapes in the cafeteria, and even made the local news once marching against a nuclear bomb test up in the Aleutian Islands somewhere.

So I went home and wrote up an angry petition on my computer, featuring buzzwords like "Late-night noise . . . drugs . . . doesn't fit in with the family character of the neighborhood . . ." Then I headed outside to knock on doors and fill my page with signatures.

But the neighborhood was virtually empty. All the kids were off at school, day care, or other child detention centers, and most of the adults were off at work. The two women I came across at the corner of Elm and Beekman were steering stolen shopping carts filled with babies and packages, and they turned their faces away as I approached them. I heard a teenage couple screaming at each other through an open window.

The West Side, usually so neighborly, felt uncomfortably hostile today. Eager for my first ally, I headed across the street to see my old friend Dennis O'Keefe. Dennis is a large, big-hearted man with a serious beer belly, which doesn't seem quite fair since he gave up beer a decade ago. He also gave up his other major vices—heroin, tobacco, and real estate work—and devoted himself to working with troubled kids, trying to save them from the addictions and other foolishnesses that had almost wrecked his own life.

Five years ago he helped some Saratoga post-post-Generation Xers form a group they named Arcturus, after a star that was shining brightly in the sky on the night when they had their first meeting. By hook and by crook (and by a government grant or two), they scraped together enough cash to buy a decrepit foreclosed house at the corner of Elm and Beekman. They fixed it up, sort of, and now they had an African drumming group on Mondays, a "young women's consciousness-raising group" on Tuesdays, a theatre improv/folk music coffeehouse on Thursdays, and "hanging out night" on Fridays.

Shades of the 60s.

They also ran a skateboarding shop there, and the streets outside the building were often taken over by teenagers whizzing around recklessly. But despite their creating a serious local driving hazard, I had a soft spot in my heart for Arcturus. When I walked in that afternoon, Dennis and three green-haired boys were performing a kazoo rendition of the Star Spangled Banner, accompanied by Jimi Hendrix's "Purple Haze" in the background. It sounded great. I felt spiritually at home, like I always did at Arcturus.

After they finished playing, and the teenagers went outside to risk death on their skateboards, I showed Dennis my petition. His blue Irish eyes lit up when he heard the word "petition"—he's always ready to take on a new political battle—but when he actually sat down and read what it was about, he frowned. "I can't sign this," he declared, shooting me an accusing look.

"Why not?"

He tossed the petition at me. "What is this nimby gentrification horseshit, Jacob? You turning Republican on me?"

Ouch! Dennis was verbalizing my deepest fears. By getting rid of the relatively low-rent apartments next door, I'd be robbing poor people of places to live. Was I betraying the socialist politics of my youth?

But on the other hand, Andrea and I needed our sleep. "Look, *you* try living next door to a bunch of drug dealers, see how you like it."

"If they're dealing drugs, then call the police—"

"I did!"

"—but that's no reason the house shouldn't be three apartments. We need affordable small apartments in this town."

I was so pissed off at Dennis's holier-than-thou attitude, and my suspicion that he really might be holier than I, that I started shouting. "Hey, I've been inside those places. What Pop did there is criminal, he ought to be shot! There's old paint flaking off the walls that has got to be lead, there's asbestos crumbling from the ceiling, there's scalding hot, exposed water pipes—"

"Jacob—"

"And the apartments aren't just small, they're pathetic—one minuscule, claustrophobic room with a kitchenette you couldn't fit a bathtub in—"

"Hey, I've got kids coming in here all the time, eighteen, nineteen years old, no money, whacked out parents, desperate for a place to stay. You wouldn't believe some of the stories I hear—"

But I was in no mood for his stories. Dennis was a loud opinionated guy, which made him a good advocate for troubled youth, but also made him a royal pain in the ass. "So I take it you're not with me on this," I interrupted.

Dennis blinked, taken aback at being cut off in mid-harangue. Then he gave me a small tentative smile, strangely at odds with his previous demeanor, and said, "Sorry, Jacob."

"No sweat. Always good to have a sixties retro around to keep us yuppie scum on our toes."

I headed out the door, with Dennis calling after me, "Man, the sixties are coming back! You oughta listen to these kids!"

I did listen as I walked up the street, but all I heard was a discussion of skateboarding techniques. I wondered, would the 60s ever really come back . . . and if they did, would an old fart like me be truly happy about it?

I wondered, also, if there might be some other unspoken reason why Dennis wasn't signing my petition. After all, Pop was one of the foot patrolmen for the beat that included Arcturus—and Pop knew how to read a signature.

I headed over to Cherry Street to try to get hold of Lia Kalmus. Maybe Dennis hadn't come through, I thought, but one signature from Lia would be worth a hundred signatures from ordinary mortals.

You see, five days a week, Lia was a mild-mannered billing clerk at Saratoga Hospital. But when she got off work, she put on her Superwoman cape and magically transformed into the president of the Save Our West Side Association.

Lia was of average height and weight, with light blond hair, but she was emphatically not a pretty woman, due to a horrible burn scar that discolored the left half of her face and gave her left eye a bloodshot, drooping look. Rumor had it that when she was a child in Estonia forty-some years ago, her house was burned down as punishment for her father's political dissidence.

Possibly in response to her scar, Lia made no effort

to look good. She cut her hair short and wore clothes that looked like they came from Kmart's half-price bin. Nevertheless, she didn't seem like an unhappy woman. S.O.S. was her family.

When she came to the front door to answer my knock, she was on a cordless phone doing her community organizing thing. She waved me inside.

I'd never been in her house before, and I glanced around. The place was chockful of velvet-covered sofas, quasi-Chippendale chairs, and ornate paintings and statues of a host of saints that my Jewish eyes didn't recognize (of course, maybe they were special Estonian saints). I've noticed this with other people who live alone: They tend to load up their houses with all kinds of *stuff*. Some of Lia's stuff was probably expensive, paid for with all the money she saved by not having kids, but I still didn't like it much.

Meanwhile she was talking on the phone. Or rather, shouting. "You *have* to come to the meeting tonight! Look, I don't give a hoot about your niece's piano recital, I don't care if she's the next *Liberace* for God's sake, this is the future of the West Side we're talking about!"

I couldn't help grinning. I pitied the poor soul on the other end of the line, feeling the brunt of a Lia Kalmus onslaught.

After successfully browbeating the other person into submission, Lia hung up the phone and started working on me. "Now, of course *you're* coming tonight, right? Eight o'clock."

"Well—"

"You've *got* to come. It's our most important meeting of the year. We're voting on whether to accept the Grand Hotel proposal."

I had to admit, this truly *was* a big deal.

Every city or neighborhood has some issue that

defines its future. For us, the issue was: What do we do with the Grand Hotel?

The Grand Hotel was a four-story affair on Washington Street in the heart of the West Side that had housed visitors to Saratoga for over a century. Now when I say "Grand Hotel," please don't be misled into imagining a *grand hotel*. And when I say "visitors," don't think "Vanderbilts." No, the hotel in question was the domicile of choice for over-the-hill prostitutes, drug-abusing pimps, and minimum-wage racetrack workers with gambling problems.

The building itself was once reasonably attractive, judging from old photographs. Even if it wasn't really grand, it wasn't an actual embarrassment to the working class families who lived nearby. But for the past three decades or so no one had bothered with maintenance, and the building had begun crumbling apart, brick by brick, roof tile by roof tile. Ever since the hotel went bankrupt five years ago, the building's decay had been even more rapid.

Two years ago some new owners bought the building from the bank for a song—well, maybe more than a song, maybe a whole CD. They were investing in the future of the revitalized West Side, I guess. But so far they hadn't lifted a finger to fix up the place. The windows were still broken, the graffitied bricks were still turning into powder, and now part of the roof was caving in. Soon, unless the owners began working on the place themselves or sold it to someone who would, the building would be beyond hope, suitable only to be condemned.

But last month, miraculously, a potential buyer surfaced: the Saratoga Economic Redevelopment Council. The SERC was a semi-public, semi-private, semi-who-knows-what nonprofit corporation that wanted to purchase the hotel and renovate it. They even had the money to back up their talk, thanks to some federal HUD grants.

The owners of the building were no doubt thrilled at this surprise windfall. And you'd think all of us on the West Side would be thrilled, too. A giant abandoned eyesore blighting our entire neighborhood would become a viable building once again.

But there was a catch. A big catch. The SERC plan called for the top floor to house *single homeless men.*

Talk about your archetypal nimby issue.

Tell me, would you want a bunch of single homeless men living right close to you? If so, then you're a better person than I.

Even worse, it felt to many West Siders like our neighborhood was being flooded with one do-gooder organization after another, bringing a huge array of screwed-up people along with them. Sometimes I felt that way too, I must confess. It seemed like every other block now contained a shelter or halfway house for drug addicts, battered women, "nonviolent" parolees. . . . Sure, these folks need help, but couldn't some of the places devoted to their welfare be located on the *East* Side for a change?

I still had enough liberal guilt that I supported the SERC plan—but without enthusiasm. We lived five blocks away from the Grand Hotel; and to be honest, if we lived closer I might have been on the other side of the issue.

Lia herself lived a mere one block from the hotel. "So how do *you* feel about it, Lia?" I asked.

"I have very mixed feelings," she said, troubled. "I mean, that building makes the whole West Side look like a dump. I feel like crying every time I walk by. If the SERC takes it over, at least they'll turn it around. But how much control will they really have over those homeless men?" She sighed heavily, then shook away her doubts. "The main thing is, the West Side has to go to this meeting in force and make ourselves heard. We're taking a vote tonight, and the mayor and city council have agreed to abide by our decision."

"That's terrific." Boy, Lia was getting more and more powerful all the time. "I do wish I could come—"

"Of course you can!"

"—but I have a meeting at seven that I was hoping *you* would come to." Then I told her all about it, and confidently handed her my petition and my pen.

But she handed them right back. "No, thank you," she said quietly.

Et tu, Lia? I stared at her. "Why not?"

She squirmed, uncomfortable. "Pop isn't a bad guy. He takes decent care of his properties—"

"Are you kidding? Every house he owns is unsafe, full of illegal apartments—"

"He's better than a lot of the other landlords around here. Look, I wish I could talk more, but I've got a lot of calls to make."

Lia didn't exactly slam the door in my face.

But she came close.

Feeling like Don Quixote on an especially windy day, I headed back to Elm to continue my one-man petition drive. Three houses down from Beekman, I stepped around a heap of mildewed boards and rusty nails and knocked on the front door of a dilapidated duplex.

Answering my knock was a runty nine-year-old boy with a stuffy nose and dull eyes that brightened considerably when he saw me. "Hi, Mr. Burns," he called out happily.

This was Tony Martinelli, a kid I was tutoring

through a Literacy Volunteers program. Andrea is on their board of directors, and she twisted my arm into working with local kids for a couple of hours per week. Tony M. couldn't read worth a darn when I started with him three months ago. Now he still couldn't read worth a darn—he just wasn't into it—but he was definitely into *me*. I was the new father figure in his life. Come to think of it, maybe I was the *first* father figure in his life.

Lately he'd been coming by our house every single afternoon after school, filling up on Cheerios, peanuts, and whatever else we had in our kitchen. I was happy to feed him, although the kid had a habit of committing petty larcenies, so every time he came over I had to make sure there were no purses, wallets, or other easily liftable items lying around. Still, I truly liked the little shrimp.

"Hi, Tony," I said. "How come you're not at school?"

"I'm sick," he told me, giving a big gooey sneeze to prove it. He wiped the snot on his sleeve and I started to say something, then remembered I was just his father figure, not his father. Besides, there was probably no Kleenex in the house, and only a fifty-fifty chance of toilet paper. Next time he came to my house, I should give him some. Actually, there were a lot of things I should be doing for this kid, and it was starting to gnaw at me.

"Where's your mom?" I asked.

Tony shrugged. I didn't push it. "What's that?" he said, pointing to the sheet of paper in my hand.

"A petition."

He wrinkled his forehead, confused. "A position?"

I explained what it was, and he instantly got so excited he literally jumped up and down. "Cool, I *hate* Pop! He's always doing a police harassment thing on me. One time he beat me up really bad!"

"You're kidding." *Was* he kidding? Or was Pop actually beating up nine-year-old kids?!

"No, for real. And I wasn't even *doing* anything. Hey, can I come to the meeting tonight so I can boo him and stuff? Maybe I could put thumbtacks on his seat!"

I started to say no, but then it hit me that having kids at the meeting would emphasize the "family character of the neighborhood." So I said, "Sure, if it's okay with your mom."

He gave another shrug. Again I didn't push it. His Mom didn't give a flying Fig Newton what Tony did or where he went, as long as it didn't interfere with her partying.

I promised to pick him up at 6:45 and said goodbye. Tony stood at the rotting doorway watching me as I walked away.

I was glad to make it back up Elm Street toward my own block, with its (except for the blot next door) well-kept homes, trimmed hedges, and mowed lawns. I finally got my first signature, from Lorenzo, the retired blacksmith across the street. Unfortunately, Lorenzo had had a stroke recently, which made his signature illegible.

It was 3:00, almost time to go pick up Babe Ruth at the bus stop. But first I played the one trump card I had left. I called up Judy Demarest, my wife's bowling buddy, who is also the editor-in-chief of the *Daily Saratogian*. Judy and I get along pretty well, especially considering that I once accused her—falsely, as it turned out—of murder. Fortunately she has a good sense of humor, and gets a kick out of the idea that she used to be a real live murder suspect.

"Jude. Major scoop," I announced into the phone. Judy tends to speak in clipped phrases, trying to sound like a hardboiled newspaperwoman I guess, and sometimes I adjust my dialogue to match. "Dishonest cop. Neighbors outraged. Tonight—live at seven."

"Dishonest cop. Neighbors outraged," Judy repeated. "We like. We like *mucho*. What's the deal?"

I told her.

"Pop?!" she asked, incredulous. "You're going up against *Pop*?!"

I stiffened. "Why the hell not?"

She hesitated. "No reason. I'll be there."

"Thanks, Jude."

"Good luck, Jake." Then she added, "You'll need it," and hung up.

You'll need it. What the hell was I setting myself up for, anyhow?

As I hung up the phone, I felt a cold shiver crawling down my spine. But hey, if Jimmy Stewart could fight City Hall, then by golly, so could I.

3

Six fifty-nine. The hearing was about to begin.

We were in a venerable second-floor meeting room in Saratoga's venerable City Hall. Portraits of famous dead politicians and racehorses covered the walls.

Six somber-faced men in jackets and ties and one somber-faced woman in a navy blue suit sat behind a long oak table up front. These were the accountants, lawyers, and businessmen who served for a nominal fee on the Saratoga Zoning Board. No doubt they were all East Siders.

To be charitable, maybe the board members were simply good-hearted folks who liked doing public service. To be cynical, there was probably money in it—and not just that nominal fee, either.

The audience, some forty strong, was sprinkled throughout the wooden pews that filled the room. In the front row, to my left, sat the man himself.

Pop.

Pop Doyle was stubble-faced and jowly, three inches shorter than me at five nine but forty pounds heavier. Some of those pounds were fat—this was not a guy who worked out at the World Gym—but some of it was leftover muscles from his younger days. He was decked out in a pinstriped, vested suit, but with his short arms, blunt fingers, flat nose, blond hair fading into pale pink cheeks, and mean, beady eyes, he looked like . . . well, there's no better word . . . like a pig.

Sitting to Pop's right was his legal eagle, Matt Wells, Saratoga's most expensive real estate lawyer. He's the gun Wal-Mart hired when they bullied their way into town. To Pop's left was Genevieve Rendell, the town's slimiest real estate broker, who swindled some friends of mine out of $3000 when they bought their house. Unfortunately, the swindle was (barely) legal.

And who was opposing this powerful threesome? Well, there was myself; little Tony Martinelli, spilling snot into the Kleenex I brought for him; Wayne Gretzky and Babe Ruth, playing with their Ninja Turtle action figures; and Andrea, who'd had to stay late at school and was now gobbling down a peanut butter and jelly sandwich for dinner.

A hell of a lobbying group.

Occupying neutral territory, on an aisle seat toward the back, was newspaperwoman Judy Demarest. The rest of the audience came in a variety of ages, clothing styles, and economic status, but they did share one thing in common: they all looked nervewracked. There was a lot of agitated whispering, nail-biting, and nose-picking.

When the hearing began, I found out what caused this frantic behavior. These folks were all petitioning for zoning changes—a new garage here, an additional bedroom there. There were so many petitions that I wondered if the board would ever get around to us tonight, but most of them sailed right through with no hassle whatsoever. All that nose-picking for nothing. So it was still only 7:30 when the chairman of the board, a smooth up-and-comer with blow-dried hair and a Boston Brahmin accent whom I disliked immediately, asked Pop's lawyer to come forward.

Matt Wells stood up, adjusting his sport jacket—not that it needed adjusting, it fit his broad shoulders perfectly—and stepped gracefully around the railing that separated the board members from the plebeians. Wells looked perfectly at ease, like he played golf on Saturdays with half the board. They were all gazing at him respectfully. My heart sank. How could I ever hope to beat this Robert Shapiro look-alike? And why hadn't I remembered to get dressed up? I was wearing blue jeans and a faded old Pogo T-shirt.

I felt outgunned, outmanned, and alone. Andrea had taken our kids for a walk around the block because they were making too much noise, so the only person I had with me for moral support was little snot-nosed Tony. I looked over at Judy, but she didn't look back; she was too busy being an impartial journalist.

"Gentlemen," Wells began in a pleasant, confidential tone, "and gentlewoman," he added, nodding pleasantly to the one woman on the board, "this is a very straightforward petition. Mr. Doyle, or as we all know him, Pop"—here Wells smiled, Pop smiled, and the board all smiled back—"wishes to officially re-zone his property on 107 Elm Street as a three-family unit. *Un*officially, the property has been three-family for over ten years, with no problems or complaints from the neighbors—"

What?! Screw you, you lousy East Side slimeball—

"—and now we're merely requesting that you formalize the arrangement. As you can see from this map"—here Wells passed around Xeroxes to the board members—"most of the other houses in this area are also two-family or three-family units—"

Wait, that's a total lie!

"—so Pop's dwelling fits perfectly into the neighborhood—"

"Excuse me," I interrupted, standing up. All seven board members turned and frowned at me. I belatedly remembered the grape juice I'd spilled on my shirt at dinner; hopefully it hadn't left too big of a stain. "May I see that map?" I blundered on, with what I hoped looked approximately like an ingratiating smile.

The board members frowned even harder, and out of a corner of my eye I saw Pop stiffen. But then Wells said, "Of course," and with the utmost graciousness handed me a copy of the map.

I had an inspiration. "Perhaps the editor of the *Daily Saratogian* would like a copy, too," I suggested.

If any of the board members hadn't known before that there was a media watchdog present, they knew it now. As Wells handed Judy the map, they all sat up straighter in their chairs. I snuck a look at Pop; he was glaring straight at me, and his face flamed bright red with anger right before my eyes.

Clearing his throat, Wells went back to the railing and resumed his confident baritone monologue. But I didn't hear what he was saying. I was busy staring at the map.

The map was baloney. It may have been true, but it was still utter baloney. There's lies, damn lies, and statistics . . . and then there's damn lying maps.

Wells's map showed a small slice of Elm Street from the cemetery northward to 107, where it stopped abruptly. And sure enough, slightly over half the houses in this carefully selected slice were indeed two- or three-families.

But.

By stopping where it did, the map obscured the fact that 107 was the only two- or three-family on our entire block. Because if you charted Elm Street *southward* to 107 instead of northward, absolutely none of the houses were multi-families.

Furthermore, though the map didn't show this, every single three-family on Elm was much, much larger than the house at 107. No other landlords had been nearly so greedy, subdividing their places into such Lilliputian apartments.

Tony nudged my shoulder sharply, and I looked up. I suddenly realized that Wells had finished his speech and the chairman was already asking for audience comments. I'd been so wrapped up in the map, I hadn't raised my hand.

"Since no one has any comments," the chairman was saying, looking pretty happy about it, "we will now proceed to—"

"Wait!" I yelled. Oops, I hadn't meant to yell. "I do have comments, Mr. Chairman," I continued, more quietly.

The chairman sighed. "All right. Please be brief."

I stood at my pew and started to speak from right there, but then went up to the railing instead and stepped around it. If Wells thought that was the best place to stand, then by God, that's where I'd stand, too.

Behind me little Tony began whistling and clapping loudly. Great, just the kind of support I needed. I looked back and scowled until he finally got the message and shut up, embarrassed, and blew his nose. On his shirt.

Meanwhile I located the grape juice stain on my own shirt. It was right above my belly button. I tried to hide it with my hand, doing the Napoleon pose.

I cleared my throat and nervously commenced with "Gentlemen," then realized I was squeaking. I was so rattled, and so intent on lowering my voice a few octaves, that I forgot to add the smooth "and gentlewoman" like Wells did.

But then somehow, out of sheer desperation, I managed to find a rhythm. Waving that dishonest map aloft, forgetting all about my grape juice stain, I attacked. I tore the map's lies and half-lies to shreds. I described the Third-World living conditions at 107—"the nightmare on Elm Street," I called it—and used all the skills I'd honed during my years as a writer to vividly depict the late-night screaming, brawling, horn honking, and drug dealing. When I happened to turn sideways at one point, I noticed Tony beaming at me proudly. On the center aisle, Judy Demarest furiously took notes. I was cooking with gas.

Maybe I was cooking with too much gas. Fueled by my eloquence, and by my two-months-long anger at being awakened nightly, I threw caution to the winds. I forgot that there must be a reason why half of Saratoga seemed to be scared of Pop. I let him have it with both barrels.

"Furthermore, gentlemen," I continued, "and gentlewoman," I added gracefully, "you all heard Mr. Wells inform you that, *unofficially,* this house has been a three-family unit for over ten years. But, Mr. Wells"—I turned to him—"and Mr. Doyle"—I turned to Pop—"and members of the board"—I turned back to them—"let's cut the crap. It wasn't just 'unofficial,' it was blatantly *illegal*. This man is a cop—a *cop* for God's sake, and yet he has broken the law with impunity for ten years. Now his lawyer shamelessly stands before you and declares that this man should be rewarded for his illegal actions. He actually wants you to approve Mr. Doyle's misdeeds, so he can sell his property at a huge profit and make even more money from breaking the law than he already has. Members of the board, on behalf of my wife, my children"—they'd come back in a moment ago, and Andrea was staring at me, astonished by my oration—"my neighbors, and the people of this city, who are represented here today by the esteemed editor of the *Daily Saratogian*"—I figured it wouldn't hurt to remind the board again that they were being observed—"I urge you to reject this man's appeal. I urge you to go even further," I proclaimed, bringing my fist down hard on the wooden railing, "and take steps immediately to force Pop Doyle to obey the law as regards his property. Thank you very much."

Then I went back to my seat.

The room was so silent you could hear Judy Demarest scribbling away in her notebook. The board members sat there stunned. Andrea, Tony, and my kids were still staring at me. The kids didn't know what was going on, but they knew it was something very weird.

Everyone else was staring at me, too. Especially Pop.

And Pop's face wasn't bright red anymore. It was dark purple.

"Mr. Wells," the chairman finally asked, "is there anything you wish to say in reply?"

Wells set his jaw. "There most certainly is." He advanced resolutely to the railing, but I noticed he stayed on the audience side of it this time. Maybe his confidence that he and the board were on the same side had been shaken.

Or maybe not. His voice sounded just as self-assured as ever. "Members of the board, I will ignore the incendiary remarks with which Mr. Burns ended his impassioned though inaccurate speech. As you know, they are totally outside the purview of this board.

"Let's move on to the *real* issue," he continued, oozing greasy sarcasm. "Since Mr. Burns claims to represent the people of his neighborhood, I have one simple question. Where are they?" He stopped, peering theatrically around the room. "I don't see them. Why aren't they here?"

"*I'm* here!" little Tony called out. Thanks a heap, kid. A wave of laughter broke through the audience, and several board members chuckled.

Wells chuckled himself, and pointed a disdainful thumb at Tony. "So this young man, members of the board, represents the total extent of the community support for Mr. Burns."

Unable to contain myself any longer, I jumped up. "There's a big West Side meeting tonight about the Grand Hotel. That's why no one's here."

Wells gave me the kind of look you'd give a mosquito. "Mr. Burns, don't insult my intelligence. You know as well as I do, that meeting doesn't start until eight. If your neighbors were truly on your side, they could have shown up here for an hour. And besides, where are the petitions? Where are the letters of support?"

"Hey, I didn't hear about this damn meeting"—no, don't cuss, get a grip—"until this afternoon. I'll bet no one else did either."

One of the board members cleared his throat loudly. He was a fat-cheeked guy with big ears, bushy eyebrows, and an officious manner who managed to look like a stuffed owl even though he was only in his mid-thirties. "Sir," he said to me, making that salutation sound like an insult, "we mailed out official notices regarding this hearing to all homeowners within one hundred yards of 107 Elm Street exactly one month ago, on September first. We followed the customary, legally mandated procedure." He held up a fistful of papers. "If you so desire, I will be glad to show you documentation."

"Hey, I'm not saying you didn't send them, I'm saying we didn't receive them. And the other thing is, my neighbors are scared to go up against Pop. They know his rep: he's crooked and he likes to hurt people."

Someone in the audience gasped. Andrea eyed me in alarm. Shit, had I just gone too far? Had I slipped into some late 60s "off the pigs" time warp? Had I been watching too much Court TV for my own good?

Was I, in short, making a total ass of myself?

Evidently Wells thought so, because he counterattacked with gusto. "Mr. Burns, you have exceeded the bounds of civil discourse. To maliciously state these reckless accusations in a public forum, when you know they will be reported in tomorrow's newspaper, is *unconscionable.* My client is a respected twenty-year veteran of the Saratoga Springs Police Department. As soon as this hearing is over, I will recommend to Mr. Doyle that he institute immediate action against you for slander."

Jesus, could I really get sued for this? I looked over to Andrea for support, half-expecting her to be glaring at me. But I got lucky—she reached for my hand and squeezed it. That gave me strength. I stood up. "Mr. Chairman, I respectfully request that you postpone your decision on this proposal until your next board meeting, to allow me sufficient time to demonstrate the unanimity of community opposition."

The chairman gave a sigh so loud I could hear it

clearly from my pew. Interestingly, all the other board members were sighing too. Why?

Then I figured it out. These were sighs of relief. With the media there watchdogging them, the board members were afraid to make any actual decisions. So they were grateful for an excuse to delay. Procrastination—the bureaucrat's best friend.

And procrastinate they did. The chairman mumbled briefly to the other board members, who rapidly nodded in agreement, and they tabled the issue until November. The battle was over . . . for now.

Andrea and I gathered up Tony and our kids and headed out. As soon as we hit the hallway, the boys immediately started jumping around and practicing their fiercest Ninja Turtle karate moves, undoubtedly their response to all the heavy tension in the air. It took Andrea and me a full minute to corral our little warriors down the stairs to the first floor.

Which is where Pop Doyle caught up with me.

4

Pop put his short, stubby, muscular hand on my arm. "Mr. Burns," he said.

I jumped, startled. His piggy eyes shone meanly, and I was afraid he'd pop me one.

But there were other people in the hallway too, coming out of meetings or just hanging out. Surely Pop wouldn't do anything violent now. Too many witnesses.

In fact, as I would learn later, there were exactly twelve witnesses, not including my family and Tony. And all twelve of them eventually wound up giving statements to the police about what they saw, which was:

They saw Pop touching my arm. As far as they could tell, he was touching me gently.

The three witnesses who were standing close to us heard Pop say, in a friendly voice:

"Just wanted to say, Mr. Burns, no hard feelings. You're entitled to your opinion."

And here's what all twelve witnesses saw and heard next:

My face exploded with fury. I yanked my arm away from Pop and instantly shoved him backward so hard he reeled, all 220 pounds of him. Now I'm no Hulk Hogan, and ordinarily Pop would beat the stuffing out of me, but I caught him by surprise and threw him down like a wet towel. Then I stood over him and started yelling.

And here's what the witnesses heard me yell:

"You motherfucker, don't you dare do that again!"

And then a lot of things happened at once. Pop tried to jump up, presumably so he could attack me, but suddenly my three Ninja Turtles leaped into the fray. Babe Ruth karate kicked Pop in one leg and Wayne Gretzky karate kicked him in the other, while Tony, more wise to the ways of the world, karate kicked him right in the balls.

Pop howled with pain. Tony kicked him again, paying Pop back in spades for having beaten him up once. Andrea, shouting, got in the Ninja Turtles' faces and tried to push them away. But they had picked up my angry adrenaline and it was carrying them to superhuman, or should I say superturtle, heights. They darted around Andrea and jumped up and down on top of various parts of Pop's body, starting with his knuckles.

I would have tried to stop them—well, *maybe* I would have—except that a lantern-jawed man in his thirties who turned out to be an off-duty police lieutenant pushed me up against a wall, away from the action. I started to explain to him the reason why I had exploded, and what had really happened between me and Pop—because eyes can deceive, and what the witnesses saw was *not* what really happened, as I'll explain to you in a moment—but the lieutenant wasn't listening. He was just repeating over and over, like a mantra, "Calm down, calm down, calm down." But it was kind of hard to calm down when the man had one hand grabbing the front of my T-shirt and another hand balled into a fist, ten inches from my nose.

It got even harder to calm down when I heard a loud clattering noise and saw, out of the corner of my eye, a gun sliding along the floor. It must have come loose from Pop's holster when the kids were mauling him.

The next thing I saw was Babe Ruth racing for the gun.

Immediately I visualized the whole thing: my six-year-old son grabbing the gun, firing at Pop and the lieutenant too, and ending up on the cover of *People.*

I ducked down so fast I left the lieutenant grabbing a fistful of air and dove for the gun, desperate to reach it before Babe Ruth did.

My hand and his found the gun at exactly the same time. I grabbed the barrel and his hand tugged at the handle, with one finger way too close to the trigger for my comfort. "Let go!" I screamed.

Thank God, he did.

I held the weapon gingerly, by the barrel, with two fingers. Then I walked up to Pop, who was still down on the floor, protecting his battered body from the continued onslaughts of Tony and Gretzky.

"Kids, stop it!" I shouted.

They looked up at me. "But, Daddy, he's a bad guy," Gretzky complained.

"Here, Mr. Doyle," I said, holding the gun out to him.

"Don't give him the gun! He might shoot us!" Babe Ruth called out.

Pop sat up and glowered at me, his relief mixed with hatred and shame. Finally he took the gun and put it away in its holster.

Instantly everyone in the hallway began breathing again, and talking nonstop. Lieutenant Lantern Jaw angrily told Pop he should press criminal charges against not just me but my children, too; Andrea started shouting at the lieutenant; Pop collected himself and yelled at everyone in sight; the bystanders put in their two cents; Gretzky whined that he was thirsty; Babe Ruth whined that he was hungry; Andrea screamed at them; Judy Demarest came down from the stairway where she'd witnessed the whole thing and tried to help us with the kids; and as for myself, I was trying to make myself heard over the din, so I could explain what Pop had done to me before that no one had seen. But no one was listening to me.

Now Lieutenant Lantern Jaw was bellowing at Andrea that the city would send in social workers to take a good hard look at our kids because they were obviously heading straight for a lifetime of crime unless there was firm early intervention. Pop was making noises like he would take the lieutenant's advice on pressing charges, so the lieutenant grabbed my shoulder roughly and said, "Come with me," to jail I guess he meant. My entire family started wailing, and Gretzky and Ruth wrapped themselves around my legs to keep me from leaving, but then right at the last moment, just as the lieutenant was leading me off, Pop called out for him to stop, and it finally became apparent that Pop's noises were just that and he had no real intention of pressing charges against me or my boys. Nervously eyeing Judy Demarest, who was standing quietly to one side, Pop stopped blustering and put a wan smile on his face. He started in about how the whole thing was just a silly little situation that got a bit out of hand, so let's not make a big deal of it, boys will be boys, he'd give us all a break, just this one time.

He was trying to play it like a nice guy, but it

didn't take a Ph.D. to figure out what was really going on in his swinelike little mind as he cast sidelong glances at Judy. He was frantic to avoid publicity for the fact that three young children, ages nine, six, and four, had overpowered him and made him lose his gun. Also, I doubt he wanted me testifying in court about what had really happened between us in the hallway.

Lieutenant Lantern Jaw wasn't the swiftest guy in the world, but he eventually figured out that Pop wasn't going to change his mind. So after giving Andrea and me a stern lecture about the responsibilities of parenthood, he let us go. His main theme was that we should take our kids to church every Sunday, and Andrea and I bobbed our heads solemnly up and down and promised to do exactly that. We figured this wasn't the right moment to tell him we were Jews, and agnostic Jews to boot.

Then Pop went downstairs to the police station and Lantern Jaw told everyone in the hallway they could go home, he wouldn't need to take their statements. It turned out he was wrong about that, though we had no way of knowing it at the time.

Andrea, the kids, and myself hightailed it out the front door and escaped as fast as we could. Finally, after endless minutes of Lantern Jaw shouting me down, I'd get a chance to tell Andrea my side of the story.

5

But Andrea, as it turned out, didn't want to hear my side of the story right then. She was far more interested in imparting some basic rules of gun safety to our children. And when I say basic, I mean basic.

"Don't *ever* touch a gun," she said to Babe Ruth and Gretzky, holding them firmly by the shoulders as we stood together on the sidewalk outside City Hall.

"But Mommy," Babe Ruth said.

"Don't *ever* touch a gun." Andrea was so riled up, the veins were sticking out all over her face. She's never shaken our kids, and I'm sure it took all of her willpower not to shake them right then. "Do you hear me? Don't *ever* touch a gun. Don't *ever, ever, ever* touch a gun."

This time the kids wisely didn't argue. They just nodded.

After Andrea and the kids got the gun thing straightened out, I eagerly told her the Real Story about what went down with Pop in that hallway. But she was surprisingly, and very annoyingly, unsympathetic. So later that night after the kids were asleep, I tried again. We were sitting together on the living room sofa, but about as far apart from each other as two people could get.

"Andrea, you have to understand, he *pinched* me," I repeated, exasperated.

"I don't *care*," Andrea replied, equally exasperated.

"He pinched me hard, on some weird pressure point. It was like getting a hundred tetanus shots at once. I'm still aching there." I pulled up my sleeve and rubbed the tender spot.

"That's still no excuse for turning into a total lunatic—"

"Okay, so I overreacted. Look, I was in excruciating pain. How about I pinch you as hard as I can on one of your pressure points, and *you* see how it feels!" I snapped, my voice and my temper rising.

"Please be quiet—unless you want to put the kids to bed all over again."

"He was *smiling*," I hissed quietly, desperate to make Andrea understand. "The prick stands there smiling like he's my best buddy, and the whole time he's squeezing me like he's studied some top-secret North Korean torture manual—"

"The prick was a cop, for God's sake. You almost got yourself thrown in jail!" She pointed a finger at me. "Don't start acting like some macho jerk!"

"Thanks for the sympathy," I said, and stood up from the sofa. I stormed into the kitchen, grabbed a beer, and guzzled it, feeding my rage against Andrea, Pop, the Zoning Board, the neighbors, and the rest of the world.

I came up with some really nasty things to say to Andrea, and started back to the living room to say them. But just in the nick of time, I decided I'd be better off going outside and walking off my anger. My impulses had already gotten me in enough trouble tonight; no need to add to it. So I put on my jacket, stepped out the side door, and took a deep breath.

The sweet smell of ripe grapes instantly surrounded me, miraculously lifting my mood quicker than pot ever did in my younger years. Maybe those aromatherapy people are onto something, I thought. Our fruitful, century-old grape arbor was in full harvest, so I grabbed a handful of big luscious purple grapes and rolled them around on my tongue, spitting out the seeds as I ambled down Elm Street, letting life's worries fade away and blithely ignoring the fact I was probably adding a few more stains to my T-shirt.

It was the kind of crisp autumn evening when you can feel both summer and winter simultaneously. I always find that strangely soothing. Way up high the North Star was beckoning, and in front of me Jupiter was strutting its stuff. Meanwhile the Nightmare House on Elm Street was dark and silent; maybe they were taking the night off from drug dealing, and Andrea and I would sleep for ten hours and wake up refreshed.

I walked down Elm and up Maple. The whole West Side was eerily quiet tonight. I whistled an old Yiddish lullaby, *Rochinkes mit Mandlen,* and it reverberated in the deserted streets. There were no cars whizzing by, no loud music, no children crying. What a magical night, I thought . . .

And then I turned onto Ash Street and realized it wasn't magic after all. Ash was lined bumper to bumper with parked cars, and the huge lot outside Pirelli & Sons, Scrap Dealers, was filled to bursting. The reason the rest of the West Side was so quiet tonight was because everyone was at the big S.O.S. meeting at the corner of Ash and Walnut. Even though it was ten-thirty already, and the meeting had started at eight, it was evidently still going strong.

I was feeling so peaceful, and the night was so

serene, I had half a mind to walk away. But the other half won out, and I soon found myself walking up the steps of the Orian Cillárnian Sons of Ireland hall.

I couldn't get any farther than the front door, though. The joint was jammed, no doubt breaking several fire laws. All two hundred folding chairs were occupied, mostly by elderly folks. The aisles were crammed with rows and rows of mainly younger people standing up and craning their necks to see over each other. A lot of them were fanning themselves with stapled handouts, because it was seriously *hot* in there. Even from where I stood at the door, I started sweating after about five seconds.

The mood in the room was just as hot as the temperature. One irate citizen after another was railing at the rank injustices of the universe in general and Saratoga Springs in particular. Their vituperations were aimed in the general direction of Hal Starette, the president of the Saratoga Economic Redevelopment Council, who sat at a table up front with a pained smile on his face and huge stains under his pits. I knew Hal, having played chess with him at the Saratoga Knights Club, so I recognized his pained smile and even his sweat—it was how he'd looked and sweated when I trapped his queen on my back rank. He was a good player, but sometimes took too many chances.

Next to poor nervous Hal sat Lia Kalmus, who was moderating the meeting and not sweating one bit. She looked absolutely at ease. She gave deep-throated laughs when the speakers made jokes, hushed them good-naturedly when they babbled on too long, and in general basked in the spotlight. With her good eye shining brightly, and her scarred cheek and droopy, bloodshot eye turned away from me, she actually looked almost pretty.

Meanwhile the air in the room was redolent with catchphrases and buzzwords. "Property values" was a biggie. So was "sick and tired." Also, "people coming in here and . . ." followed by some clause like "messing up our neighborhood!", which inevitably inspired wild applause.

Half of me agreed heartily with these folks, but the other half thought they were narrowminded right-wing pains in the ass. I was doing an awful lot of splitting in half lately; part of turning forty, I guess.

"Why don't they just stick all these homeless people on the East Side for a change!" one feisty old gent shouted, and two hundred other feisty old gents cheered as one.

A sweet grandmotherly type got up and said, "You know, a lot of homeless people are perfectly normal folks, just like you and me. All they need is a little helping hand." Then she added, "But let's face it, most of them are diseased, drug abusing, mentally insane criminals!" More clapping and cheers.

Half of me agreed with her, but half . . . et cetera. And I wasn't the only one who seemed torn. As I stood on tiptoes and gazed around the room, I noticed a lot of people biting their lips and looking like they wished they were somewhere else. Most of them were about my age, and I guessed they were just like me—ex-hippies feeling ex-hippie guilt.

There were also a bunch of people at the meeting who actively supported the SERC plan for the Grand Hotel. One suit-wearing, professional-looking woman in her forties stood up and identified herself as "Jennifer Hopkins, a longtime West Sider who's lived in this neighborhood for ten years." (I saw two old women share a look—"She thinks *ten years* makes her 'longtime'? Phooey!") Then Jennifer began what sounded like a prepared speech. She was probably a lawyer, but I tried not to hold that against her.

"People," she declared, "with every passing month, the Grand Hotel is falling even deeper into decrepitude, disgracing our neighborhood and driving down these very property values we're all so concerned about. Now instead of just sticking our heads in the sand, why don't we take a serious look at this SERC plan, instead of getting caught up in ill-considered scare tactics?"

"Scare tactics?!" an outraged old-timer yelled, pointing his cane at Jennifer. "You'd be scared too, if you were an old fart like us and you couldn't run away from these sons of bitches when they mug you!"

The other old-timers hooted and hollered, and Lia had to work her ass off to quiet them down. She finally succeeded, but then a woman with a thousand wrinkles on her face stood up and screamed, "And what about these teenage kids skateboarding on our streets every hour of the day and night? I can't even go outside my house anymore, I'm so scared they'll run me over!"

The old-timers went berserk all over again. Finally Lia restored order and Jennifer continued on determinedly. "As I was trying to say—before I was interrupted—this plan calls for the bottom two floors to be SERC office space. Surely no one objects to that?" She paused; no one objected. "The third floor will have computer training and G.E.D. classrooms. Surely no one objects to that, either?" She paused again, very smoothly. Definitely a lawyer.

"Now it's true," she said, "that the fourth floor would house homeless men, and I know a lot of folks have problems with this. But how many homeless men are we really talking about?"

"Too many!" someone shouted, but before the place could erupt into applause, Jennifer shouted back, "Twelve! Only *twelve* units for homeless men! And the SERC will be right there in the building, keeping an eye on them! So tell me, what is so gosh-darn horrible about this plan?" She jabbed the air with her index finger. "How could this plan be any worse than what's happening right now, which is that this abandoned building is a boarded-up haven for crack users! Is that what you people really want for our neighborhood?!"

Suddenly, as if on cue, the room burst into frantic applause. But it was a different set of folks cheering this time: the younger set, the ex-hippies, the thirty- and forty-somethings who'd been uncomfortably chewing on their lips for the whole meeting.

Without even noticing, I started clapping myself. Well, at least now I knew which side I was on.

But as the debate raged on, I realized there were still a lot of people who *didn't* know which side they were on. The room was full of people—Irish, Italian, black, old, young, middle-aged—who were scratching their heads, shifting their feet, and generally looking confused, not clapping or cheering or saying anything at all.

Then one of them did say something. It was a five-foot-tall white-haired woman with a standard-issue little old lady voice but surprisingly large ears. Lia had to shush people three times before the hall got quiet enough for everyone to hear this female Ross Perot.

"Lia," she said, "I'm sitting here and just feeling more and more mixed up. First I think no, and then yes, and then no again." She threw up her hands. "I'm in such a tizzy. So my question is: Lia, which way are *you* going to vote?"

BOOM!

Three hundred people stopped moving.

Three hundred people stopped whispering.

Three hundred people turned their eyes to Lia Kalmus.

Lia cleared her throat. She scratched her chin thoughtfully. She rubbed her eyebrows. She had the power here—and she was loving it.

The sweat stains under Hal Starette's pits instantly grew another six inches. His smile was so grim, he looked like someone was sticking needles into him under the table. No doubt he assumed, as I did, that when push came to shove Lia would show her true colors as a dyed-in-the-wool reactionary nimby.

"Well," Lia finally uttered, in a deceptively casual tone, "as you all know, I want what's best for our community. But in this case, I have to admit to you, I can't *tell* what's best. We're caught between a rock and a hard place. Either we leave that disgusting building the way it is, and maybe wait another five years or even longer until someone else comes in and offers to fix it up, or we go with the SERC plan, with everything that brings. I'm like you, Helen," she addressed the elderly Ross Perot, "my head can go either way. And when that happens . . . there's only one thing to do. You have to listen to your heart.

"And my heart tells me, when I have two choices that seem pretty equal—but one choice will provide homes to twelve people—then there's no question what's right. Because when I was growing up, my whole family was homeless!" Lia's voice had been growing almost imperceptibly louder and stronger, and now it suddenly exploded in the hot Orian Cillárnian air. Her good eye somehow seemed to be looking directly at every single person in the crowded room. "Friends, if you're positive the SERC plan is bad for us, then vote against it. But if you're like Helen and me, and you're not sure, then you have to vote *for* it! Those twelve men tip the scales! Speaking for myself, I'm not just a West Sider. I'm not just the president of this S.O.S. Association. I am also a Christian! And Jesus Christ teaches me that every man is a child of God, and as much as I love the West Side, there are things in this world—and the next—that are more important than *property values*!"

Then Lia sat down.

At first no one moved, but then one person clapped, and then more people, and more, and by the time the applause finally died down, it was obvious that Lia Kalmus had just single-handedly swung the room to the SERC. Hal Starette's sweat stains didn't suddenly shrink, but they did stop getting bigger.

A little while later Lia called a vote. Several politicos I hadn't noticed before, because they were blocked from my view in the front row, stood up and started counting hands. I recognized four of them: the commissioner of public works, two city councilmen, and last but not least, the confirmed sleazoid who's the mayor of Saratoga. The hall was so packed that tallying the exact totals was laborious, but when all was said and done, the SERC plan won 182 to 133. With the councilmen nodding in agreement by his side, the mayor announced that he and the council would vote tomorrow to approve the plan.

Yes, by gum, despite all its flaws, we still live in the greatest country in the world. This S.O.S. meeting was an inspiring demonstration of good old-fashioned American democracy at its finest. It took the stench of that zoning hearing out of my head, with its pompous bureaucrats, amoral lawyers, and crooked violent cops.

Lia Kalmus, with her stunning speech, had just replaced Harold Stassen as my favorite all-time public statesman. (H.S., for the uninitiated, was a one-time Minnesota governor who spent the last forty years of his life running increasingly deranged campaigns for the presidency.) I was feeling so patriotic that when I got home I watched the last inning of the baseball playoffs on television.

Even better, the Yankees got whupped. Another triumph of good over evil.

I brushed my teeth and went to bed. Andrea shifted in her sleep and spooned me. Subconsciously at least, she had forgiven me for my outburst at City Hall. Snuggling next to her, I closed my eyes and fell sound asleep.

But not for long.

I was woken up from dreamland by a car door slamming—or maybe two car doors slamming, my head was still fuzzy. Those damn neighbors again, I thought. Then the night was shattered by an ear-piercing shriek. Pierced *my* ears, anyway. Andrea and the kids were amazingly still asleep.

It was past midnight. I swung out of bed and reached for the phone. But then a car backfired outside, followed by another shriek, even more desperate than the first. I couldn't tell if these shrieks came from a woman, child, or even a man for that matter; they were ageless, genderless shouts of pure pain and terror. To heck with calling the cops—they'd take half an hour to get here. An attack of middle-age macho came over me, and I put on my slippers and threw a robe over my pajamas, preparing to go forth and do battle.

But macho man though I was, I didn't go forth to battle just yet. First I stopped off in the john, following my number one rule for success and happiness in life: Never begin an important project with a full bladder.

Then I went outside.

Unfortunately, the fifteen seconds it took me to find relief made all the difference. Because by the time I got outside, the night was eerily silent again. Nothing but distant car sounds and a far-off street lamp buzzing.

But then I heard that agonized, low-pitched moan.

And that's when I found Pop Doyle bleeding to death behind 107 Elm.

And that's when I got arrested for murder.

6

What happened was, I stood there staring down at Pop's body, pulling my robe around me and shivering, when suddenly—

"Put your hands up!" someone behind me yelled.

I turned. It was Dave Mackerel, the cop from across the street. He was wearing sweat pants and a windbreaker. How'd he get here so fast? "Dave—"

"Hands up!" He had a gun pointed straight at my chest. His voice was shrill and panicky.

I moved forward into the light where he could see me. "Hey, it's me, Jacob—"

"I know it's you. Don't move!" He lifted his gun and pointed it at my head.

I stopped in my tracks and put my hands up. "Look, this is crazy. I didn't shoot Pop—"

"What?" He waved his gun at the dead man lying there in the darkness. "That's *Pop*?"

"Yeah, he's dead," I said helpfully. "Someone shot him in the neck."

Dave stared at me. Even though he was still holding the gun high, his shoulders drooped and he looked sad. "Jesus, Jake, why'd you have to go and kill him?"

"I didn't kill him!" I yelled hysterically, and was

going to yell some more when Dave stopped me with "Get on the ground!" I just stood there. *"Lie down!"* he shouted, waving his weapon.

I lay down.

"Arms to the side," Dave told me.

I put them to the side. "Dave, don't be an idiot. You know me. I trim your hedges. We're friends."

"Where's the gun?"

"How can you possibly think I did it?!"

"Oh, come on, Jake!" he sputtered furiously. "I heard all about your stupid little episode at City Hall tonight!"

"But that had nothing to do with this!"

"Where's the gun?"

"I just came outside to—"

"Where's your fucking gun?"

I sighed, exasperated. "There's a gun right next to his body. But I always keep a second gun in my special custom-made ankle holster."

"Don't make jokes." He stood over me and patted me down, being pretty darn thorough about it, even checking for that ankle holster.

"Oh, and before I forget," I said, "I have a World War Two hand grenade sewn into a secret pocket of my bathrobe—"

"I told you, don't make jokes!" And damned if he didn't slap me on the back of my head.

I wanted to jump up and punch him out. But it wasn't a hard slap, and it wasn't even out of anger really, more out of frustration, trying to knock some sense into me. So I just smiled and said, "Thanks, I needed that."

Dave shook his head. "Another joke, huh? Well, here's a joke for *you*: Anything you say can be used against you, you have the right to a lawyer, and all that other crap you've seen on TV. Now lay right there and don't move a single damn muscle because I'll be covering you the whole time."

I was lying on my belly with my robe hanging open. *How did I get into this mess?* The ground was cold and damp, and sharp pebbles dug into the side of my face. Dave took a cell phone from his jacket pocket, started dialing a number—

And that's when I saw it: a shadowy flicker of movement coming from the other side of 107 Elm.

"Dave," I said urgently.

But he was talking into the phone, and ignored me. Meanwhile the shadow turned into a person, crouching low and running at full tilt away from 107 and down the street.

"Dave, look!"

"What's your problem?" he asked irritably.

I paused. Then finally I said, "Nothing."

Because at the last moment, I'd recognized that fleeing figure.

It was little snot-nosed Tony.

What was *he* doing here? *Did my nine-year-old pal kill Pop?*

"There's been a homicide at 107 Elm," Dave was saying into the phone. "It's Pop—Pop Doyle. I have the suspect right here. I need immediate backup."

And then Andrea screamed.

Neither of us had noticed her. She must have come out the front door, and now she appeared out of the darkness about three yards away from me. *"My God!"* she said, her voice quavering.

"Back up, Andrea," Dave broke in.

"Jacob—"

"Back up—"

"Did you kill Pop?" Andrea asked frantically.

I tried to laugh. It sounded hollow. "No, of course I didn't kill him."

She stared deep into my eyes, and I stared back. But I couldn't tell if she believed me or not.

And it looked like she couldn't tell, either.

Sirens blared. Cop cars stormed up. Two large men handcuffed me behind my back without saying much, just a brief snarl here and there. The neighbors all came out to watch, including Dale and Zapper, the drug dealers next door. They stood on their front porch together and observed me with folded arms and detached, faintly ironic expressions. Was their irony really a mask for something else?

Lorenzo, the old guy from across the way, shuffled out to the street and waved at me. I couldn't wave because of the handcuffs, so I nodded weakly back. My other neighbors stood on their porches and avoided my eyes. I could see they felt guilty about enjoying themselves, but they were anyway. This was almost as much fun as watching someone's house burn down. Someone *else's* house, that is.

I was shoved into the backseat of a cop car that stank heavily of cigars. A middle-aged cop with a busted nose leaned against the car as he watched over me. There was hate in his eyes.

Feeling claustrophobic, I awkwardly tried opening a door with my cuffed hands just to get some air, but the car was locked from the outside. Busted Nose unlocked it for me. Before I could thank him, though, he slammed me in the gut with his nightstick. "Siddown, you fucking cop killer," he growled as I sat there crumpled over, with the wind knocked out of me. Then he slammed the door shut.

Meanwhile Babe Ruth and Gretzky came out onto our front steps, bewildered. Andrea intercepted them before they could see my handcuffs, thank God, and shepherded them back inside. Before she went in, though, she shouted something to me. I couldn't hear her through the closed car windows, but it looked like she was shouting, "I love you!"

At least, I *hoped* that's what she was shouting.

More vehicles drove up, police cars and other cars too, filling the block. The cops put up yellow crime scene tape, flashbulbs started going off, and men in suits stooped down over Pop's corpse. Through an opening in the curtains of my sons' room, I saw Andrea leaning over their beds and tucking them in. She gave them a big, desperate hug.

I should tell these damn cops about Tony. Give them another suspect, take the heat off me. Maybe then they'll let me out of this lousy, smelly cop car.

But I couldn't bring myself to blow the whistle on the kid. *Did Tony really kill Pop? But why would he . . . ?*

My mind raced. Those horrific shrieks I'd heard—maybe they were Tony's. Maybe Pop was beating up Tony big time tonight, as revenge for the kid karate kicking him to the floor at City Hall.

And then . . .

Then Tony grabbed Pop's gun and shot him in self-defense.

It all fit perfectly.

Or did it? What was Tony doing outside 107 Elm at one a.m. in the first place?

I wasn't thinking all that clearly, I just knew I had to talk to Tony first, before the cops. After all, it was partly my fault he got into that big brouhaha with Pop at City Hall. I owed it to the kid to help him. If the killing was self-defense against police brutality, I couldn't just sit back and let the cops railroad him.

I mean, I was the only person alive that Tony could count on. God knows his mother was about as useful as a dried rutabaga.

My thoughts were interrupted when Busted Nose threw open the door and yanked me out of the car. An Asian woman photographer came up and clicked away at me. "Be sure to get my good side," I said, trying to impress them with my suave Cary Grant bravado. Then I happened to glance in the car's side-view mirror and realized I didn't *have* a good side. My nose was covered with blood.

No wonder I'd looked like the murderer to Dave. For an insane moment I wondered if I really *did* kill Pop. Then I remembered Pop's bloody arm jerking at my nose. I shuddered.

A cop in a wrinkled uniform who looked like he'd just gotten out of bed swabbed my nose with three Q-tips and put them in a plastic bag. Then Busted Nose—from his conversations with the other cops, I learned his regular name was Manny Cole—shoved me back into the car and got in the driver's seat. My erstwhile buddy Dave got in beside him. "Where are we going?" I asked.

"Where do ya think, scumbag?" Cole answered. "Jail. Your new home."

Evidently Cole had attended the same charm school as Pop. I waited for Dave to tell him to lighten up, but he didn't. "Dave," I said, "you're gonna feel awfully silly when you find out I didn't do it."

Dave sighed, tired. "Tell it to the judge, Jake."

"Let's make a bet. If I'm innocent, you have to trim my hedges *and* snowblow my driveway for a full year."

Dave gave me a ghost of a smile. "And what if you're guilty? You gonna trim *my* hedges?"

"Fat chance," Cole snorted. "They don't let faggot cop killers out on work release until they've done about thirty years first. 'Course," he added cheerfully, "the judge might just say the hell with it and put you in the chair. Killing a cop, that's a capital offense."

"Depends which cop gets killed," I said. I was scared shitless, but refused to act that way in front of this jerk. "When the cop is a zero-IQ turdball like you, then killing him is barely a misdemeanor. Sometimes they hold public parades down Broadway to celebrate."

"Is that what you were thinking when you killed Pop?" Cole asked.

"Yeah, that's exactly what I was thinking when I killed Pop," I said, then pretended to get all flustered. "Oh gosh, you just tricked a confession out of me! How clever you are, Mr. Policeman, sir!"

Childish, I know, but it did shut him up. No one said another word until we got to the Saratoga police station, which is located in the City Hall basement. Dave got out of one side of the car while Cole got out the other, so I'll give Dave the benefit of the doubt. From where he stood, maybe Dave couldn't see what Cole did to me while he took me out of the backseat.

Cole jabbed my eyeballs, *hard,* with his thumb and forefinger.

That eyeball-gouging trick is one of the self-defense techniques they teach women, and believe me, ladies, it works. Instant *killer* migraine. My eyes shut tight, and I couldn't get them to open back up. All I could see were tight black circles of pain. Walking blindly, my hands cuffed behind me, I tripped on the curb and fell face first on the concrete.

Cole pulled me up roughly. Then he and Dave guided me by the elbows as I stumbled through a door and down some stairs. I wanted to scream, but hated to give Cole the satisfaction. I heard him say gruffly, "Here he is," and then a new voice said,

"Good," followed by, "What's wrong with your eyes?"

That had to be me he was talking to. "This pathetic excuse for a human being stabbed them with his fingers. I want to press charges," I said.

Someone chuckled. I was so mad a surge of adrenaline ran through me, and my eyes started clearing up a little. I made out some blurry faces hovering near me, and a barred window. Meanwhile a man came up behind me and unlocked my cuffs, but before I got a chance to massage my aching wrists, I was cuffed to a metal ring on the wall.

"Okay, pal, what's your name?"

I didn't answer.

"I said what's your name?" the voice snapped threateningly.

"Sorry. You said 'pal,' so I figured you weren't talking to me." My eyes cleared some more, and I was able to make out two cops standing close to me, Cole and a young guy with a crewcut. A redhead in his forties with bad acne scars leaned against the wall, giving me the evil eye. Dave was gone.

Young Crewcut was the guy who'd been firing questions at me. Now he balled his hand into a fist, and I braced for a punch. But none came. "What's your name?" he hissed.

Suddenly I flashed back to a vicious game I used to play as a kid, during my brief career as a junior high school hooligan. We called the game "Gestapo." A couple of friends and I would back some nerdy seventh grader up against a wall in a deserted corner of the school and ask him, "What's your name?" And when he told us, we'd shout, "You lie!" and slap his face.

Maybe now God, or Someone similar, was extracting karmic revenge on me. "My name's Jacob Burns, pal," I said. "What's yours?"

Still no punch. No slap on my face either. By now I could see the whole room, if a little hazily, and I noticed a video camera above Young Crewcut's head. As he wrote down my name, address, and date and place of birth (Why do so many forms ask what state you were born in? What difference does it make if you were born in Rhode Island or Delaware?), it dawned on me that this was the world-famous booking area where the night manager of Roosters Pub got roughed up by a Saratoga police sergeant. I say "world-famous" because a videotape of the event made it onto a couple of national shows like *Nightline* and *60 Minutes.*

That video camera on the wall explained why I wasn't getting punched. At least, not here anyway. I could only hope the rest of the police station was videotaped, too.

"Take off your belt," Young Crewcut ordered me.

"Oh, come on—"

"Take it off."

Since I was cuffed to the wall, I only had one hand free. I used it to remove the belt from my robe. Then I looked down at myself.

I was wearing ancient blue and yellow striped pajamas that some barely remembered girlfriend had bought me half a lifetime ago. The middle button on my fly was missing, so with my beltless robe hanging open I had to adjust my pajama bottoms just right, or my johnson would come flopping out into full view.

If I'd known I was going to jail, I would have worn spiffier PJs.

Even worse, I was wearing slippers that my wife got me for a joke when I turned forty last year. They were purple fluffy jobs with the words "World's Greatest Lover" printed on them in bright orange.

Cole and Young Crewcut were eyeing my slippers, too. "You can keep your footwear if you want," Young Crewcut said, deadpan.

Cole busted out laughing for what felt like a full minute. The acne-scarred redhead, who'd been silently malevolent this whole time, laughed, too. Then he stepped in front of the videocamera and, hidden from the lens, spit at my face.

Maybe the fun would have lasted longer, but a door opened and the lieutenant in charge of the investigation stepped into the room. My heart sank. Lieutenant Foxwell was the same lantern-jawed lieutenant that the Ninja Turtles and I had fought with earlier that night.

He thrust that impressive jaw forward and gave me a hard stare. Then he unsnapped my cuffs, said, "This way," and pushed me through the door.

I was fingerprinted, not just once but three times—for the city, the state, and the FBI. Well, heck, I'd always wanted to be famous. Then Foxwell wiped the blood off my nose with a wet paper towel and took my mug shot with a Polaroid Mini-Portrait camera. I was prisoner number 274013. I vowed that if I ever got out of this mess, I'd play the lottery with those numbers.

I wanted to smile for my mug shot, just to be different. But Foxwell ordered me not to. I asked him why, without expecting an answer, but he gave me one. "Mug shots should look the way people usually look, and people don't usually smile. Especially douchebags who've been busted for killing cops."

I raised my eyebrows reproachfully. " 'Douchebags?' Isn't that rather a sexist term?"

This time Foxwell didn't bother to favor my remarks with a reply. He grabbed my arm and pushed me into the chief of police's office.

The chief was sitting behind his desk waiting for me. "Please sit down, sir," he said pleasantly.

They were the first pleasant words I'd heard since this whole ordeal began. I sat down. My chair was comfortable, and the old-fashioned, leather-covered desk gave off an earthy smell. Pictures of the chief and his family adorned the walls and bookcases. Like me, he had two sons, and several of the pictures showed them playing baseball. I tried to relax and pretend I was there on a social call. After all, this whole thing was just a silly little mix-up. It shouldn't be all that hard to clear up.

Chief Walsh was smiling at me. It was a warm smile. The chief had a thin white mustache and distinguished silver hair and he reminded me of someone; I wasn't sure who but it was someone good. I immediately wanted him to like me.

"Coffee?" he asked.

"Thank you, sir," I replied.

The chief nodded to Foxwell, then added, "Oh, and could you turn on the videocamera before you go?"

Foxwell pushed a button on the wall and left, and the chief turned back to me. "You've been treated well, I hope?" he asked.

I started to tell him about the spitting and eyeball-gouging, but then decided to let it go. Why make waves? "Yes, thank you," I said.

"Excellent." The chief beamed with satisfaction. "I'm glad to hear that. And I hope someone has adequately explained to you that anything you say may be used against you, and you're entitled—"

"Yes, sir. No need to do it again unless you feel it's important." Mr. Agreeable.

"Okay, good, I'm glad we got that all squared away. Now if you just want to sign this card for us . . ."

"No problem." I signed the Miranda card.

Foxwell returned with two cups of coffee, then left again as the chief reached into a mini-refrigerator behind his desk. "Cream or sugar?"

"No, thanks. Black is fine."

He nodded approvingly. "Cowboy style, huh? That's how I drink it myself. I grew up out in cowboy country."

"Oh, really?" I asked politely.

"Wallace, Idaho. Ever been there?"

"I drove through once. Big lead refinery."

He grinned knowingly. "Stunk pretty bad, didn't it?"

I grinned back. "I can still smell it."

He rolled his eyes. "Tell me about it." Then he leaned forward and gave me a solemn look. "Actually, what I'd *really* like you to tell me about, unless you feel more comfortable waiting for a lawyer, is what happened tonight."

I had nothing to hide—well, *almost* nothing—so what the heck, I told him. About the car door (doors?) slamming, and the shrieks, and the gunshot. About Pop's arm jerking at my face, and his dying words. I told the chief everything.

Almost.

Desperate though I was, I still kept little Tony out of the story.

When I finished, Chief Walsh tented his fingers thoughtfully. "You know," he said, "I believe you."

I had to fight to keep from crying. I would have kissed his feet, except they were under the desk. "Thank you, sir," I breathed. *"Thank you."*

"The only thing that screws it up a little," he said

unhappily, "is this whole crazy business that happened in the hall upstairs, where you and Pop were really going at each other."

"Oh, *that*," I said hurriedly, waving my arm. "That really wasn't such a big deal." And this time I *did* tell him everything: about the late-night noise, the drug dealing, the zoning hearing, the North Korean pressure-point torture . . .

Chief Walsh nodded sympathetically. Finally, someone who *got* it. "I totally understand," he said. "Listen, I'm aware that Pop was not always a . . . shall we say, model policeman. So here you were, already feeling upset because of the neighbors, and not being able to sleep for a couple of weeks—"

"More like two months. It's been a nightmare."

"I'm sure it has been. And then to add insult to injury, this guy pinches you in a sneaky, vicious way, so you were quite legitimately angry at him."

"Yeah, I was furious." I shrugged self-deprecatingly. "I guess I kind of lost it there. I went a little wild."

"Uh huh," the chief said, and looked at me over those tented fingers. Then he gave one of his little smiles.

But this time I didn't smile back. Instead I looked at him in horror.

Because it finally hit me—too late—what had just happened. I had just handed Chief Walsh a murder motive, all neatly gift-wrapped for his convenience.

The cops had the what, where, and how . . . and now, thanks to me, they had the why.

I stared at Chief Walsh, and realized at last who he reminded me of, with his thin mustache and distinguished silver hair. It was my father. No wonder I'd been so desperate for the chief to believe me. God knows I'd spent large portions of my life desperate for my father's approval.

As I sat there, horrified, I suddenly also realized why I had overreacted so fiercely to Pop's pinch. It wasn't just the pain. My big brother used to pinch me when I was a kid, and my parents never believed me. Drove me nuts.

I felt all of about four years old. First Pop's pinches, and now the chief's smiles, had snuck past my adult defenses.

"I want to make a phone call," I said through clenched teeth.

"By all means. Would you like to use my phone?" the chief asked pleasantly.

The bastard could afford to be pleasant.

He had everything he needed.

7

Andrea answered in the middle of the first ring. "Hello?" she said breathlessly. She'd been crying.

"Honey, I'm okay, but I need a lawyer."

"Where are you? I called the police but they wouldn't tell me!"

"They're a bunch of peabrains. Right now I'm in the office of the chief peabrain of them all." The chief gave me a fake hurt look. How had I ever let this jerk sucker me into liking him?

"Jacob, what in God's name happened tonight?"

"I can't talk right now. I need a lawyer."

Andrea gave a sharp intake of breath, and there was a moment's silence before she asked, "Who should we get?"

"I have no idea. Do we know any lawyers?"

"How about my Uncle Harold?"

"Your Uncle *Harold*? In *Buffalo*? Come on, his specialty is parking garage law."

"Yes, but he might know what to do."

"Only if Pop was killed in a parking garage!" I yelled.

"You don't have to be sarcastic!" she yelled back, then started to cry. "I'm sorry, I'm just so—"

I was in no mood to be a sensitive modern guy. I

interrupted her. "Come on, we *must* know a good lawyer. We're Jewish, for God's sake."

"How about the fat guy who runs that chess club?"

Malcolm Dove. What kind of law did he practice? And was he any good?

I didn't have a clue.

On the other hand, anyone who played chess as well as Malcolm did had to be at least a half-decent lawyer. I'd been trying to beat his Muzio Gambit for over a year now. "Okay," I said, "give Malcolm a call."

"Where will you be tonight?"

I turned to Chief Walsh. "Where will I be tonight?"

"City jail," he replied. "Right down the hall. You'll love it."

And then he smirked at me.

I found out the reason for that smirk several minutes later, when I was escorted to the jail. The maximum security prisons I'd taught in were veritable Club Meds compared to this hellhole. I couldn't believe a jail this barbaric existed in the same building as that venerable meeting room where I'd been earlier tonight—though it now felt like eons ago.

The jail consisted of six identical cages, jammed together against one wall. They were built back when people were shorter, so I couldn't stand up straight in my cage; I had to stoop. The cage was four by six feet, barely big enough to do pushups in. My bed was nothing but a narrow wooden shelf, without blankets or sheets.

Not that I could have slept anyway. The bright fluorescent lights stayed on all night, and the other five cages were full of loud, angry men who'd been busted for "drunk and disorderly" and other lifestyle crimes.

My toilet had no seat, and no flush handle either, so there was nothing that even the most dedicated inmate might be able to break. Instead there was a flush button that you had to kick real hard before it would work, and then it flushed so loud that any drunks who had thankfully fallen asleep would wake up again, yelling about bugs or dental work or whatever else was on their minds. One of them howled incoherently all night long about the Dalai Lama.

A couple of sad sack derelicts were brought in after me, and since the six cages were already full, they spent the night handcuffed to the outside of the cages and crapping in their pants. For entertainment I tried to determine which crap smell came from which derelict.

There wasn't much other entertainment to be had. It was hard to write graffiti, because all of our pens and pencils had been confiscated, I guess so we wouldn't stick them into our foreheads. One guy did manage to scratch "Habib was here" on the wall of his cage with a shirt button, talking to himself in Arabic the whole time; but it took him several hours. I didn't have his stamina.

A couple of my comrades spent the night drunkenly tossing toilet paper through their bars, aiming for the video cameras that pointed toward each cage. They were trying to cover up the lenses. Personally I was grateful to have a lens pointed at me, protecting me from police abuse. But maybe some of the other guys wanted privacy to jack off or something. Anything to pass the time.

Every half hour a cop would come through to make sure no one was slitting his wrist with a pants zipper. The cop and the inmates would trade a few "motherfuckers" back and forth, which was fun for a while, but by around four in the morning it got kind of old.

At 5:30, though, we had fresh excitement. Some cop with bad breath came in, stopped at my cage, and sneered, "So you're the big, tough cop killer, huh? Not feeling so big and tough *now*, are you?"

Immediately the rest of the guys wanted to know all about it. I wasn't really in the mood for sharing, but one of the drunks who came in after me had heard some talk, so he filled everyone in. Suddenly they all brightened up. Habib called out in an Arabic accent, "Two points for our side, my brothers, we *nailed* one of them motherfuckers," and the guys all burst out laughing and cheering.

Somehow they got the idea it was my birthday, so they all sang "Happy Birthday" to me, which segued into "For He's a Jolly Good Fellow," followed by "Take Me Out to the Ballgame." Then the Dalai Lama guy started chanting "Hare Krishna," and we all joined in.

Their happy mood was infectious, and by eight a.m. or so, I was feeling pretty darn good for a guy whose whole world had just fallen apart. Our jailers brought us breakfast, and I never knew that greasy eggs, Wonder bread with margarine, and cold instant coffee could taste so delicious.

An hour later the cops let us out of our cages and marched us up to the courtroom on the first floor to be arraigned. I looked around at Habib and the rest of the fellas. I'd been listening to them ranting, raving, and laughing all night long, but except for the two drunks cuffed outside the cages, I hadn't seen their faces. I was amazed by how young most of them looked. They couldn't have been a day older than twenty-two. Their voices at night were hard and angry; but their faces in the morning light were soft and scared. I tried to guess who had been calling out to the Dalai Lama for help, but it could have been any of them. They all looked like they needed help, and they all looked like the Dalai Lama was as likely as anyone else to help them in this sorry-ass world.

I'd never been to an arraignment before, and I didn't know what to expect. They herded us upstairs through an empty stairway, then opened the back door to the courtroom. I stopped in my tracks and blinked. After a night spent in a tiny cage, this huge, spacious courtroom was a shock. Not only that, there were a hundred or more people sitting in the pews. Who were all these people? What were they doing here?

And where was my wife? Where was my lawyer?

Just then I saw Andrea peeling herself out of a pew and running toward the front railing. My heart filled, and I came forward to embrace her. But the bad-breath cop got in my way. "*Back,*" he barked, and Andrea and I gazed at each other longingly as he corralled me into the jury box with my fellow crimies. I sat down on the hard wooden bench and looked around. Some of my new pals were cracking their knuckles, others were scratching their crotch hairs, and others were giggling insanely. All of us were scared out of our wits.

Meanwhile everyone in the pews stared at us like we were animals in the zoo. I heard a buzz going through the audience, and a bunch of index fingers started pointing in my direction. I guess the word was out on the street, and I was a celebrity now: rich writer turned cop killer. Who knows—maybe I'd get lucky and everyone would break into "For He's a Jolly Good Fellow," then carry me out of the courtroom on their shoulders.

Or maybe not. The front pew was occupied by seven cops with seven identical stone faces and seven identical pairs of well muscled arms folded over seven identical uniformed chests. They were there in force to make sure I got my butt kicked—legally or otherwise. *Where was my lawyer, already?* If someone didn't show up soon, I'd have to represent myself. A frightening prospect.

I gazed at the audience, restraining an impulse to shout, "Is there a lawyer in the house?" None of them looked like lawyers anyway. There were lone men with impossibly greasy hair, burnt-out moms with crying kids, teenage boys wearing earrings and eyebrow rings . . .

And *Tony*. Little Tony, wiping his nose on his shirt in the far corner of the very last pew. I stared at him.

He stared back briefly—*very* briefly—and then turned away from me. What was going on here?

"All rise!"

We all rose. The judge came in and sat down, and we did, too. His Honor was a bald little man; even in his gorgeous to-die-for black robe, he was still a bald little man. But he had a deep bass voice. "The City Court of Saratoga Springs, New York, is now in session. The date is . . ." He squinted at a calendar on the wall, which had "America, Land of the Free" written on it in big letters. *America, Land of the Free.* I had nothing to worry about, did I? I'd get a fair trial, wouldn't I? From the front row, I got seven identical glares. ". . . Friday, October second, and the time is . . ."

The judge kept talking, but I quit listening. *October.* I gazed out the window at the orange and yellow maple leaves fluttering in the distance. I vowed that if I ever made it out of here alive, I'd take time to smell the trees. Or the flowers; whatever I was supposed to smell, I'd smell it.

And I'd make sure to watch *Law & Order* religiously, so if I ever got arraigned again, I'd know what the heck I was supposed to do.

"The People versus Ray Adamson," the judge called out in a stentorian tone. One of the greasy-haired loners slithered out of the audience and stepped nervously in front of the judge, head down, hands folded meekly behind his back. Someone I hadn't noticed before, a tired man in a tired suit, stepped up beside him.

The judge nodded to the tired man, then turned back to the defendant. "Mr. Adamson, I take it you're represented by the public defender's office?"

Adamson shrugged in response. The tired man, evidently the public defender, shrugged too.

"Sir, you're charged with driving while intoxicated, failure to stop at a red light, and driving without a seatbelt. How do you plead?"

Adamson shrugged again. So did his defender.

"Guilty," Adamson mumbled.

"Bail is twenty-five dollars. Pay the city clerk on your way out."

Adamson and the public defender both shrugged yet a third time, then Adamson shuffled out of the courtroom.

"The People versus William Bell," the judge announced. Alphabetical order. That meant I'd be soon. A teenage boy with black, pink, and green striped hair stepped up to the judge and assumed the meek head-down, arms-folded-behind-the-back position. I studied it, to make sure I got it right when it was my turn.

"Mr. Bell," the judge declared, after the public defender stood up too, "you're charged with . . ."—he checked a piece of paper on his desk, then rolled his eyes—". . . rollerblading where you're not supposed to."

A titter went through the audience. Even us hard cases in the jury box smiled.

"How do you plead, Mr. Bell?"

"Guilty."

"Bail is one dollar. Pay the city clerk on your way out. And Mr. Bell, please . . . next time commit a more interesting crime."

The audience tittered louder. "Yes, Your Honor," Bell said, then gave a couple of other teenage boys sitting by the aisle a high five as he highstepped out of the courtroom.

Hey, I thought, this wasn't so bad. I could handle it. Even if they set my bail higher than a buck, it was no sweat, that's what being rich was for. I'd be smelling those trees in no time.

"The People versus Mr. Burns," the judge then announced.

I stood up.

Instantly the courtroom went silent. No more tittering, no more knuckle-cracking. Even the babies stopped crying.

I can handle it.

I stepped up to the judge, trying so hard to feel confident that I forgot to put my head down and act meek. Instead I gave the judge a friendly smile. He frowned at me. "Do you have a lawyer?" he asked.

"I'm not really sure, Your Honor," I replied, smiling even wider, as if it was the funniest thing in the world.

From the pews, Andrea called out, "Your Honor—"

"Silence, please!" the judge's voice boomed angrily.

"But, Your Honor—"

"Silence! Or I'll have you thrown out!"

My wife sat back down in her seat, stunned. Hey, whatever had happened to the wry funny judge who'd kidded the teenage rollerblader? Without even meaning to, my hands went meekly behind my back and my head went down.

As it went down, I saw those ridiculous slippers. I put one foot on top of the other, trying to hide the bright orange "World's Greatest Lover."

But then my penis came flopping out of my pajamas.

Oh, Lord. I quickly hitched up my pajamas to get myself back in there. Had the judge seen it? The last thing I needed was for my shlong to be held in contempt of court.

Fortunately, though, the judge's attention was elsewhere. "Mr. Frick?" he said, and the public defender stepped up. *Frick.* The name fit him like a glove. He gave me a shrug. He was good at that.

The judge turned back to me. His face had gone sour, and he looked like a guy with a killer toothache. "Mr. Burns, you are charged with homicide in the first degree. How do you plead?"

"Not guilty," I said, trying to make my voice ring strong, but all that came out was a sickly little squeak. From the corner of my eye, I saw seven smug smiles.

"Mr. Hawthorne?" the judge said, and another man came up and stood next to Frick. He was wearing a blue suit, nothing fancy, but compared to Frick he looked like an Armani model.

"Mr. Hawthorne, does the D.A.'s office have a recommendation in this case?"

"Yes, we do, Your Honor," Hawthorne declared. "Given the severity of the crime, the overwhelming evidence against the defendant, and the fact that he recently received one million dollars for a single screenplay and thus has sufficient wherewithal to begin a new life elsewhere, the People believe the defendant poses a significant flight risk. We therefore request that bail be set at *ten* million dollars."

"But—" I said.

The judge put out his hand to shut me up, then turned to my intrepid lawyer. "Mr. Frick?"

And darned if Frick didn't just stand there and shrug. I stared at him, openmouthed. A little first-degree homicide sounded like an excellent idea to me right then. *How could I possibly raise ten million bucks?!*

If I understood how bail worked, I'd only need to give the bail bondsman a tenth of that sum. But even so, three hundred K was my absolute upper limit. Three twenty tops, if we took out a second mortgage on the house. This was unbelievable. Was I doomed to spend the next year of my life awaiting trial in some urine-soaked jailhouse basement, sharpening my choral skills with a bunch of hopeless men wearing droopy pants and dabbling in Eastern religions?

"Your Honor!" someone called out, and I spun around.

It was my lawyer at last!

Malcolm Dove came racing up the aisle toward us, all three hundred pounds of him, the floor shaking beneath his weight. The judge raised his thick black eyebrows in annoyance, but before he could speak, Malcolm barreled on. "Your Honor, I have been unconscionably detained by the chief of police on an utterly bogus security check. I was forced to actually remove my shoes to check for a hidden knife. *Preposterous.* Now may I consult with my client, please?"

The judge wrinkled his nose in distaste, but he had no choice. "You have three minutes," he said irritably.

While the judge made a big show of checking the clock, Malcolm pulled me aside.

"Malcolm," I began, "I didn't do it—"

"No time for that," he replied, briskly wiping his forehead with a handkerchief. He was sweating after his long run up the courtroom aisle. But even sweating, red-faced, fat and winded, he still looked somehow dignified—more dignified than that guy Frick would ever look on the best day of his life. Some folks have it, some don't.

"How much money have you got?" Malcolm asked.

I eyed him in amazement. They say lawyers are a money-hungry breed, but this took the cake. "Enough to pay you quite well," I said, fighting to keep my temper.

The fat on Malcolm's chins jiggled as he shook his head impatiently. "Skip that. How much?"

"Three hundred thousand," I answered, still nonplussed.

"Okay. All I need to know." He clapped me on the back. "By the way, *of course* you didn't do it. No one whose favorite chess opening is the Hedgehog Defense would ever have the guts to commit murder."

"Thanks. I think."

Malcolm turned to the judge. "We're ready, Your Honor." The judge eyed him in surprise, then gave a flicker of a smile. It looked like Malcolm had scored points by coming in under three minutes.

"Your Honor," Malcolm intoned, "the People's bail request is way out of line. My client does not represent a flight risk, far from it. He has no police record. He has a wife and two small children. He is a longtime resident of Saratoga Springs with deep roots in the area . . ."

The judge looked bored, like he'd heard this *shpiel* a thousand times before, and I guess he had. He let Malcolm go on for a while longer, then interrupted. "How much money does the defendant have?" he asked.

"Three hundred thousand dollars," Malcolm replied.

"Bail is hereby set at three hundred thousand dollars," the judge declared, rapping his gavel when the District Attorney protested. So I would actually be able to raise the bond money! "Thank you, Your Honor," I said, heaving a huge sigh of relief.

"Hare Krishna!" one of my crimies sang out.

"Hare Krishna!" the rest of the gang shouted.

The judge rapped his gavel again. "The prisoner is ordered remanded to the county jail until such time as bail is posted." The seven cops all stood up at once and grimly escorted me from the courtroom, with three in front of me, two beside me, and two behind. A special honor guard, designed to intimidate. But Andrea somehow broke through their ranks and embraced me.

Just for a moment, though. Then the cops pulled her away.

"I'll go get the bail money together," she called out as the cops led me off. "You'll be out of jail before tonight."

"I'm sorry, sweetie," I called back to her, trying to keep my voice from breaking. "I guess there goes all our fuck-you money."

"That's the least of your worries, *sweetie*," one of the cops said, and the others all snickered. I was about to make a snappy retort when I suddenly spotted Tony, just a few yards away.

It was only for a moment. But from this distance, that moment was long enough to see a hideous black eye and several other cuts and bruises on the boy's face.

Somebody had manhandled him—and I was pretty sure I knew who.

Then Tony ran away and disappeared down the stairs, his floppy tennis shoes beating out a speedy rhythm.

Damn it, I had to talk to that kid.

And soon.

8

But I didn't talk to him soon. And I didn't get out of jail that day, either.

We could have paid some bail bondsman from Albany a thirty-grand fee and I'd have gotten sprung right away. But I managed to reach Andrea from the one public phone that was accessible to prisoners, and I told her I refused to let some inane, trumped-up murder charge eat up thirty thousand dollars of my hard-won nest egg. Even though I was rich now, I still remembered all too well the days when thirty grand represented my entire income for two or three years.

So Andrea had to pull together the whole 300K, and that took her until the next day. Our green stuff was spread among three different mutual funds, meaning three different sets of bureaucrats and factotums for Andrea to nag and yell at. I hope you never need to get money out of mutual funds in an emergency. It ain't pretty.

In retrospect, I shouldn't complain too much about the one night I spent in scenic Ballston Spa County Jail. I wasn't gang raped, and I was only beaten once—painfully but professionally, so as not to leave any marks. I'm not planning to put this event on my highlight reel, so suffice it to say that those guards knew exactly what they were doing. They weren't going to let this rich "cop killer" get off easy.

I had other excitement, too. My boss called from the state prison where I taught and fired me. "As someone who's been arrested for homicide," he explained, "I don't think you'll be a good role model for the men." I didn't attempt to fight him legally, even though I might have had a case. I doubted I'd have the stomach for prison work anytime soon.

It was depressing: First I'd given up writing, at least temporarily, and now I was giving up my teaching job.

I got even more depressed when I opened the *Daily Saratogian* on Saturday morning and read their account of the murder investigation. As I'd surmised, Pop had been shot with his own gun. The police theory went like this: The suspect, Jacob Burns, was awakened late at night by loud noises next door. Furious, he stormed outside to confront the tenants. Lo and behold, he ran into Pop instead. They got into another knock-down, drag-out fight. Having seen Pop's gun come loose from its holster earlier that same night, Burns knew exactly what to do—and he did it. He grabbed Pop's gun and shot him.

I had to admit, it was a good theory.

"But what about fingerprints?" I asked my lawyer, when he came to visit.

Malcolm and I were facing each other in the prison's small, windowless, cinderblock conference room. He shifted his large butt around on the tiny plastic chair. "There were no prints on the trigger," he said, "just smudge marks."

I sensed he wanted to say more, but he didn't, he just sat there fidgeting. "What are you not telling me?" I asked.

"Well," he answered hesitantly, "they did find your prints on the handle."

I started shaking. The cops had actually *planted* my fingerprints on the gun?! But then I remembered. "That's *easy,*" I said excitedly. "The prints are from earlier that night, when I took the gun away from Babe Ruth."

Malcolm sighed. "Yeah, it's just one small detail that we could probably explain away—except there's a whole wagonload of *other* small details. And they add up. The thing is, that confession of yours doesn't help any."

That confession of mine.

The night before, on the 11:00 news—right before I was beaten up—some vacant-faced reporter with a silly mustache had quoted Chief Walsh as saying I'd confessed.

"I told you, Malcolm, *I didn't confess*. It was just some Geraldo Rivera wannabe misquoting the chief!"

"The chief was quoted pretty much the same way on every channel."

I banged my head in frustration. "But why would Walsh lie? Won't he look like an idiot when it comes out I never confessed?"

Malcolm tapped his fingers on the low plastic table. "Even if you didn't exactly confess to the *homicide,* you *did* confess—very stupidly, and on videotape—to having deep-seated homicidal feelings. So like it or not, the chief isn't completely off base. Also, you have to remember what he's doing here. He doesn't care about the truth; it's like with any other high profile case, he just wants to poison the jury pool."

Poison the jury pool? My stomach churned. "You really think this will go to trial?"

"Unless they come up with another suspect, yes."

"But there's all kinds of other suspects! What about his wife and kids? God knows if *I* was stuck living with him, I'd have killed him by now!"

"He didn't have any kids—and his ex-wife is married to a home shopping network mogul in Arizona."

"Okay, then what about Zapper and Dale, the drug dealers? And what about—" I was going to say, "What about Tony?" but stopped. I still wanted to talk to the kid myself first, before the cops or Malcolm or anyone else got to him. "What about all the other people who hated Pop's guts? Maybe the killer was some homeless guy that got sick of Pop popping him all the time!"

Malcolm just shrugged. But I wasn't finished. "Besides, the cops' theory about me killing Pop has huge holes in it! Like, what was Pop doing in that backyard in the wee hours of the morning?!"

Malcolm put his hand on my shoulder. "Don't worry, Jake," he said reassuringly. "We'll get you out of this mess."

But I didn't feel reassured. Malcolm may have been a good lawyer, but he wasn't going out and beating the bushes trying to find the real killer. And God knows the cops weren't doing that either.

Malcolm kept on talking to me, but I stopped listening. It was like he wasn't even in the room anymore. My mind hardened.

I was in deep, deep shit—and there was only one man who could get me out. That man was me.

Screw these bozos. I don't need Malcolm or *the cops.*

I solved that other murder by myself. I can solve this one, too.

Just let me out of jail and I'll do it.

My twenty-nine hours at county weren't totally devoid of entertainment. I got phone calls from several local TV stations and newspapers, as well as *The New York Times, The Los Angeles Times,* and *Variety*. I was flattered to learn that as the screenwriter of the upcoming blockbuster movie *The Gas that Ate San Francisco,* my legal problems were national news. Okay, just a couple of paragraphs on the inside pages, but still.

Maybe I'd have rated more paragraphs, or even cracked Page One, except that I obeyed Malcolm's orders and said my "no comment" mantra to one and all. The only reporter I might have trusted enough to talk to was Judy Demarest from the *Saratogian,* but oddly, she never called.

I did get a call from my agent, though. Andrew and I hadn't talked much in the past several months. He was pissed at me for turning down all the opportunities that had come my way lately, including a highly lucrative offer to rewrite a movie about mutant killer beetles, of all things.

For my part, Andrew represented everything I loathed about Hollywood. And, I suppose, loved.

The last time we'd spoken, Andrew had called me a "fucking nitwit," if I remembered correctly, and I had called him a "pathetic Hollywood whore." But he seemed to remember none of that now. "Jacob, how you doing, buddy?" he boomed into the phone.

"Not too good, Andrew," I replied.

"Yeah, I read all about it, kid! This is *fabulous*!"

"What is?"

"You know how much dough you're gonna make off this murder situation of yours? It'll make that million bucks you got for your last screenplay look like chickenfeed. I've even got the title for your new movie figured out already: *West Side Gory*. What do you think?"

"Look, Andrew, I'm too busy working on my legal defense to think about writing any screenplays."

He didn't miss a beat. "Hey, you'll need money for your defense, right? And if you get convicted, you'll need money for your kids. So you better start working on that screenplay right away. I've already had calls from three studios—"

I hung up on Andrew and asked the guard not to call me to the telephone anymore, just say I wasn't available. I was already getting dirty looks from the other inmates for hogging the phone. I didn't want to give anyone any more excuses for attacking me.

Another good reason for refusing phone calls was that it limited my teary conversations with Andrea. Each time we talked, I just got more upset. Also, my phone boycott enabled me to avoid talking to my father or my three siblings. I wasn't ready to open that whole kettle of emotional worms.

Andrea finally got me out of jail on Saturday afternoon, at 3:59. Just in time, too. One minute longer and I'd have been stuck in there all weekend. When I made it outside, I forgot all about smelling the trees. I just hurried into the safety of our car and buried my face in Andrea's neck. She held me tight and we just sat like that, practically without moving, for about five minutes.

Neither of us spoke. I think we both had a feeling words might reveal something we didn't want revealed. From the undercurrents of our phone conversations, I'd gotten the vibe that she was aggravated at me for getting into this whole mess. And I was aggravated at her for blaming me. I mean, hey, it wasn't my fault Pop got whacked.

Fortunately, Andrea and I had ten years' worth of love in the bank that we could draw on. So we sat there in the parking lot silently holding each other, and we might have sat there even longer except that a van from Channel 6 pulled up and Max Muldoon, my favorite Geraldo Rivera wannabe, knocked on our window.

We immediately drove off, but he followed us home, where two other TV vans were waiting for us, too. It was awfully disconcerting, having those fat microphones shoved in our faces. I tried to say "no comment" in as boring a way as possible, though it was hard to keep a straight face when Muldoon called out, "Jake, is it true Pop Doyle was having an affair with your wife?"

In a way it was good to have the TV guys bothering Andrea and me, because they gave us a common enemy to rant at companionably.

Babe Ruth and Gretzky were at home when we got there, being baby-sat by Lorenzo from across the street. Ordinarily, because of his recent stroke, Andrea wouldn't have trusted him with our kids, but this was an emergency. As soon as I came through the door, both boys ran to me and hugged me so hard my heart almost broke.

I hugged them back so hard their ribs almost broke. "Babe Ruth and Gretzky, I love you guys so much—"

"I'm not Babe Ruth," Babe Ruth said.

"And I'm not Gretzky," Gretzky added.

"You're not?" I asked, befuddled.

"We're Ninja Turtles! I'm Leonardo!" Babe Ruth shouted, and karate chopped me.

"And I'm Raphael!" Gretzky announced, karate chopping me from the other side.

This Ninja Turtle thing was getting out of hand. I mean, their heyday had to be at least a decade ago. Why couldn't my kids be into Pokémon and Power Rangers like all the other kids? I put up my arms to defend myself from their fierce karate moves while Andrea explained, "I forgot to tell you, the boys changed their names."

"We're gonna *get* those bad guys!" Babe Ruth sang out.

"Yeah!" seconded Gretzky. "Let's *kill* 'em!"

I shushed them. "Guys, enough. There's been too much killing and talking about killing lately."

"But we'll *protect* you, Daddy!" declared Babe Ruth, and his little brother chimed in, "Yeah, we won't let them take you back to jail! Watch my new Ninja move!" He did a one-two karate punch combination, and Ruth joined in with some kicks, and between the two of them they smashed an imaginary opponent to bits on the living room floor.

"Boys, come here."

But they weren't listening. They were too busy stomping another invisible bad guy.

"Come here!"

They came. I gathered them in my arms.

"Sweethearts, Daddy's okay now," I said. "I know you're just trying to help me, and that's very sweet, but you don't need to worry anymore. Daddy's not going back to jail again."

"You promise, Daddy?" Babe Ruth asked.

"Yes," I lied. "I promise."

9

And I lied again an hour and a half later. I told Andrea I was going for a little walk around the neighborhood before dinner, to give my legs some post-prison stretching. Where I was really going, though, was Tony's house.

I felt guilty about leaving Andrea and the boys so soon after I came back. But if I wanted to keep that promise to my boys about not going back to jail, I'd better get cracking.

Muldoon was still in front of our house, probably waxing his mustache while he waited, so I slipped out the back door. I vaulted the back fence and cut through our neighbor's yard, then started down Ash Street, planning to double back to Tony's house. But as I passed the Orian Cillárnian Sons of Ireland Hall, I saw Hal Starette of the SERC coming out. I stopped to chat with him.

"Hi, Hal," I said.

He turned toward me and his face instantly turned white, like he was seeing a ghost. Or a murderer. "Hi," he mumbled.

Beyond playing chess together, Hal and I didn't have much of a relationship. But I was starved for some plain old ordinary, uncomplicated human contact. "You gonna play in the Capital District Open next month?" I asked.

"Yeah," he said monosyllabically.

"Me, too. Which division?"

"Dunno," he grunted, and headed for his car.

I tried another conversational gambit. "Everything going okay on the Grand Hotel project?"

This time Hal didn't even favor me with a monosyllable, just nodded his head up and down a couple of times as he quickly got behind the wheel and took off.

Evidently being labeled a murderer was not going to do wonders for my social life, I thought, as I headed for Tony's house. I stepped around the rotten planks on his front porch, with their rusty nails standing tall and shouting *"Watch out! Tetanus!"* as loud as they could. Which of course wasn't very loud. I rang the doorbell, but it was no louder than the nails. So I knocked. Some peeling paint flaked off the door, but except for that, I got no response.

The sky was growing dark, with a full moon hanging down low. It was a perfect night for werewolves and madmen. My recent jail time must have made me jumpy, because I suddenly had an awful premonition. *"Tony!"* I shouted, pounding on the door. *"To-nee!"*

But still I got no answer, except for an urgent pounding in my chest. I threw my shoulder at the door. No go. I threw my other shoulder at the door—still no go.

I ran to the front window and pushed upward. It made a token effort at resistance, but then it gave. I quickly climbed in.

I found myself inside a darkened living room that smelled like death. Or not death exactly, more like a mixture of stale socks, stale cigarettes, stale excrement, and . . . what was that other odor? *Peppermint?* Some kind of air freshener, I guess. Nice to know someone cared. But even the air freshener smelled stale, and it did nothing to ease my premonition. A sliver of light showed underneath the door to the kitchen. I hurried to the door, opened it, and went in. Then I stopped.

Three people were sitting on the kitchen floor. One of them was Tony's mom. She was thin as a rail and buck naked, and she must have been awfully cold on that chipped linoleum floor. But maybe she was too high to notice. Right now she was taking another hit off a glass crack pipe.

Sitting beside her and eagerly reaching out for the pipe was a scruffy-looking man of indeterminate age with an eye patch, a dirty leather jacket, and heavy boots. Next to him was another man who looked about the same, except his pants were down around his ankles. Interestingly, he was wearing boxer shorts.

Looked like a great party.

As Tony's mom handed the pipe to Eye Patch, she looked over at me. Surprise, then fear, then annoyance registered in her bloodshot eyes. She waved at me to get the hell out of there.

Which I would gladly have done, except the guy with the rolled-down pants picked that moment to turn his head. He spotted me.

"Fuck you want?" he snarled, no doubt vexed that I might want to share the crack, or the woman. Then he pulled a gun from his jacket pocket and pointed it at me.

"Sorry, guys, just passing through," I said, as cheerily as I could. "Guess I'll be on my way."

"Fucking answer me!" Gunman yelled, jumping up and waving his weapon. Meanwhile Eye Patch was glowering at me with his one good eye, obviously furious that I had interrupted him just when he was about to take a hit.

I turned to Tony's mom for support. She was still sitting there on the floor. "Hi, Mrs. Martinelli," I gulped. "Or Ms. or Miss," I added inanely. "I was looking for Tony."

Gunman glared at me, then at her. "Tony?! Who the fuck is Tony?"

"Nobody. Just my son," his mom said impatiently. "He's not here."

"Do you know where he is?" I asked, not expecting an answer really, but not knowing how to get out of the conversation gracefully. If I ever run into Miss Manners on the street, I'll have to ask her what to do in a situation like this.

Fortunately, Gunman was able to rise to the social occasion. "No, she don't know, fuckface. Now get out before I bust your ass!" he said, advancing on me.

I backed up. Tony's mom didn't say anything, and neither did Eye Patch. He just fired up his pipe.

As I started out the door, Gunman turned back toward his friends and put away his gun. He curved his lips into a tight, hard smile, looking forward to his turn with the pipe, and with the local sex goddess.

I was glad Tony wasn't at home right now to witness this. I had to get that poor kid out of this hellhole. Permanently.

Eagerly sucking in the fresh outside air, I stepped around those nails on the porch and started searching the neighborhood for Tony. I looked in Arcturus, the local pizza joint, and a couple of other likely places, but he was nowhere to be found.

Then it occurred to me that Tony might actually

be at my house, since that seemed to be his home away from home these days. So I headed back there. I was happy to see that all the TV vans were gone; probably the media folk were out enjoying nice expense account dinners on Broadway. I'd be able to sail right through our front door without harassment.

But when I came to the infamous house next door, I stopped. One of our friendly neighborhood crack dealers, Zapper, was sitting on the front steps drinking beer. His eyes hit mine briefly, and then he aimed them over my head, just like always. With his Tyson-like muscles and sullen, dead-eyed scowl, Zapper would make a perfect henchman in a Ninja Turtle video.

Zapper. Interesting name. Who or what had he zapped in order to get it?

And what exactly did "zapping" mean, anyway?

Sometimes he shared his tiny apartment for days at a time with a black woman in her early twenties and two small infants. I hadn't seen them the night Pop got murdered, but I sure remembered seeing Zapper. When the cop sirens filled the street, he'd come out on his front steps along with his twitchy colleague, Dale.

Had either of these two fine, upstanding young men seen anything that night? I was desperate for Zapper to open up to me. If only I could do some male bonding with this drug dealing creep. I pointed at his beer. "Colt 45. My favorite."

Zapper just kept staring vaguely over my head. I followed his gaze. "Nice moon," I said.

Silence.

"You see that bright star?" I prattled on. "That's a planet, actually. Jupiter."

Zapper didn't seem overly impressed by my astronomical knowledge. So much for male bonding.

Maybe if I watched more Miller commercials, I'd be better at it.

But what the hell should I do now? Goddamn it, I *needed* this scumbag. He might know something that could keep me out of jail. On a sudden impulse, so sudden I didn't even know I was doing it until it was already done, I stepped right up to Zapper, real close, so close he couldn't look over my head anymore unless he put his neck so far back he'd get whiplash. Then I hissed between my teeth, "What did you see that night?"

Finally Zapper looked at my face. Score one for my side. But his voice stayed blasé. "What night?" he said, bored. Then he took a vicious-looking knife out of his pocket, some kind of hunting knife. He opened it up and began ostentatiously cleaning his fingernails.

Talk about overkill. I mean, with those monster muscles of his, what did the guy need a knife for? I was so mad, I ignored the darn thing. Hey, after staring down so many gun barrels lately, the knife seemed downright nonviolent. "Listen, *asswipe,*" I said, "you were home that night, and your window faces the backyard. I think you looked out there when you heard screaming. I think you know who killed Pop."

Zapper just lifted his thumb and inspected the nail for dirt. His forearms were thicker than my thighs. If size was all it took, he could have hit more home runs than Mark McGwire.

"Or maybe you killed him yourself," I went on. "Maybe that's why you're scared shitless." He didn't actually look scared, shitless or otherwise, but hopefully I could rile him into talking.

And the truth was, maybe Zapper really *did* kill Pop. After Tony, he was my best suspect. What if

Pop caught Zapper selling crack and tried to bust him?

Or what if they had a landlord-tenant dispute that turned physical?

Or—

"I know you," Zapper said quietly, and finally focused straight into my eyes.

We gazed intently at each other for a few moments. What the heck, maybe I should give the male bonding thing another whirl. "Sure, you know me. I live right next door. My younger boy is just a little older than your kids."

Zapper nodded thoughtfully. "Yeah, I know you. You the dickhead keeps calling the cops on me."

I nodded politely back. "Yeah. And you're the dickhead sells drugs and abuses his wife and children." I suppose this *was* male bonding of a sort, though it would never make it as a beer commercial.

"Bitch ain't my wife. Think I'd marry that ho?"

"Let me ask you something. Do you hate me so much that you want me to go to jail for a murder I didn't do?"

"Don't hate you, man. Just plain don't give a ladybug's ass about you."

"What about my kids? You've seen them around, playing hockey on our driveway. You want them to grow up fatherless?"

"Fuck your kids." He grinned at me, showing a couple of gold caps. "Yo, bro, you mind getting out of my way? You blocking my moonlight. An' Jupiter, too. *Shee-it.*" He slapped his knee and started chortling. "Man tries to be my friend, tells me about fucking *Jupiter.*"

He thought that was utterly hysterical, and his body shook with laughter—which was his mistake. I was beyond desperate, and hearing this pimple on the face of humanity get witty at my expense just sent me over the edge.

Zapper was so busy cracking up, he let down his guard. Using the roundhouse karate kick my children had taught me, I thrust my leg out sharply—and kicked the knife right out of his hand.

It went flying into the bushes. Zapper jumped up to grab it, but I was already standing and it was no contest. I grabbed the knife and pointed it at his chest. My Ninja Turtle sons would have burst with pride. My wife would have flipped. *Macho man returns!*

Zapper backed up, eyes widening with panic. I had a sudden flash that for all his trash talking and all his henchman muscles, the guy was still nothing but a punk. Maybe he was a brave man with a gun in his hand, I couldn't say, but without it he was just a 250-pound weakling. "Sit down, turkey," I spat out. He stumbled on the steps and sat down.

I stood there brandishing the knife and panting with rage, feeling like I was foaming at the mouth. What the hell had gotten into me? Leftover adrenaline from getting beaten up by those guards? Whatever, it sure was fun being the one holding the weapon for a change. Poor Zapper better hope my kids weren't watching out the window, or they were liable to come outside and stomp him into the sidewalk.

"Yo, chill, man," Zapper whimpered. "I was just funning you, that's all."

"You better tell me what happened that night," I snarled, "or I'll stick this knife from your belly button straight through to your asshole." *Not bad,* I thought to myself. That time in jail had clearly sharpened my dialogue.

"I didn't see *nothing,* man!"

"Then you're one dead motherfuck—" I began, but I was stopped by a voice from behind me. "What's going on here?" it rumbled.

I didn't need to turn around to recognize that voice. Shit, it was *Dave the cop*. And here I was, holding a lethal knife and threatening murder.

This probably wouldn't do wonders for my legal defense.

My back was still to Dave. Had he seen the knife? I wasn't sure. Holding it close to my body and out of his sight, I sidled up next to some overgrown juniper bushes. "What're you doing?" Dave demanded hotly.

I flicked my wrist, and the knife flew deep into the brush and disappeared. Then I turned back around. "Hey, Dave, what's up?"

Zapper found his voice again, big time. "Officer, this muthafucka had a knife!" he screamed.

"A knife?" I said incredulously. "What in the world are you babbling about?"

"He just threw it over there, Officer!" Zapper yelled, pointing. "And he talking some crazy shit, about he gonna *kill* my ass!"

I rolled my eyes. "Dave, I don't know what this guy's problem is—"

"Jake, you *idiot*!" Dave snapped. "Intimidating a witness?! Where do you think *that's* gonna get you?!" Waving his arm disgustedly, he motioned for me to follow him across the street. "Come here."

Come *where*?

I didn't move. My feet wouldn't let me. *Intimidating a witness*—that sounded bad. Real bad.

Was I going back to jail?

Was I going back to jail, less than two hours after promising my boys it would never happen again?

"Dave, I'm not going back to jail."

Even in the dim light from the street lamp, I could still make out Dave's ice-cold glare. "Get over here. *Now.*"

Terrified and zombie-like, I moved slowly across the street toward him. Macho Man was a distant memory. Behind me Zapper laughed.

Dave opened his car door and got in. I was supposed to get in, too. I wondered, was he carrying his gun? I hadn't seen it. Suddenly I had a wild, overwhelming urge to run away as fast as I could down Elm Street. There were forty bucks in my pocket—one buck for every year of my life. Maybe I could escape down to Mexico. I'd write another hack screenplay and sell it under a pseudonym, live in comfort in some forgotten Mexican beach town. Now was my last chance. *Run, Jake, run! Just do it!*

I opened the door to Dave's car and got in. He started up the engine.

"Where are we going?" I stammered.

Dave pulled out of his driveway and headed down the street. When he finally spoke, I was thrown by the fury in his voice. "Why'd you do it, you fool? We're talking class-A, no-fucking-around *felony*. I got no choice. I have to bring you in."

He turned right, heading down Washington Street toward the police station—and jail.

"But, Dave—"

"And not only that—"

"I was just—"

"You should've read the fine print on your bail agreement. Because if you intimidate a witness, your bail is immediately revoked."

What? Revoked?!

A year or two awaiting trial in the Ballston Spa County Jail, surrounded by bored, sadistic guards? I'd hang myself by my bathrobe belt.

This was just too bizarre. I mean, I was a *millionaire,* for God's sake, an honest-to-God Hollywood hotshot. In less than three months, a major motion picture that I wrote would be opening in malls all across America . . . and I would never get to see it.

Or maybe I'd see it in three years, if whatever prison I was in at that point got HBO. "*Dave,*" I said, my voice shaking, "I did not commit this murder."

"That doesn't matter—"

"But your brilliant little police department thinks I did! They're not even bothering to look for other suspects, that's why I have to do it myself! And I wasn't *intimidating* the guy—"

"Cut the crap, Jacob, I *saw* you throw that knife!"

Oh, jeez. "It wasn't my knife," I said plaintively, "it was his, he was threatening me with it."

"Sure, the whole thing was his fault—"

"Look, what do you want me to do?!" I exploded. "Lie down and roll over and let the entire Saratoga Springs Police Department fuck me up the ass?"

"That's not—"

"Sure it is! Admit it, if by some fluke you and your buddies screwed up and actually found the real murderer, the chief would have a heart attack! He's on record saying I *confessed* to the killing. Don't tell me that doesn't put a little *damper* on your so-called *investigation*!"

Dave stared straight ahead. Except for a grimly set jaw, he gave no sign that he even heard my outburst. He turned onto Broadway. The police station *cum* jail was just three blocks away.

"If I don't find out who really killed Pop, I'll spend the rest of my life in a small cage!"

Two blocks.

"Will you please *look* at me, and tell me to my face that you believe I committed murder!"

But he didn't look at me.

One block.

"Come on, I'm just a regular guy with a wife and two kids and a minivan! I even helped you *solve* a murder, Dave! Or have you *forgotten*?!"

We were there. He parked at the police entrance.

"You lame excuse for a cop, LOOK AT ME!"

Finally he looked. And then he spoke—softly, almost tenderly. "Jake, I've been a cop for a long time. And I've learned the simplest, best thing for everyone is to just play it by the book."

"Dave," I whispered, "I'm innocent."

"You don't know how many people have told me that—"

I touched his arm. "But this time it's true."

He moved his arm away. "What can I tell you? A cop's been killed. I'm taking you in."

He got out of the car and came over to my side, to get me out. I sank down into my seat. Maybe if I sank low enough, he wouldn't find me.

Then I saw someone with distinguished silver hair come walking up the sidewalk toward us. Oh great, the chief—just what I needed to make my day complete. I sank even lower.

"What's the word, Dave?" Chief Walsh asked. "You looking for dirt on Burns, or you just sitting on your ass as usual?"

Christ, here it comes. I waited, trembling.

Dave didn't answer right away. Then finally he said, "Yeah, I'm working on it, Chief."

I blinked. What the . . . ?

Dave got back in the car. *"Stay down,"* he ordered me in a low hiss, out of the side of his mouth.

I stayed down, all right.

He pulled away from the curb. "Fuck the chief," he said. "I'm bringing you home."

10

"Thanks," I said, when my voice returned.

"Yeah, yeah, I'm a damn idiot. Just don't tell the chief, he'll can my ass in a second. Be fifteen years' pension shot to shit, and I'm still not sure you didn't do it."

"*I'm* sure."

He grunted and turned right on Washington, toward the West Side and home. I started breathing a little more normally.

"So who do you think *did* do it?" I asked. "If it wasn't me, that is." Personally, my money was still on Tony, but I kept that to myself.

Instead of answering, Dave asked, "How about offering a reward?"

I snorted. "You mean like O.J. did? Or JonBenet Ramsey's parents? If I offer a reward, it'll just make me look even guiltier."

Dave nodded thoughtfully and chewed on his lips as we drove past the Grand Hotel. I noticed a couple of construction trucks and a big sign: CURRENTLY UNDER RENOVATION. It sure hadn't taken them long to get started.

Meanwhile Dave was silent for so long I wondered if he'd forgotten my question. But at last he said,

"The truth? About who killed Pop? Could've been a lot of people."

"Like who?"

We turned onto Elm. The media types were still off at dinner. We parked in front of Dave's house, and he lit a cigarette. "I didn't know you smoked," I said.

"I don't." He took a deep drag. "Look, do you know how many houses Pop owns—owned—on the West Side?"

I added them up in my head. "Four?"

"No. Seven. And three of them have crack dealers for tenants. Far as I can tell, there's no other dealers on the entire West Side. Interesting, huh?"

It took a moment, but then I caught on. "So you're telling me the dealers who rented from Pop got a break? Like, bribing him for protection was part of the rent?"

"No, I'm not telling you that. I'm a cop. I would never say something like that about a fellow cop." He flicked an ash into the tray. "You, on the other hand, can say anything you want."

All my available brain cells raced into action. This would explain what Pop was doing at Zapper's house that night: collecting his payoff money.

And it could explain some other things, too. My head swam with possibilities. Say Pop and Zapper got into an argument—maybe Zapper didn't have the money ready. Pop gets pissed, and pops Zapper one. Zapper screams. Pop pops him again.

Just like me, Pop figures out that musclebound Zapper is really nothing but a scared punk. So he has fun with him. Only Pop makes a big mistake: He gets careless with his gun. Zapper grabs it—

Dave was talking again. "Now Pop's other houses, well, one of them has three girls living there. With a wide variety of men stopping by for about thirty minutes at a time, if you catch my drift."

"You're kidding. I didn't know Saratoga was big enough to have prostitutes."

"They're the only ones I know of in the whole town."

"Interesting. Another monopoly."

"Right. And then Pop owned another house where trucks pull up at strange hours of the night and load and unload boxes."

"So that makes five crooked houses so far."

"Right again. As for houses six and seven, your guess is as good as mine. Who knows, they might even be kosher. Though I doubt it."

"Can I bum a cigarette?" I asked.

"I didn't know you smoked."

"I don't." He gave me a cigarette and we went through the lighting ritual. I took a drag and felt the nicotine go to my head, reminding me of my younger days. Then I asked, "Have you done anything about all this?"

His voice took on a mock-formal tone. "I reported all suspicious activities to the foot patrolman responsible for the area."

"In other words, to Pop."

"Correct. When he failed to act, I spoke to the lieutenant in charge of the Investigative Division."

Lieutenant Foxwell. "What did he do?"

"He also failed to act. So I went to the chief."

We sat in the dark car smoking. "Let me guess. He didn't do shit."

"No, he *did* do shit. He reprimanded me for making scattershot accusations of my fellow men in blue. Said I was obviously just jealous that Pop got the community patrol job and I didn't. Then he informed me my behavior was bad for department morale, and

I better shut up and walk straight or I was history." Dave coughed. "I hate cigarettes," he said, and put his out in the ashtray.

I put mine out, too. Babe Ruth—I mean, Leonardo—knew that cigarettes kill people, and if I took up smoking again, he'd freak. "So the chief and the lieutenant were getting a piece of Pop's action, huh?"

"I would never say something like that about a fellow cop—"

"Yeah, I get the picture. But then who do you think killed Pop? Was it Zapper? Or some other sleazy tenant?"

"That's one possibility." Something about the way Dave said this made me stare sharply at him. His face had twisted into a sarcastic grimace with curled lips and bitter eyes. I didn't get it. What was that look saying? What was I missing?

Then his face changed again. It filled with fear.

"Dave—"

"Shh! Under here!" he barked out, and threw a coat on top of me. I wondered if he'd gone loony tunes all of a sudden, but as I started to remove the coat I spied a cop car approaching on my right. I ducked back under the coat and slumped down as low as I could while the car pulled up alongside.

Dave rolled down his window. "How's it going, big guy?" he asked.

"Just cruising," the other cop said, with a familiar, hateful drawl. It was Manny Cole, the cop with the busted nose who had almost gouged my eyeballs out. "They let that cop-killing bastard out of jail today."

"Yeah, I heard," Dave answered.

"Fucking pathetic. We're gonna keep an eye on him, drive by his house a hundred times a day. We catch him intimidating witnesses, drinking beer on his porch, hell, we even catch him *jaywalking,* we'll throw his sorry ass back in jail, *keep* him there this time."

"Sounds good. I'll look out the front window of my house, see if I can nail him at something."

There was a hard edge in Cole's voice as he said, "Good man. I told the chief we could count on you."

"Damn straight."

"Yeah, I told him, I don't care what color the man's skin is, he's still a team player."

"We're all wearing blue, my man."

Finally Cole drove on. When he turned left and disappeared, Dave said, "Get out of the car."

I opened the door, then paused. "Look, what did you mean before by 'That's one possibility'? What are you hiding from me?"

"Get out already. He might turn around and come back."

Good point. I jumped out of the car and headed across the street. Then Dave called out, "Listen, Jacob."

I turned. "Yeah?"

"Just so we're clear. If we ever get in a situation where it's my ass or yours . . ."

I nodded. "It's mine. Thanks for the tip," I said, and walked back to my house.

When I came in the front door, Andrea looked like she didn't know whether to hug me or wring my neck.

"I thought you were just going on a little walk! You've been gone more than an *hour*!" she snapped. The boys were quarreling loudly in the other room about who got to play with their favorite Donatello action figure. "We've been waiting dinner for you. The kids are *starving*. Where the hell were you?"

"I was just stretching my legs and airing my brain. After all that time in jail, I needed it."

She glowered at me. "You're lying, aren't you?"

I was the picture of innocence. "What do you mean?"

"You were out somewhere playing Colombo!"

"Hey—"

"Look, the last time you played this game, you almost got yourself killed! Don't be stupid, let Malcolm do his job! Isn't it bad enough that you . . ."

She paused. And it hit me like a five-ton weight: Maybe what she wanted to say was, *Isn't it bad enough that you killed Pop?!*

"Isn't it bad enough that you beat up Pop in the first place?" she said.

I took a deep breath, as the five tons fell away from me. I wondered, should I tell my faithful wife what was *really* going on?

No—there was nothing she could do to stop me, and it would just make her worry even harder.

I touched her arm and looked earnestly into her eyes. "Andrea, I just needed to go for a walk. That's all. You don't know what it's like, being caged up for two whole days."

She fell for it. Immediately contrite, she threw her arms around me. "I'm sorry, honey. Wait 'til you see dinner. I made you salmon, artichokes, and fresh cornbread."

I felt like a jerk for making Andrea believe my lies. But all I said was "Mmm."

And there, at least, I was being truthful. Dinner was *mmm* in the first degree. After the kids got food into them, they were on their best behavior, and we had a pleasant evening playing with Ninja Turtles, drawing Ninja Turtles, and wrestling like Ninja Turtles.

My sons' fascination with the Turtles could be wearying. But on the positive side, I had to admit that those pizza-loving amphibians were definitely cool—much cooler than all the other protectors of the universe that have come along since then. You can tell just from the names. I mean, who would you rather have saving the world: "X-Men," "Power Rangers," "Beetle Borgs," or "Teenage Mutant Ninja Turtles"? Clearly there's no contest. Turtle power forever!

It was a surprisingly peaceful night, largely because Andrea had changed our phone number and kept it unlisted to ward off Hollywood agents, media mugwumps, and other undesirables. I decided not to let my father and siblings know our new number until tomorrow or the next day. Hopefully, by then I'd have the energy to talk to them.

We let the kids stay up late, so when Andrea and I finally hit the sack I was dog tired. I hadn't slept much in jail, and I wasn't really in the mood for lovemaking, I just wanted to be held.

Or so I thought. After a few minutes of being held, I started feeling differently. We made love for a long time, first with great gentleness but then fiercely, as though we were trying to break through all the anger and guilt that had arisen between us.

I didn't want it to ever end. I wanted to be inside Andrea, safe and loved, for the rest of my life.

But that was impossible, of course. After we finished making whoopee, despite my wild raw emotions I fell asleep instantly.

And woke up with a start at four a.m.

No, for once it wasn't the neighbors waking me up, or gunshots either. It was a nightmare, about being stuck in a deep muddy swamp and thrashing around like crazy but sinking lower and lower into the goo. I called out desperately to the Teenage Mutant Ninja Turtles to save me.

Sure enough, a giant Turtle did rise up out of the muck, but he looked suspiciously like Chief Walsh, with gray eyes and distinguished silver hair above his green Turtle nose. He saw me sinking into the goo and laughed. Then his face transformed into a regular snapping turtle without any hair, but with teeth as big as an alligator's. He snapped his iron jaws at me, making a deep *BOOM* sound like someone beating a drum. I flailed my arms wildly, struggling to escape the mud, but I just got stuck even worse. All I could do was watch in terror as the snapping turtle crawled closer, working his huge jaws and *BOOM BOOM BOOMING* until he was just inches away and I woke up, damp with sweat, and realized it was my own fiercely beating heart I'd been listening to.

I lay in bed for a while with my nerves all jangled up until I figured out there'd be no more sleep for me tonight. Then I put on my jacket and headed outside. It was still dark. Good—I didn't want any cruising cops or news hounds to spot me.

It was freezing cold, the coldest it had been since last March, so I stuffed my hands in my pockets as I walked briskly toward Tony's house. In the moonlight, I saw the rusty nails on his porch and stepped around them.

Was the crack-fueled orgy still going on, or was everyone postcoital and mellow? Only one way to find out. I tried the door but it was still locked. So I lifted up the window, hopped over the sill into the putrid-smelling living room—

And immediately tripped over Tony's mom's nude body.

Damn! Why does it always have to be me *finding the dead bodies?*

I bent over her but didn't hear any breathing. I put my hand on her neck but didn't feel any pulse. I gave her a little kick in the gut.

"Ugh," she said, then went back to sleep.

Thank God. I left her lying there and did reconnaissance in the rest of the house, stepping softly in case Eye Patch and Gunman were still in residence. But I didn't see them. No Tony, either.

I went back to the living room and shook Tony's mom on the shoulder, averting my eyes from her emaciated-looking breasts. She didn't move, so I shook harder; still nothing. Then I went back to my old standby and kicked her gently in the gut. She went back to *her* old standby, saying "Ugh" and falling back asleep. But this time she threw in a new twist: While she was sleeping, she puked on the rug.

Call me heartless if you want, but I kicked her yet again. At last she opened her eyes slightly.

"Where's Tony?" I asked.

"Hell should I know?" she mumbled, and fell back asleep. I slapped her face. Her eyes reopened, a tad wider this time, but still zonked-looking.

I put my face close to hers, hoping she wouldn't throw up again. "When did you last see him?"

"Who?"

"Tony."

"Why you want him?" A hint of craftiness crept into her hollow eyes. Now that she was opening her mouth more, her breath almost knocked me out—a fascinating combo of puke, potato chips, and rotten teeth. "You a fucking pervert?"

How sweet. She was actually showing some protective maternal instincts. Would wonders never cease?

I tried to act very matter of fact, as if reasoning with a drugged-out, depraved sicko was no big deal to me. "Mrs. Martinelli," I said, moving even closer, but wrinkling my nose so I wouldn't breathe in too much of her decay, "your son is in big trouble."

She gave me a perplexed look, and I reminded myself to speak in short, simple sentences. "Someone may be trying to hurt him. He may have witnessed a murder." *And he may have* committed *a murder,* I thought, but didn't say it out loud. "I need to know where he is. I want to help him." *And myself.*

Tony's mom lay there for a while opening and closing her jaw. I thought she was trying to say something, but then vomit came forth and spilled on her chin.

I looked around in the darkness for something to clean her off with. I found an old one-eared stuffed bunny rabbit, and used the ear to wipe her. Some of the puke had dribbled off of her chin onto the top of her breast. I gingerly wiped that, too.

She opened her mouth again. I stepped back, expecting more puke. But this time she said, "Cemetery."

"Cemetery?!" Jesus, was the kid *dead*? Had he died while I was in jail, and no one even told me?!

"Sleeps there . . . sometimes," Mrs. Martinelli said weakly, using every last bit of her strength getting those three words out.

I eyed her in disgust. How could she let her young son go sleep in the cemetery while she sat around getting high?

She seemed to know what I was thinking, and she looked up at me from the floor. It was a look that if you painted it everyone would say it was brilliant, and it would be displayed prominently in some big-city museum—but nobody would ever in a million years want it on their living room wall. Her look was composed of equal parts guilt, fear, exhaustion, and an overwhelming sorrow. Like she knew she was a shitty mother and a shitty person to boot, and she hated it, but she also knew she could never change it.

Then she closed her eyes and fell asleep.

I tore the puke-covered ear off the bunny and threw it in the overflowing garbage can. I found a towel on top of the refrigerator that was only partly dirty, and draped it over Mrs. Martinelli's thin breasts.

Then I stepped out the door and headed for the cemetery.

11

The historic Gideon Putnam Burial Ground is Saratoga Springs's oldest cemetery. If it were located on the East Side, it would be a major tourist attraction. Since it's not, it isn't.

But even though the city spends virtually no money on upkeep—or maybe because of that—the cemetery has a wonderful disheveled charm. When you push aside the overgrown weeds and read the crumbling gravestones, the names instantly transport you back to an earlier time: "Hosea Samuel Prescott" . . . "Hester Eliza Budd." My personal favorite is "Edward Augustus Rutledge," a Baptist minister who shot himself at the Adirondack Springs Hotel in 1846. Now he's buried across the street from Rite-Aid.

Sometimes I cut through the cemetery on my way to town in the morning. If it's before eight o'clock I usually come across a derelict or two curled up asleep, using a gravestone for shelter from the wind. By eight-thirty or nine, you can generally find the derelicts sitting propped up against the stones, having their first cigarette of the day, or their first drink. I guess these were the same folks who would be sleeping at the Grand Hotel, once it got renovated.

Right now it was a little before five, still dark, and even colder than before. The wind knifed right through my denim jacket. I walked from one corner of the cemetery to the other without spotting Tony or anyone else. I guess the derelicts had felt the weather turning last night, and found shelter indoors.

The wind was attacking the trees, and leaves were committing hari-kari all around me. Shivering, I crisscrossed the cemetery twice more with no luck. The sky was slowly lightening. It looked like Tony's mom was wrong—the only people here were the dead ones.

Unless . . .

Old Gideon Putnam himself was buried atop the highest hill in the cemetery, in a large family plot surrounded by a ten-foot-high stone wall. There was a locked gate that I'd tried to get through once and found impossible. But had Tony, petty criminal that he was, somehow found a way to break in?

I walked up the hill and peered through the gate. I didn't see anyone, but maybe Tony was huddled against a wall out of view. I rattled, pushed, and pulled the gate, then gave up on that and circumnavigated the wall in search of a decent foothold. But there were none; the wall was made of smooth stone, and impregnable. No way Tony could have climbed in. I took one last look through the gate and started to leave.

But then the wind let up for a moment and I heard a tiny noise coming from inside the Putnam family plot, a repetitive *click click click.* It was so faint that at first I wasn't even sure I was hearing it. *Click click click.* What *was* that, anyway? Just a trapped leaf flicking against a tombstone, or something else?

"Tony!" I called out. "Tony, are you in there?"

There was no answer, just more *click click clicking.*

Then the wind picked up again and I couldn't hear it anymore. I stood there straining my ears, so cold my teeth started chattering.

When they chattered, they made a sound. *Click click click.*

I shouted Tony's name some more. Then I circled the wall again and found a corner where the stones were a tad rougher and the masonry work a tad sloppier. I scrambled upward, squirming, clawing, scraping my palms raw, and falling flat on my ass five times. But eventually, somehow, I hoisted myself to the top of the wall. I looked down.

Tony Martinelli lay on the ground beneath me, sleeping.

I jumped ten feet down and bent over him. All he had was a sweatshirt and a thin cotton blanket. His teeth were playing a cha-cha. I touched his hand. Ice-cold.

With sleeping conditions like these, no wonder the kid had a perpetual runny nose. I sighed and did the noble thing, taking off my jacket and setting it on top of him. Then I lay down beside him, as much for my own warmth as for his.

Tony's eyes opened. He saw me, and turned wide awake in about a hundredth of a second. He sat up.

"Mr. Burns! How'd you find me?"

"Your mom told me."

At the mention of his mother, Tony's face darkened. Then he turned away from me and started picking his nose. In the pre-dawn light I could see that most of his bruises were gone. But the discoloration from that black eye remained.

"Tony," I said softly, "I saw you that night. I saw you running away from the house."

He took his finger from his nostril and examined

it. "I know." He sounded very far away. "When you looked at me in the courtroom, I could tell."

"Tony . . ." I took his hand. "What happened that night?"

"I'm cold."

I covered him up with the blanket. It was torn and full of holes. I put my jacket back over him too, then put my arms around him. His body stiffened. I rubbed his back.

He gazed up at me. "Do you want to put your thing in me?"

I wasn't sure I'd heard him right. *"What?"*

"You can put your thing in me if you want."

Oh, Lord.

What unspeakable horrors had this boy been subjected to in his nine years of life? No doubt they made my two days in jail look like a springtime walk in the park.

"No, Tony, I don't want to put my thing in you."

His body relaxed. I gave him a hug. He started to cry, then he sneezed, and pretty soon his face was full of snot and tears. He wiped them with the blanket.

"I'm so sorry, Mr. Burns." He begged me for forgiveness through moist brown eyes. "I'm so, so—"

"It's okay—"

"No, it's not!" he blurted out vehemently. "I know you didn't kill him! You went to jail because of me!"

You went to jail because of me. Was Tony about to confess to murder?

I felt joy and terror at the same time—joy for my sake, terror for his. My voice shook. "Tony, what happened that night?"

He blew his nose into the blanket.

"You need to tell me. I promise I won't hurt you."

Like hell I wouldn't. If he confessed, I'd rat him

out to the cops. I'd pay for his lawyer and visit him every week—but I'd turn him in, no question.

This was incredibly screwed up.

"Okay, Mr. Burns," Tony said gravely, "I'll tell you."

Tony, watch out, I'm your enemy! part of me screamed. But silently, of course.

"What happened, I went to that house next door to you to buy some . . . some . . ." In the thin gray light, the boy's face flushed with shame. "Some crack. For my mom." His words poured out in a torrent. "Look, I *know* it's bad, I *know* drugs are terrible and everything, but you don't know how she gets. She runs around screaming like some kind of animal, and I'm scared she'll kill herself, or maybe me! She'd do it, too! I *have* to buy the drugs! I *have* to!"

"It's okay, Tony, I understand." *Sure, I understand, now spill your guts to me, kid.* I felt like an utter slimeball.

"See, my mom doesn't like to buy the crack herself 'cause she's embarrassed. And she gets, like, afraid to leave the house. So I do it for her."

I nodded, as if that sounded like the most sensible arrangement in the world. His face held something I couldn't decipher at first, then realized it was *pride.* Pride that he was taking good care of his mom. That he was being such a good son.

"So that night I went over to Dale's apartment . . . do you know how him and Zapper work it?" I shook my head, so Tony proceeded to enlighten me. He looked proud again, this time of his knowledge. He might not be too hot when it came to reading and writing, but at least he was getting a solid education in drug dealing. "On odd days, like the first or third of the month, you go to Dale's apartment and give him five dollars. Then he goes over to Zapper's apartment and gets the rock and brings it back to you. On even days it's the opposite—you go to *Zapper's* place, and he gets the rock from Dale. I guess keeping the money in a different place from the drugs is better somehow, if the cops come and try to arrest them."

Some other time I might be interested in the inner workings of the street-level drug economy, but not now. "So you went to Dale's place?" I prodded.

"Yeah. I gave him four bucks, and promised to give him the other dollar tomorrow from empty cans and stuff. He gave me a hard time but then he said okay. So he went over to Zapper's place for the rock, and he was gonna give it to me. But then we got in a fight."

He shuddered and pulled the blanket around him. "Dale said he'd forget about the extra dollar if I . . . if I would . . ."

"If you would what?" I asked, then immediately regretted it. After that business about putting my thing in him, I was pretty sure I knew the answer, and I didn't really want to hear it.

But Tony stunned me by answering: "If I would rob your house."

Then the torrent of words started flowing again, as he gazed at me earnestly. "But I'd *never* do that to you, Mr. Burns. I mean, I know I've stolen from people, but not for, like, *years*"—yeah, sure, I thought to myself, but I didn't stop him—"and besides, I never robbed from people I *knew.* All it was, see, I was just trying to talk big. Telling him how you and me are friends, and you're a rich famous movie writer and everything, and I got all carried away. I didn't mean to tell him you have a safe with lots of money in it—"

"What?"

"—and I know where you keep the combination—"

"Tony, are you *nuts*? I don't have any safe!"

"I know, I made it up! And I kept *telling* him I made it up, only he didn't believe me, he thought I was just too scared to rob you. See, he was really lifted—"

"Lifted?"

"You know, stoned. And he kept saying over and over how if he had enough money he could buy enough dope to move down to Schenectady and be a big shot, and he'd take me with him. And when I said no, he got crazy pissed off and he said he wouldn't give my mom any rock until I told him where the combination to your safe was. Then he closed the door and wouldn't let me leave and he started punching me in the face, and it really hurt and I was running away from him, and then all of a sudden we heard someone screaming. And then the gunshot. I didn't know who was screaming or who got shot and I was real scared but Dale just laughed. He said no one would ever hurt him because he had his own gun, and if I didn't do what he wanted he'd shoot my puny little ass full of holes and throw my body in the cemetery. And he opened up a drawer to get his gun and turned his back on me for, like, half a second, so I grabbed the rock, opened the door, and ran outside. And that's when I saw you running toward the body. So I know you didn't do it, because if you did, why would you run *toward* the body instead of *away* from it? Right?"

I nodded, reeling from the onslaught of his words. *So little Tony didn't do it after all.* I was relieved—and disappointed as hell. There would be no simple, tidy solution to my legal problems.

Meanwhile he was saying, "I wanted to go over there, when you were standing by the body, but then that cop came. And I had the drugs on me, so I had to wait real quiet until he wasn't looking and then I ran away. Only I felt real bad about you getting arrested and everything, so that's why I went to court the next day, but I kept my mouth shut because my mom would get in trouble if I told about the crack and she'd get super mad at me, and she gets real scary when she's mad, but I know I did the wrong thing and if you want me to tell the cops I will. I really want to."

He finally stopped for breath, and to hear my answer. I wanted to hear my answer, too. Should I ask Tony to tell the cops? It couldn't hurt.

But would it help?

Would the cops pay any attention to this pipsqueak? Not only was he a known thief and a drug middleman, but even worse, he was a friend of mine. Maybe if he had actually *seen* the murder, and could name the murderer, the cops would listen. But as it was . . .

If Tony told the cops, probably all that would happen was his mom would beat the tar out of him.

His teeth were *click-click-clicking* again. Dawn was breaking but it wasn't getting any warmer.

"Let's go get something to eat," I said.

Tony's face brightened instantly. "Okay."

I looked up at the stone wall. "Oh phooey, now we have to climb this thing all over again."

"No, we don't," he announced cheerfully. From behind old Gideon's tombstone, he produced a long rope with a noose at one end. He threw it way up to the top of the gate, and on his very first try the noose settled around a spike at the top. Then he scampered up the rope, swung onto the wall, and jumped down to the ground on the other side. "Come on, Mr. Burns," he called out triumphantly, "it's a piece of cake!"

As I began the slow ascent up the rope—not the quick scamper that Tony had managed—I thought to myself: *This kid's a resilient little bastard. A survivor.*

At least I hoped so.

12

At that time of day—six a.m.—the only place where you can chow down in Saratoga is the Spa City Diner, on Route 9 next to the Greyhound station. Not exactly a four-star joint, but what the heck. We went back to my house, looking around to make sure no cop cars or TV vans were lurking. Then I grabbed my car and we zoomed on out.

I ordered pancakes, and so did Tony. Then we ordered some French toast for good measure. After we finished all that, we scarfed down a couple of jelly doughnuts. Hanging out in cold, dark cemeteries is a great way to build up an appetite.

By the time the jelly doughnuts had met their destiny, Tony and I were feeling warm and cheery, the world seemed like a happy place, and best of all, we had come up with A Plan.

Actually, two plans. One of our plans was a sneaky little hustle that we'd try to pull off tonight, if possible. The other, more immediate plan was to find Tony a temporary safe haven where he wouldn't have to live in fear of his mother's crack-induced mood swings. Or her boyfriends' sexual perversions, I thought to myself, remembering his comment in the cemetery.

Since it was already seven when we left the diner, I called Andrea. I figured the kids would be up already, and they'd be wondering where I was. And I was right. When Andrea picked up the phone with a tense "Hello," I could hear Babe Ruth and Gretzky—Leonardo and Raphael—bawling in the background. The kids had come into our bed at six-thirty, and when I wasn't there they decided I must be in jail again. They'd been freaking out for thirty minutes straight.

Andrea, her own voice edged with hysteria, yelled at me—totally justifiably, I knew—for not leaving a note saying where I was going. I said "I'm sorry" several times, in several different ways. But I still didn't tell her about Tony and the investigating I was doing. I figured that would just rile her up even more.

Then Andrea put our four year old on the phone. "Hi, Raphael," I said.

His frantic crying stopped, replaced by heavy breathing. Then I heard a gulp, then more heavy breathing, as he tried desperately to make himself relax.

"Sweetiepie," I told him, "I'm not in jail. I'm in a restaurant having breakfast. I'll be home just as soon as I finish eating."

Another gulp came over the phone, then Raphael said, "Daddy?"

"Yes, honey?"

"Do you think God made me love Ninja Turtles?"

What? If men are from Mars, and women are from Venus, then children are from some other galaxy entirely. "I don't know, kiddo. What do you think?"

"I think first God made me love dinosaurs, and then robots, and now Ninja Turtles. Because he has a magic invisible hand that makes you love things. And I think I'm going to love Ninja Turtles forever."

I had no idea what to say to that. But as so often happens when you don't know what to say, I ended up saying the exact perfect thing. "I love *you* forever, Raphael."

His breathing changed, and I could feel him turning calm. "And I love you forever, Daddy."

After Raphael and I got that squared away, and Leonardo got on the phone and asked me to bring him back a cinnamon doughnut, I took Tony to his new temporary home—Dennis O'Keefe's house.

Besides running the Arcturus youth group, Dennis also ran an emergency shelter for kids out of his home, a few blocks away from us on the West Side. He had two extra bedrooms for that purpose. I felt funny ringing his doorbell at seven-thirty on a Sunday morning, but hey, what are friends for?

When Dennis finally answered the door, he gave me a perplexed look. He scratched his beer belly—or given his years on the wagon, maybe I should say coffee belly—and declared, "Jacob Burns, I thought you were in jail." Tired though he must have been, his voice was startlingly loud in the early morning quiet. His T-shirt was loud too, with the old 60s slogan CHALLENGE AUTHORITY written in canary yellow on a magenta background.

"No, they let me out on bail. This is my friend Tony—"

"Hey, Tony, what's up?" Dennis greeted him heartily, then turned back to me. "Jake, I want to be up front with you. The cops came around asking me questions, and I had to tell them the whole thing."

Now it was my turn to be perplexed. "*What* whole thing?"

"You know, how you came around with the petition, and you were saying Pop was criminal and ought to be shot—"

"What are you talking about?! I never said that!" Dennis just gave me a sad look. "If I *did*, I didn't mean it!"

"Hey, I had to tell them the truth—"

"For God's sake, Dennis—"

"My sobriety is dependent on it!" he announced firmly. I stared at him, exasperated. Sometimes I can't stand twelve-steppers—they get so sanctimonious. Dennis switched into earnest lecture mode, like I was an AA newcomer he was proselytizing. "If I start being deceitful and telling lies to people, then my mind gets all twisted and messed up. Pretty soon I'll be back to a pint of bourbon and a line of coke every morning when I wake up!"

I stepped forward into his face. "Dennis, screw you, and screw your sobriety."

I was so steamed up, I'd already begun walking away before I even remembered about Tony. "You got room for a kid?" I asked Dennis through gritted teeth. "Abuse, drugs, family in crisis, the whole megillah."

To his credit, Dennis was able to shift gears immediately. He stooped down to Tony's level. "Pretty bad, huh?" he asked the kid.

Tony nodded, his lower lip quivering. Dennis patted his shoulder. "Yeah, I got room. Come on in, Tony."

Then he opened the door for Tony and me to enter. "No, I'm going home," I told him.

"No hard feelings, Jake." He stuck out his hand. I didn't take it, but he seemed oblivious. "So what's the story anyway?" he asked. "Did Pop pull you out of bed and start popping you or something?" I just stood there, incredulous, and Dennis nodded to himself, as if my silence was confirming what he had just said. "Yeah, I figured it had to be something like that. Even with all the stuff you said to me about Pop, I knew you wouldn't just murder the guy in cold blood."

"Thanks for your confidence," I said dryly.

My sarcasm didn't seem to register. "No problem. Listen, buddy, if you want me to testify at the trial about what a nasty, violent sonufabitch he was, I'll be more than glad to. You gonna try for manslaughter?"

I searched my mind for an incredibly snappy retort, but my internal hard drive crashed on me. Fortunately Tony stepped in. "Mr. Burns didn't kill Pop. He *didn't*."

"Thanks, kid," I rubbed his head. "I'm glad *somebody* believes me."

"I'll see you later," Tony said, anxious about my leaving.

I bent down and hugged him good-bye. "Don't worry, little guy, Dennis will take good care of you. He may have his head up his ass—but at least his heart's in the right place."

It wasn't a bad line to leave on. So I left.

I'm not a big fan of Wal-Mart. In fact, I hate everything about Wal-Mart—their ubiquitousness, their union busting, their bright fluorescent lights, their inanely smiling robotic employees.

So why is it that at least twice a month I find myself shopping there?

Today I had no choice. I mean, where else can you buy a video camera in small town, U.S.A., first thing on a Sunday morning?

To inflame my Wal-Mart fear and loathing even further, when I came in that day the store robots were in the middle of their morning cheer. From inside the manager's office, I heard the master robot call out, "Give me a W!" A chorus of perfectly synchronized robot voices shouted as one, "W!" Then the master called out, "Give me an A!" And the cheer continued until everyone yelled *"WAL-MART!"* in one wild robotic orgasm.

I bought the cheapest Taiwanese piece of junk I could find, since all I needed it for was tonight, for the sneaky hustle that Tony and I had concocted back at the Spa City Diner. An elderly woman robot showed me how to work the thing. "Will you be using it to videotape your children?" she asked, with an approving robot smile.

Just to knock her out of automaton mode, I told her the truth. "No, I'll be using it to blackmail my next door neighbor."

She didn't even blink. "How nice," she said. "Well, I'm sure you'll be happy with it. Is there anything else you'd like to purchase today?"

Yes, they train them well at Wal-Mart.

The camera and accessories came to $350, which I paid for with a credit card, feeling wistful. Our $300,000 nest egg had dwindled down to about negative $800. If things kept up like this much longer, I'd have to find an actual job.

What a horrid thought.

Of course, if I went to jail my job worries would be over. Permanently.

On my way home I decided to stop at Judy Demarest's house, a restored Victorian a couple of blocks off Broadway—on the East Side. When I drove up, she was outside picking up *The New York Times* and her own paper, the *Daily Saratogian*, from her front steps. Her eyes narrowed as she watched me get out of my car.

"Hey, Jude," I said, hoping a little Beatles reference would get us off to a friendly start.

But she just nodded noncommittally. I came straight to the point. "Judy, I've been meaning to ask you something. All the TV stations said I confessed, but you never put that in the *Saratogian.* How come?"

Judy shrugged. "The chief said you confessed, but I didn't want to publish it until I got your side of the story."

"So why didn't you just call me up and get my side?"

She silently looked down at her fingers, so I answered for her. "Because you were afraid I'd tell you it was true."

"Hey, what did you expect me to think?" she said defensively. "I saw you fighting Pop that night, you scared the hell out of me. You were like the Wild Man from Borneo."

I nodded, and tossed her a smile. "Well, now we're even."

"What do you mean?"

"Last time around, I wrongly suspected you of murder. This time you wrongly suspect me."

She nailed me with a look. "Wrongly?"

For some reason I couldn't help laughing. "Jacob, this isn't funny," she said.

"I know. Look, can I come inside for a minute?"

A little more reluctantly than I would have liked, she opened the door for me to come in. After I got settled at her kitchen table, I asked her to tell me everything she knew about the murder. As editor of the town newspaper, I figured she must have heard some good gossip.

And she had. Unfortunately, all of the gossip pointed to me as the killer. There was even a story making the rounds that the cops had found some skin with my DNA under Pop's fingernails.

Come to think of it, the way he'd pinched me, that story might turn out to be true. Yet another crooked nail in my legal coffin.

"What about Pop?" I asked. "You hear anything interesting about Pop?"

"Just that he picked the wrong time to die. He was about to make a shitload of money off of selling the Grand Hotel to the SERC."

What? "Pop was one of the owners?"

"You bet. Majority owner."

Interesting. Dave hadn't mentioned that; I guess he didn't know it. The Grand Hotel building, even foreclosed and in disrepair, must have cost Pop and his partners serious dough—a couple hundred grand, at least. Where had Pop gotten all that green stuff? Not from his cop salary, that's for sure. Apparently his bribery scams had done him proud.

"Judy, thanks for the info," I said, getting up to go. "And listen, please don't tell Andrea I came by asking questions. I'm kind of handling this on my own."

"I hope you know what the hell you're doing."

"I don't. As usual. But if I ever figure it out, you'll get an exclusive. And if I ever really do confess," I added, "you'll be the first to know."

Judy gave me another piercing look, probably still trying to figure out if I was guilty. I gave her a lighthearted thumbs up and walked out.

Then I drove back home to the bosom of my family. But there was a TV van parked out front, lying in wait for me. I was glad I'd stashed my Wal-Mart purchase in the trunk under an old towel. I didn't want any eager beaver media people asking me why I'd bought a new video camera.

When I pulled into my driveway, Max Muldoon jumped out of the van along with a five-foot-tall camerawoman. Camera rolling, they blocked my way. He shoved a microphone in my face and asked, "Mr. Burns, where were you this morning? Meeting with your lawyer?"

I started past them, but Muldoon and his sidekick stuck with me step for step, crowding me away from my house. "It looks like an open and shut case, Mr. Burns. Why don't you give us your side of the story?"

I stopped. If I weren't afraid of "poisoning the jury pool," I'd have jammed that microphone down his throat. "Actually, I do have a comment I'd like to make."

Muldoon's eyes glinted, and his well-waxed mustache positively gleamed in the cold morning sunshine. I could almost hear what he was thinking: *"MSNBC, here I come."* But what he said out loud was, "Yes, Mr. Burns?"

I waited to make sure the camerawoman had a good shot of me. Then I cleared my throat and declared, "I would like to say to the people of Saratoga Springs, Albany, and surrounding areas . . . I honestly believe that Geraldo Rivera's facial hair looks good on him, but on this guy here, don't you think it looks kind of goofy?"

Muldoon just stood there looking stricken. His sidekick started giggling. I took the opportunity to stroll away from them toward my house.

But before I went in, I took a quick gander at the Venetian blinds that covered Zapper's tiny side window. Just as I'd remembered, the slats were uneven, leaving plenty of empty spaces to look through. Perfect for tonight's blackmail scheme, I was telling myself, when suddenly the door banged open, my kids poured out, and I was greeted by hugs, kisses, and the alarming smell of pancakes. Alarming, because there was no way I could possibly eat another bite after that epic pig-out at the Spa City Diner.

Or so I thought. I guess two days of jailhouse food had left me feeling pretty ravenous, because I attacked my family's pancakes like they'd been cooked by Julia Child herself. Babe Ruth and Wayne Gretzky had been excellent pancake makers; it was good to see that Leonardo and Raphael were, too.

Andrea and I decided that with all the stress the kids had been going through lately, it might be soothing to them if we carried on with our lives as normally as possible. So following through on some plans we'd made last month, we went out after breakfast for the Fifth Annual West Side Make-a-Difference Day. My favorite TV reporter was gone, hopefully to a barbershop to get those facial hairs clipped.

The Make-a-Difference Day was a program sponsored by S.O.S. (who else?), where young, able-bodied West Siders would help their elderly or disabled neighbors with leaf raking and other fall chores. We had signed our family up to work for an old man named Joe McGillicuddy who lived on Cherry Street. Joe was blind, which turned out to be a big break. He didn't recognize me from the TV news, so he didn't ask me any tough questions. Instead we talked about grapes. He pruned his arbor himself every spring, totally by feel. "It's not so hard," he told me. "Close your eyes. I'll show you how."

We stood under the arbor and I closed my eyes. With his own calloused hands, he moved my hands from one branch to another so I could feel their different textures. He showed me how to tell the dead old branches from the new ones by their roughness.

"You must go slow," he said softly, "very slow." So I let my unseeing hands take their time, as I breathed in the smell of the sweet grapes and listened to the old man's calming voice.

It took us all morning and most of the afternoon to rake Joe's leaves, clean his gutters, and do a lot of *et cetera* stuff, but I didn't mind. By the time we left there, I felt like a new man.

Best of all, Joe took the kids inside for lunch while Andrea and I spent a whole hour digging in the dirt together, planting bulbs and chatting about things that had nothing to do with Pop's murder. She told me about all the obscure mail-order bulbs she was planning to plant in our own garden, and somehow we got into singing all the songs we knew that had the word "rose" in the title. One thing led to another, and we started laughing and groping each other behind the hedges. It definitely was a good thing Joe was blind.

Heading home, Andrea and I held hands while the kids skipped along in front of us, making sure to avoid stepping on any cracks. We took a roundabout route through the West Side. The afternoon sun was slanting down and the autumn leaves were glowing. Our West Side neighbors were out in force helping each other put down storm windows, spread winter fertilizer on their lawns, and touch up their paint jobs.

This was what the West Side was all about. Good people. I couldn't let one crooked cop and two lousy crack dealers ruin my affection for the whole neighborhood.

A lot of the West Siders recognized me as we walked by, and I got some startled looks and stares. But no one made any nasty comments that would have made my family uncomfortable. And when I waved, they waved back pleasantly enough, then went back to their work.

We passed a group of young mothers and toddlers cleaning up the litter on Pine Street. Then we saw three purple-haired teenagers raking leaves for a white-haired old lady who was bringing them cookies and milk. Even in the West Side's more downtrodden areas, folks were out mending broken fences and pulling weeds from sidewalk cracks.

Andrea and I were so inspired by all this that when we walked past the Orian Cillárnian hall, we dropped in to tell Lia Kalmus how much we appreciated her organizing this day. We could see her through the window talking to two junior high school girls with rakes, no doubt giving them their next assignments.

Lia looked up when we came in, and her scarred face immediately assumed the same startled expression I'd seen on many of the other West Siders. I determinedly ignored it. "Hi, Lia," I said with an upbeat, oblivious smile. "I just wanted to thank you. I think it's totally great what you're doing here."

"It really brings the community together," Andrea put in.

"I raked three billion infinity leaves!" Raphael announced.

"And I found four pennies and two nickels! That's fourteen cents!" Leonardo crowed.

By now Lia had recovered her equanimity. "Wow, that's a lot of leaves and a lot of money," she said.

Raphael wrinkled his nose. "What's that *thing* on your *face*?" he asked, pointing at Lia's disfiguring scar.

Thanks, Raphael. I stuttered with embarrassment, and the two junior high schoolers slipped out the door to avoid the awkward scene. Meanwhile Andrea was shushing Raphael, but Lia put a comforting hand on Andrea's shoulder. "It's okay, honey," Lia told her.

Then she turned to Raphael. "This is a burn mark. I was in a fire once when I was a young child. It hurt for a long time, but now it's okay."

"Were you playing with matches?" Leonardo asked. His first grade class was in the middle of a unit on fire safety.

I stuttered some more, and Andrea did her shushing thing, but once again Lia stayed composed. "I used to live in a country called Estonia," she explained gently to Leonardo, "where sometimes the government would set fire to your house if they were mad at you. That's why we're lucky to live in America, where things like that don't happen."

Then Lia straightened up and picked up her cell phone. "Well, I better check with the Open Space people and see how the bike path cleanup is going."

I was still feeling bad about my sons' rudeness, so I tried to fix it by showering more compliments on her. "Lia, I have to tell you." She paused in mid-dial. "I thought that speech you made at the Grand Hotel meeting was the most beautiful expression of the need for morality in politics that I have ever heard. Listening to you made me feel good again about being an American."

Maybe my language was too flowery, because Lia eyed me suspiciously, like I must be putting her on somehow. "Well, thank you," she said cautiously.

"I have to admit," I babbled on, talking too much because I was nervous, "I expected you to vote the other way on that issue. Just goes to show, you can never prejudge people."

She nodded uncomfortably. The boys had dragged Andrea away to show her a video game in the hallway. Now that I was alone with Lia, I got an idea. Judy Demarest hadn't been able to give me much useful information, but she was an East Sider, whereas Lia was hooked into a whole different pipeline. "Lia," I began, "maybe you could help me."

She lifted the phone again. "I'm kind of busy right now—"

"I'm sure you know about my legal troubles."

She waited, holding the telephone like a shield.

"Listen, you know everyone on the whole West Side. And I'll bet people tell you things they'd never tell the cops. You think you could ask around and see if anyone heard something that night, or since then? About the murder?"

Lia gave me a strange look. I couldn't tell what it signified; her droopy, bloodshot eye threw me off. But there seemed to be some kind of . . . *fear*?

But why would she be afraid?

Did Lia know something about the murder? Something she was scared I might find out?

I forced myself to look directly into her disfigured face. Then it hit me: That's not fear I'm looking at, but horror.

Like everyone else in Saratoga who watched the TV news, Lia must be certain that I'm a coldblooded killer—and here I am asking her for help.

She must feel the same way I'd feel if O.J. Simpson came knocking on my door. I blushed hotly. Even though I hadn't killed anyone, I was embarrassed. What right did I have to impose on this good woman's trust? Mumbling "I'm sorry," I left the Orian Cillárnian with my tail between my legs, not even saying good-bye.

13

The rest of the day passed excruciatingly slowly, but finally it was night time. Show time for Tony and me. The moon was full, the stars were doing their thing, and we were about to do ours.

By God, we were going to make Zapper talk.

I was sure of one thing: Zapper knew a lot more about Pop's murder than he'd told me yesterday. If he wasn't the killer himself, then he knew who was.

I mean, when you're in a high-risk profession like drug dealing, and you hear screaming and shooting in your backyard, you don't waste any time before you peek out through your Venetian blinds to see if someone's about to bust into your house and shoot you.

Now if Tony and I could just work this hustle the way we wanted it . . .

Tony had snuck out of Dennis's house after midnight, and I snuck out of Andrea's arms at about the same time. Now we were huddled behind the yew bushes in my backyard, spying on 107 Elm and waiting for the local drug traffic to die down. It took a while, because even though it was a Sunday night, a steady parade of happy-go-lucky partiers was knocking on Zapper's back door. Zapper's and not Dale's, since it was October 4, an even number.

It's a good thing Tony and I had each other around to keep us awake, because we both kept nodding off. We'd only gotten maybe four hours of sleep the night before. Finally, around three a.m., a full half hour had passed by with no drug purchasers. We made our move.

I gave Tony five bucks to buy drugs with. I did one final check of my video camera, and Tony did one final check of the old microcassette recorder I'd given him. Then he turned the recorder on, put it in his pants pocket, and walked up to Zapper's back door. I went up to Zapper's side window and placed my camera against it, in the spot where the Venetian blinds were most twisted and easiest to see through.

Hopefully no late-night partiers would happen along right now, because they'd practically bump into me on their way to Zapper's back door. If they spotted me videotaping drug buys, that old happy-go-lucky spirit could disappear in a hurry. And if Zapper found the microcassette recorder in Tony's front pocket, well, I didn't even want to think about it. I tried to tell myself the recorder had been Tony's idea, not mine, but it didn't make me feel any better. I was putting the little guy in serious danger.

Through my camera lens, I saw Zapper lying down on a sagging brown sofa, watching *The Three Stooges* on TV. Curly was clobbering Moe on the head with a frozen fish. Meanwhile Zapper had his hand down his pants, either scratching himself or masturbating, I couldn't tell which.

Tony knocked on the back door. Zapper yawned and got up. As he took his hand out of his pants, his loose-fitting black T-shirt lifted up slightly. A big black knife handle stuck out of a holster on his hips.

This one looked even scarier than the hunting knife he'd pulled on me earlier. The guy must have a fetish for knives. I had an urge to yell to Tony to run away. But before I had a chance, Zapper opened the door, Tony came in, and Zapper closed it again.

Now everything happened fast. They spoke for only ten seconds, maybe less, before Tony handed him the fiver. Zapper stuffed it in his pocket, threw on his coat, and went out the back door. I knew he was going straight over to Dale's apartment to retrieve the crack, so I didn't worry about him coming around my side of the house and spotting me. Meanwhile Tony sat down on the sofa and watched *The Three Stooges.*

Some of this drug deal was hidden by the blinds, but I was getting most of it on tape. Any moment now, I'd capture Zapper coming back inside and handing a vial of crack to a nine-year-old boy. Coupled with the audio from the microcassette recorder, I'd have Zapper right where I wanted him. Either he spilled the beans about the murder to me, or I'd spill the beans about the drug deal to the D.A.

Of course, if Zapper had done the killing himself, then getting him to talk would be tougher. But even so, if I pushed him hard enough I was confident I'd trip him up. This wasn't a rocket scientist I was dealing with here.

Yes sir, I congratulated myself, this nifty hustle was going smoother than a Hollywood movie—

But then a cop car drove up. It stopped right outside my house.

Shit, go away already! But the car idled there, less than fifty feet away. Then the driver cut the engine, opened the door, and got out.

In the light from the street lamp, I saw a familiar busted proboscis pointing toward the sky. It belonged to Manny Cole. He was looking up at my bedroom window. If he happened to turn and glance in my direction, he'd see me.

Oh, God. Did taping a witness's drug deals count as intimidating him? Cole shut his car door and started for the sidewalk. His face was still turned to my window, but he was coming closer to me . . . closer . . .

Three yards away from me there was a juniper bush that would hide me from Cole's sight. Should I make a quick dash for it? But maybe the sudden movement would make him look over and see me—

Cole began whistling as he ambled toward me. I couldn't take it anymore. I did the quickest three-yard dash in history.

With dry leaves and twigs crackling under my feet the whole way.

Cole stopped whistling and came off the sidewalk. He headed straight for my juniper, arms swinging confidently at his sides. Backlit by the streetlight, with his nightstick and gun, he looked like a Saratoga Springs version of Darth Vader. I watched him, breathless and paralyzed, knowing that I was about to get my ass kicked and thrown in jail—

He walked right by me.

He went past my juniper and around the side of the house, then knocked hard on Zapper's back door.

The door opened, and I heard Cole say, "Yo." Then the door closed again, followed by silence. Finally I caught my breath and got up the nerve to creep back to the window and look in.

Cole and Zapper were talking. Or rather, Cole was talking, Zapper was just nodding. I aimed the video camera at them, almost without thinking, as Zapper reached into his pocket and pulled out a wad of bills. He took about ten of them and handed them over to

Cole, who stuffed them in his own pocket with a big shiteating grin on his face.

Holy tamale—I had just recorded a *police payoff*!

I could have danced all night. This was way cool—much cooler than the pissant drug deal I'd been aiming for.

Too bad I didn't have the audio for it, since Tony and the microcassette recorder were gone. . . . Speaking of which, where *was* Tony? His jacket was still on the sofa, but he wasn't there.

Suddenly I heard another knock on Zapper's back door. It had to be Tony, wanting to come back in—but why? For his jacket? *Jeez, forget the stupid jacket, kid, let's get the hell out of here before our luck runs out!* Cole didn't look too pleased either. He stood to one side and watched as Zapper answered the door.

"Forgot my jacket," I heard Tony say. He slipped past Zapper and grabbed it off the sofa. Then he pointed at the TV and said something I couldn't hear. But Zapper and Cole must have heard him, because they both glanced over at the TV . . .

And in that millisecond when they were occupied with *The Three Stooges*, Tony snuck his hand under the sofa cushion, pulled out the little recorder, and stuffed it in his pocket.

So we had audio for the bribe after all—the sneaky little guy had left my recorder behind! With his street wisdom, he must have guessed that the drug dealer and the cop were about to engage in some kind of nefarious deal.

Tony bid them a friendly good-bye and took off. A moment later he was at the window beside me, and a few moments after that we were both sitting in my darkened kitchen, quietly celebrating.

"How'd I do?" Tony whispered excitedly.

Rewinding the microcassette recorder, I let Cole and Zapper answer for me.

"So you gimme a hundred bucks every week, long as you're in business, you got that?" Cole said on the tape.

"Yeah, I got it," Zapper answered.

We had those suckers *nailed*.

Two minutes later I was pouring glasses of milk for Tony and me when I heard Andrea's voice. "Jacob?" she called.

Yikes! Andrea's footsteps were hesitantly coming downstairs. Tony and I looked at each other. He slipped out the side door without a word. I stuffed the video camera in the cabinet under the sink and slammed the door shut.

"Jake, is that you?!" Andrea called again, in a frightened voice.

"Yeah, it's me," I called back, as casually as I could manage. "What's wrong, honey?"

She came in from the dining room. "I thought I heard you talking to someone."

"No, just to myself, as usual," I joked.

She looked past me to the table. "How come you poured two glasses of milk?"

I forced a laugh. "Jeez, I must be really tired. You want a glass?"

She didn't say anything for a few seconds, then she sat down. I tried to fill in the uncomfortable silence. "Sorry if I woke you up. I was having trouble sleeping, so I got out of bed."

She eyed me solemnly and said, "Jacob, ever since Pop got killed, I've felt like there's something you're not telling me."

No kidding. Maybe I should've told her about

Tony in the first place. I mean, we'd always been a team, Andrea and I. It was time to come clean.

But before I could get the words out of my mouth, she asked, "Did you . . . *see* anything that night?"

Something about the way she said it made my body tense up. What was she asking me exactly? "Like what?"

"I don't know. Anything."

My face suddenly got hot. "Are you asking me whether I *did* it?"

Her fingers fluttered nervously. "No, it's just, I mean . . ."

"You mean what?" I asked angrily.

The fingers stopped fluttering. "I don't *know* what I mean. You sneak off in the middle of the night doing God knows what, and you won't tell me. Jacob, I don't know who you are anymore."

She was gazing deep into my eyes with an unfathomable expression. Something inside of me snapped. It was bad enough I was facing a lifetime in jail, now on top of that I was supposed to Work on Our Relationship, too? Forget it. I didn't know what unspoken message she was giving me, and I didn't want to know. I just wanted to get the heck out of the house before I said or did something I might regret.

"I'm going out for pancakes," I said through gritted teeth, and headed for the door.

As I stormed out she called, "Jacob, don't walk away mad!"

Heck, I wasn't mad. I was furious. I was so sleep-deprived I got an attack of galloping paranoia. Except for little snotnosed Tony, I thought, there wasn't a single soul in the world I could trust.

I drove out to the Spa City Diner. But this time their pancakes didn't taste so good.

* * *

Andrea and I did patch things up later that morning, when my paranoia subsided. She said I'd misunderstood her, and *of course* she knew I was innocent. And I told her I believed her.

And I did, I truly did. But I also had a gut feeling that things would never be quite right between us until I found the killer.

My strained conversations with Andrea were veritable models of emotional clarity, though, compared to the phone calls I had later that day with my father and my three siblings. They all decided many years ago that my wanting to become a writer was proof I was completely nuts (and of course they were right). But then when I hit my thirties, I crossed them up by doing all kinds of incredibly normal things. I married a nice Jewish girl, had two kids, and bought a house and a minivan. My family of origin tentatively began to wonder if my sanity was perhaps not a totally lost cause. Especially after I struck it rich with that hack movie.

But now that I was accused of murder, all of their original doubts about me resurfaced in a hurry. Our phone calls were filled with tears, protestations, and strained silences. My father, as usual, didn't have the foggiest idea what to say. He rarely does, which is ironic because he's a professor of linguistics. My older brother wasn't much better. My younger brother said some blithely encouraging words and got off the phone as fast as he could. My sister cried so hard, *I* got off the phone as fast as I could. Screw it. The only good thing I'll say about these little chats is, I managed to overcome the childish desire to tell my family that my older brother's pinches had started this whole mess.

But enough dwelling in the past. In the late afternoon, after indulging myself in a desperately needed nap, I told Andrea I was going to spend a couple of hours by myself taking a peaceful walk in the state park. She didn't believe me, but she let me go. What else could she do?

I hopped in the car and drove down to a video store in Clifton Park, fifteen miles south, where they'll copy videotapes for you without asking any embarrassing questions about copyrights. I made a copy of the payoff videotape, then headed over to an audio store in Clifton Country Mall and got the microcasette tape copied too.

I put the copies in a large brown envelope and wrote on the front TO BE OPENED IN THE EVENT OF MY DEATH. Then I drove to a Federal Express dropoff point, where I sent the copies off to Judy at the *Daily Saratogian.*

I felt silly. Melodramatic.

On the other hand, I reminded myself as I knocked on Zapper's back door at six-thirty that evening, these weren't exactly Boy Scouts I was messing with.

Still wearing the same tight jeans and loose shirt he was wearing last night—and presumably still wearing the same knife, too—Zapper opened the door.

As soon as he saw me, he tried to shut it again. His muscles were about five times larger than mine, but I had the drop on him. I barreled through the door, knocking him backward, and headed straight for his VCR. "What the fuck—" he began, but I cut him off with "Shut up, chump," and by the time he recovered from his shock I had the tape in the slot and the TV on. I pushed the play button. The power of TV is so great that Zapper lay off me and waited for the show to begin.

But once it began, Zapper didn't seem to enjoy it much—even though he himself had the starring role.

On the TV screen, Zapper was either scratching his balls or masturbating. Then he answered the door and took five bucks from Tony.

Meanwhile, live and in person, Zapper bared his gold caps at me and snarled, "You fucker, you and that little punk set me up!"

"No, Tony didn't know anything about it," I lied quickly. "Hey, if you're not having fun, I tell you what. I'll fast forward to—"

"Hold up!" he said, staring at the screen. It was blank, because the videotape had reached the point where I was hiding in the bushes from Cole and just taping the ground. "What is this shit? You pecker-head," he chortled, poking me jovially—and painfully—on my shoulder, "you ain't got squat! Ain't got me laying the rock on him. How you gonna prove the kid ain't just paying me back for some pizza?"

He was right. I'd been hoping he wouldn't notice that. But fortunately I had my ace in the hole. I poked him jovially—and as painfully as I could—on his shoulder. "Keep watching, my brother. The best is yet to come."

Feeling like one half of some bizarre dysfunctional Siskel and Ebert team, I stood beside Zapper with my arms folded and watched. The blank screen was suddenly replaced by an image of Zapper and Cole. The on-screen Zapper was taking cash out of his pocket, counting it, and handing it over to the cop.

The live-and-in-person Zapper stiffened with fear as I piled on the pressure. "I'm thinking of selling the video to one of those real-life cop shows on Fox," I said conversationally. "Or maybe I'll just give it to a real-life D.A. down in Ballston Spa, see how he feels about you bribing an officer of the law. Should be worth a couple of years in a state facility, don't you think?"

I had to hand it to Zapper, he kept his cool. "Fuck you, you still got the same problem. How you gonna prove I ain't just paying him for a used TV set?"

Without saying a word, I took the microcassette recorder out of my pocket and turned it on.

"So you gimme a hundred bucks every week, long as you're in business, you got that?" Cole said on the audiotape.

"Yeah, I got it," the Memorex Zapper replied—

But then the live Zapper lashed out with his arm and banged the recorder out of my hand. It hit the floor and went silent. In a flash, Zapper's knife came out of its holster. He pointed it at my chest.

My knees turned to jelly. But there was no turning back now. "I have other copies of that tape—" I said in a terrified, high-pitched voice.

He backed me up against a wall, his long, curved knife wiggling in front of my eyes. *"Fuck you want from me, muthafucka?"*

I took a deep breath, but my voice still sounded disturbingly like Tiny Tim's. "I want to know what happened that night."

His knife point touched my left nipple, right above my heart. "I don't know nothing, dickweed! I was sleeping!"

"Bullshit," I squeaked.

Zapper stared at me briefly, then his eyes flicked away. And in that moment when his eyes flicked, I knew it really *was* bullshit—he was lying through his caps. And I also knew, somehow, that he didn't have the balls to stab me. I reached out and pushed his hand away—the hand that was holding the knife.

"Listen, moron, I'm not playing," I said, and although my voice wasn't back to normal, at least I no longer sounded like I was getting ready to sing "Tiptoe Through the Tulips." "I'm facing a murder charge. You don't help me, I'm taking you down with me—"

"It weren't my goddamn night!" Zapper burst out wildly. We were both taken aback by the suddenness of it. Then he made an effort to pull himself together. He spoke carefully, his eyes begging me to believe him. "See, Dale be doing the selling that night, not me. I be sleeping, I *swear*. I didn't wake up 'til I heard the yelling and the shot. Time I found my knife and got up, you was already out there, with your hands in the air and that cop on your ass."

I almost believed him. But then he gave me that tell-tale eye flick again. Ignoring the knife, I stepped up and put my face two inches from his. Aside from the caps, his teeth were white and well kept, which surprised me; somehow you don't expect drug dealers to have good dental habits. "Buddy, I'm giving you five seconds to get real. Then forget it. Pack your bags. You're going to Coxsackie Correctional for an extended visit."

An angry light flared up in Zapper's eyes, and his grip on the knife handle tightened. *Uh-oh.* Had I fatally overestimated Zapper's punkiness?

But the moment passed, and he sagged and sat down on the sofa. "All right," he said wearily. "Yeah, fuck it, I'll tell you."

He sighed heavily. I waited, goosebumps rising all over me. *The truth at last.*

"Like I told you, I heard some screaming, and the gun. But then I heard a car."

I waited impatiently for more.

"I heard a car start up."

I waited again. But this time nothing else came. So I prodded, "Yeah, and then what?"

"That's it. When I looked out the front door, the car be driving off real fast. So I figure that's who killed Pop."

"What kind of car?"

"Fuck should I know, man, it was dark outside," he said irritably. "The car was, like, medium size, and some kind of dark color. Yo, I make up some extra stuff if you want, just to get you to leave my house, but anything else I tell you be a lie."

I stood there trying to stare into his soul, as he gazed up at me innocently from the sofa. Was that *it*? Was that all I would get out of this creep? I had just pulled off an incredibly clever undercover operation, suitable for *NYPD Blue*, and all I'd get for my trouble was some half-ass story about a barely seen, darkish, medium-size car?

I tried a new tack. "What was your relationship with Pop?"

He lifted his thick shoulders. "Man was my landlord. I wouldn't say we had no deep *relationship*—"

"Come on, you were bribing him, just like you bribed that cop on the video."

"No way. Pop didn't go for that kind of shit—"

"Do I look like a fucking idiot?!" I ejected the tape from the VCR and held it up. "See you in a few years. Don't forget to pack your toothbrush—"

"Yo, yo, keep your pants on!" Zapper smiled ingratiatingly. "Man, you one tough motherfucker. You want some Coke or something? I mean, like Pepsi type of Coke?"

Well, what do you know—male bonding at last. "Sure," I said, and sat down in a coffee-stained metal folding chair.

Zapper got two cans of Coke out of the refrigerator, tossed me one, and sat back down on the sofa. We popped the tops and had a sip. Then he cocked his head at me. "So tell me about this big-ass Hollywood movie of yours," he said. "Got any brothers in it?"

"Yeah, the main character's buddy is black."

Zapper rolled his eyes, annoyed. "How come the hero dude is always white and the buddy's always black? Why don't they ever do the other way around?"

"It's screwed up, what can I say? So what was the deal with Pop?"

Zapper took a long swig, then burped. "Yeah, man, I bribed him, all right. Top of the rent, I had to sling him a hundred a week, just like with this new guy Cole." Zapper shook his head with grudging approval. "That cracker Pop had him one hell of a setup. Was getting grease from me, and some more grease from his other houses, and Arcturus—"

I was so surprised I spilled Coke on my pants. Maybe I could wear them with my grape-stained shirt. "*Arcturus?* How was he getting money from Arcturus?"

"Man was a mastermind at getting paid. That was his thang."

"Are you positive he got money from them?"

"Yo, it's what he told me. Boastful motherfucker. I don't play like that myself. I believe in keeping my private business private, know what I mean?"

"What did he say to you, exactly?"

"Hey, I didn't write it down. Man come over here one Friday night to get his money, and I'm having trouble finding it in all my different pockets, so he be yelling at me to hurry up 'cause he got four other collections to make that night, and he name the places and one of them was Arcturus."

I sat there trying to put it all together, but Zapper beat me to it. "See, Jacob—that's your name, right?—

Jacob, my man, be all kinds of people would want to kill Pop. In some kind of financial dispute, know what I'm saying?"

I nodded. "But what I don't get, why would any of those disputes have happened *here*? Behind your house? That doesn't make sense."

"Maybe they got pissed off and followed him here."

"And another thing I don't get. I bet it took me a full two minutes after the first scream before I made it out to your backyard. I don't believe it took you that long to just get up and look out your window."

"What can I say, man? When I get woke up in the middle of the night after some serious partying, I ain't no Deion Sanders."

I looked hard at Zapper.

He flicked his eyes.

He was lying to me again. Why?

I took another sip of Coke. "I'll bet you're half right," I said. "I'll bet Pop did die in an argument over bribe money." Then I set the Coke down on the floor. "But I don't think it was someone else. I think it was you. I think you killed Pop."

I'd made this accusation once before, the last time Zapper and I chatted. But that time I hadn't totally meant it, because I still had my money on Tony as the murderer.

This time, though, I meant it. And Zapper knew I meant it.

There was a silence in the small room. Zapper sucked in a scared breath.

Then he laughed. "Yo, didn't your mama never teach you no manners? Here I invite you into my home, give you something to wet your lips, and now you gonna go and accuse me of murder? Shame on you," he said, wagging a finger at me. "Shame on you."

Usually I like to have the last line. But his line was so nicely done, I didn't think I could improve on it. Especially since being in the same room with a guy I thought was a murderer kind of interfered with my powers of speech.

So I just picked up my videotape and my busted microcassette recorder and walked out.

14

But now what? How could I get solid evidence against Zapper?

Or was I jumping to conclusions too quickly, just like the cops did? Might the murderer be someone else Pop had extorted money from, someone like . . .

Dennis O'Keefe?

My heart skipped a beat. Was Zapper right about Pop getting grease from Arcturus? And if so, could my old hippie friend have killed Pop?

No, impossible; homicide wasn't one of the Twelve Steps.

And yet . . .

Maybe killing a crooked cop would appeal to Dennis's "Challenge Authority" philosophy, especially if that crooked cops was shaking Dennis down for money he didn't have. And especially if that crooked cop was popping him hard enough to make him scream that horrific scream I'd heard, and he grabbed the gun in self-defense.

As I walked back home from 107, I stopped in my backyard. I closed my eyes and tried to hear that scream again. It had been high-pitched, like a woman's or a child's shriek. But as I'd seen in my recent tête-à-tête with Zapper, when you're scared silly your voice does funny tricks. Also, I was half asleep when I heard the scream, and my aural memory was blurry. The scream could easily have come from Dennis.

It suddenly struck me that I had taken little Tony to a possible murderer's house for safety. Not the most brilliant of moves. Maybe I should go there now and confront Dennis, and move Tony elsewhere.

Or maybe I should go right over to Cole's house and show him the incriminating tape. That way I could blackmail him into helping me with the investigation. I'd get the cops to actually do their job for a change.

My thoughts were interrupted when I somehow got the sense I was being watched. I turned. It was true. Zapper was eyeing me malevolently through the busted slats in his Venetian blinds. I waved. He withdrew from the window and disappeared.

I could theorize about Dennis all I wanted, but I'd bet my credit card limit that Zapper was the killer. After all, Pop died only fifteen feet from Zapper's house, and like they say, *location, location, location.*

The major reason to doubt Zapper's guilt was that he was a musclebound, cowardly punk. But hey, even a cowardly punk can kill, if he's pushed to the wall. And Pop pushed people, no question; look what he'd done to me that night. Turned me into a stark raving lunatic.

Some words got stuck in my brain—"if he's pushed to the wall." That was exactly what I was doing to Zapper right now. What if he sold himself some crack tonight and filled up with pharmaceutical courage? He wouldn't suddenly take it into his head to kill me . . . would he?

I stood under my grape arbor, gazing through the busted slats of Zapper's blinds as if that would help me understand the busted slats of Zapper's mind, when my six year old ran out of the house. Or, as he would immediately correct me, my six and one-quarter year old. He jumped into my arms, calling out "Daddy! Daddy!"

I kissed him. "Hi, Raphael."

He threw me an exasperated look. "No! I'm Leonardo!"

"Sorry, I keep getting it mixed up."

"That's because we never see you." *Ow!* Stab in the heart. "You can tell I'm Leonardo because I'm wearing blue. And you know what Splinter says?"

"Hey, Leonardo, why don't we go inside? Then you can tell me all about Splinter."

And that's what we did. I decided that spiriting Tony away from Dennis's house could wait until tomorrow, especially since I couldn't think of a safe place to take him to tonight. God knows my own house didn't feel real safe these days.

So I took Leonardo inside, double locked all the doors, closed all the curtains and windowshades, and put the kid on my lap. By the end of the night I hadn't gotten any further in my hunt for the murderer, but I did learn everything there is to know about Splinter, who, for those of you not in the Ninja Turtle loop, is a big rat. But not just *any* big rat: He's a true spiritual leader, the wise old guru of the sewers.

I wish I'd had some of Splinter's wisdom myself that night. Maybe then I would have foreseen what was about to happen in just a few hours. Maybe I could even have stopped it from happening.

That's a thought that will stay with me until I die.

I was awakened by the sound of a car backfiring. But it didn't take me long to remember what that sound really meant the last time I heard it. Hot prickles raced up and down my spine. Andrea, annoyingly true to form, was still asleep. I jumped out of bed, opened the curtains, and peered out the window.

Nothing but darkness and déjà vu.

Someone could be bleeding to death outside. I had to go and help them. I might be able to save their life.

But there was a teensy little downside to going out there and doing the Good Samaritan thing: I might get busted for murder again.

What would *you* have done? Been a hero or covered your ass?

Me, I stayed inside and dialed 9-1-1. What can I say?

"There's been a shooting at 107 Elm Street," I spoke into the phone.

"Who's calling, please?" a woman asked. I hung up and waited in my house for the cops to come, wondering who had been shot and if they were still alive or dead. In my mind's eye, I saw someone's life's blood flowing out as they lay there helpless and alone because I was too scared to get involved.

I felt full of self-loathing. Youthful Idealism meets Middle-Age Cowardice. And Middle-Age Cowardice kicks butt.

Maybe I'm being unfair to myself. The thought of getting jailed again and leaving my children fatherless was just too painful to deal with. So is that cowardice, or love?

I wish all the moral choices were simple again, like when I was younger and you were either for the Vietnam War or against it. When we were always right and our parents were always wrong.

Fortunately for my conscience, the cops came pretty quickly with their blaring sirens and squealing tires. Through our front window I saw my new pals

Manny Cole and Lieutenant Foxwell, along with about four other cops I recognized from my recent misadventures. I noted with disappointment that Dave was nowhere to be seen. Well, he probably wouldn't be any help to me anyway; he was too busy covering his ass with the chief.

The sirens finally woke Andrea, and she stood beside me at the window. "What's going on out there?" she asked.

"Let's go find out."

"We can't leave the kids."

"Okay, you stay here. I'll be right back—"

"*No.*" Andrea shoved me backward, practically throwing me onto the bed. "You're not going anywhere. *I'll* go."

"But—"

In the other bedroom Raphael started wailing, then his older brother joined in. "Get in there *now*," Andrea ordered. "Your kids need you."

So I went to their room and lay in bed with them.

And that's how I missed seeing Zapper keeled over in his open doorway with his head blown off.

From Andrea's description, and from the vomit odor she emitted when she returned home, I gathered that the dead man was not a pretty sight. In a way, I was relieved that he was so emphatically dead. It meant that even if I'd dashed outside the moment I heard the gunshot, there's no way I could have saved his life.

But that still didn't stop me from feeling guilty. Because I had a strong suspicion that the hustle I pulled on Zapper was somehow the reason behind his head getting blown off.

Not that I harbored any special love for the man, but still. We'd drunk Coke together. Classic Coke, no less.

I didn't feel inclined to share this information with the cops, who rang our front doorbell ten minutes later. By now Andrea, the kids, and I were all cuddling in our queen-sized bed, while I told them a story about the Ninja Turtles helping the Red Sox win the pennant. Obvious fiction, of course. Even if Ninja Turtles really *do* exist, the Red Sox will *never* win the pennant.

I ignored the doorbell at first, since I knew it was cops. But when they rang a second time, and a third, and the kids started getting upset, I threw on some clothes and opened the front door.

"We'd like to ask you some questions," Lieutenant Foxwell began, as Cole stood beside him glowering at me with pure hatred. Judging by his expression, he wouldn't be content to just gouge at my eyes this time. Instead he'd scoop them out of my face and eat them raw for a midnight snack.

Why was Cole so enraged at me? Was it because he thought I was a cop killer, or was something else going on here, too?

Wait a minute. *How much did Cole know?* Had Zapper for some reason *told* him about my incriminating videotape?

I gasped inwardly. What if Cole learned about the videotape, figured it was on its way to the D.A., and got scared Zapper might cut a deal to save his own skin.

"Why don't you come with us to the station," Foxwell said flatly. It was an order, not a question.

But I couldn't tear my eyes away from Cole's furious scowl. What would this bad seed do if he thought he was facing jail time? *Would he kill Zapper to shut him up?*

It made sense. And there was something else scratching away at my brain, too. What was it?

I tried to track it down, but Foxwell was saying, "Mr. Burns," and firmly taking my arm.

I yanked it away. "You got questions, ask 'em right here and now."

"You can come with us voluntarily," said Foxwell, "or we can arrest you."

"Hey, let's bust the shithead anyway," Cole threw in.

"Your call," Foxwell told me, his face expressionless, a mask. "Which way you want to go?"

I stared fearfully at Foxwell's blank face. Did he know that Cole was a crook? Were they in on this together?

Would they kill me on our way to the police station, and say I was resisting arrest?

Or was I ascending new heights of paranoia?

"Don't hurt my Daddy!" Raphael screamed from the top of the stairs. I looked up; my family was looking down at me and the cops in horror.

Leonardo shouted at the cops, "If you hurt him, you're dead meat!"

I gritted my teeth, then forced myself to laugh. "Don't worry, kids," I said, "these are *good* policemen, not bad ones. I'm going with them for a little while to help them out. I'll be back in a couple of hours."

"Can you finish the story about the Red Sox first?" Leonardo asked.

I eyed Foxwell. He shook his head no.

"Ask Mommy to finish it," I said, and walked out the door. I'd have gone upstairs to kiss the kids good-bye, but I was afraid I'd break into tears.

I walked over to the cop car with my head down, avoiding the eyes of Lorenzo and my other neighbors who were watching from their porches. But I did look over toward the front steps of 107, where I saw Dale, Zapper's crimie.

He was sitting on the steps with his head between his knees, distraught. A policewoman had her arm around him, trying to calm him down. I briefly entertained the idea that he might have shot Zapper in some drug dispute—hadn't Tony mentioned that Dale had a gun?—but his grief seemed too genuine.

I looked away from him and searched the sidewalks and porches for Dave. I didn't see him, though. Where was he?

I got hit by a new dread: Now that Zapper had been killed, Dave might feel compelled to come forward and say he saw me holding a knife on Zapper yesterday. Then I'd be in deep swamp goo for sure.

I got in the backseat, as Foxwell and Cole got in front. Cole turned and threw me a nasty grin—

And finally my wayward mental synapses hooked up, and I found the source of that insistent scratching in my brain.

It was something Dave said to me yesterday . . . or rather, something he *didn't* say. When I asked him who he believed had killed Pop, and he suddenly made like a clam.

Now I was pretty sure I understood why. Dave had been too loyal to his fellow cops, or too scared of retribution from the chief, to say out loud what he suspected.

Which was that Pop was killed by another cop. Some cop who wanted a piece of his lucrative extortion scam.

Some cop like Manny Cole.

15

"So we meet again," Chief Walsh greeted me cheerfully, as Foxwell escorted me into his office. Though it was the middle of the night and he must have just gotten out of bed, the chief's silver hair was perfectly coifed and his pinstripe suit was immaculate. "Have a seat. Coffee?"

I stayed standing. "What's this I hear on TV about me making a confession, you lying piece of shit? I'm speaking to my lawyer about bringing a libel suit against you."

The chief gave me a rich, manly laugh. "Mr. Burns, I always get special pleasure from interrogating a suspect with money and privilege. Makes it more of a challenge. You sure you wouldn't like coffee?"

I gave him a rich, manly sneer, and tried out a theory of mine on him to see how he'd react. "Chief, you knew about Pop extorting protection money from drug dealers and prostitutes, but you didn't lift a pinkie finger to stop it. I wonder why. How big a percentage did *you* get?"

But I didn't get a rise from him. He just nodded in his usual pleasant way and said, "Very interesting." Then he turned to Foxwell. "Mr. Burns certainly does have a deep seated hatred of police officers, doesn't he? Verging on pathological."

"Go ahead, twist my words, I've *got* your ass. You want the word to get out about widespread police corruption on the West Side? S.O.S. will have you fired before you can finish blow drying your hair."

"Libel suits can go in both directions, my friend." He lifted a speculative eyebrow. "Unless you have some kind of proof?"

I knew exactly how to wipe that silly smirk off his face. "As a matter of fact, I do have proof. I have a—"

A videotape, I was about to say, but stopped.

"A what?" the chief asked, his eyes flashing greedily.

Should I tell him? There was no way that tape could be used against me . . . was there?

I was eager to tell him. But the chief was a master at this game—he sure beat me the last time we played. I better watch myself.

Once again, it was Mister Discretion versus Macho Man.

"I'm not saying another word until I speak to my lawyer," I said, and instantly felt very wise, very discreet . . . and very old. Maybe I was doing the right thing, but still. If this was middle age, I didn't like it much.

"If you have any information about police corruption, I'd like to hear it. Who knows, it might even help your murder case."

"So who do you think will win the World Series?"

The chief held out open palms. "Look, I'm not your enemy, you know. If you really didn't kill Pop, I want to know who did. Pop was one of my men."

"He was my man . . . but I done him wrong," I sang. The chief and the lieutenant looked at me like

I was a bad sardine. "That's from *Frankie and Johnny,*" I told them.

"When's the last time you saw Waldo Alexander?" the chief barked at me.

"Waldo who?" I asked, genuinely baffled.

"Don't get cute with me. He was your next door neighbor—before you killed him." *Waldo?* No wonder he called himself Zapper. "Were you trying to get him to testify for you and he said no? Is that why you did him?"

"No, I just didn't like his hairdo. Too short on top."

Foxwell stepped in. "You didn't really mean to *kill* him, did you, Mr. Burns? You just brought your gun over there to intimidate him a little, right?"

I felt panic seizing hold of me. How much did they know about my attempts at intimidation? Were they just playing with me? Had Dave already told them about that little episode with the knife?

Sensing my fear, Chief Walsh stepped around his desk and stooped down so his face was right in front of mine. His breath smelled like Colgate. The lieutenant crowded me from behind. I felt like a very thin slab of meat stuck in the middle of a very large sandwich.

I turned my head to the side to avoid the chief's eyes. He spoke softly in my ear, "Waldo pulled his knife on you, didn't he? We found it in his hand. So you had to shoot him. You *had* to. It wasn't your fault. It was just self-defense."

The way he said it, it sounded so logical I almost believed it myself. My throat was so tight, I could barely whisper, "I want my lawyer."

"Here's the deal," the chief whispered back, seductively. "You give us this one, and we'll drop the charges about Pop."

Suddenly he clapped me on the shoulder, throwing me a broad wink. "Screw Pop anyway. Like you say, he was a crooked cop. Could've been a million people wanted to kill him. Hell, *I* wanted to kill him." He leaned forward, confidential. "So here's what I'll do for you, Jake. You cop to this drug dealer shithead, all we'll hit you for is involuntary manslaughter, that's it. Two years max. And hey, you plead self-defense, considering the guy was a convicted felon with a hunting knife in his hand, and you got the resources to buy Barry Scheck if you want, you'll probably do no time at all. Which sure beats hell out of facing the electric chair for killing a cop."

He leaned back and rubbed his hands together, ready to close the deal. "So what do you say? You gonna be smart about this?"

"You got this offer on videotape?" I asked.

The chief and the lieutenant gave each other a happy look. "Yes, we do. My offer to you for involuntary manslaughter is right there on tape. So you can be confident the offer is for real. I'll even give you a copy, if you want."

"Good. I *would* like a copy."

"No problem, you got it. So now why don't you tell us what really happened with that scumbag Waldo—"

"Of course," I interrupted, "this so-called 'offer' of yours isn't worth a bucket of piss, because as any idiot knows from watching Court TV, cops are allowed to lie while interrogating suspects. But what you're *not* allowed to do is continue interrogating someone after he's already asked for a lawyer. *Twice.* You two clowns are stone busted on that. So yes, I *would* like a copy of the tape, thank you very much."

I gave them a big fat grin. Suddenly I wasn't feeling so old and tired anymore.

But I guess the chief was, because he sighed wearily and sat back down in his chair. There were frown lines at the corners of his mouth I hadn't noticed before. "Lieutenant," he said, "erase the tape."

"Yes, sir," Foxwell replied.

"But my gosh, Chief," I asked breathlessly, putting my hand on my heart, "are you sure that's *legal*? I wouldn't want you to get in *trouble*."

"And when you're done with the tape," the chief told his lieutenant, "throw this prick in jail. Murder one, take two. And *this* time," he said, straightening his back as he turned toward me, "lots of luck getting out on bail. What with being a repeat murderer and all."

Then the chief smiled.

I didn't.

There was a commotion out in the hall. At first it didn't register. I was too busy gulping for air as I contemplated spending a year or two without bail, dodging from large under-educated men with bad teeth. But then I heard someone call out, "Hey, stop!" and suddenly Chief Walsh's door crashed open. My favorite three-hundred-pound lawyer burst into the room.

Young Crewcut raced in right behind. "I tried to stop him—" he began.

"Jake, your wife called," Malcolm said. "Are you all right?"

"Not exactly. We're booking him for murder," Chief Walsh replied. "Right now, I have to ask you to leave. You can see him after he's processed—"

I broke in, speaking loudly over the chief's attempts to interrupt me. "They kept interrogating me even after I asked for my lawyer." I pointed at the video lens. "The whole thing is on tape. That's why they want to get rid of you—so they can erase it."

Malcolm's eyes gleamed ferociously as he turned on the chief. "Is this true?"

"We hadn't yet arrested him," the chief replied smoothly, "so we weren't legally required to let him call his lawyer."

"He was doing *something* illegal, or pretty damn close," I threw in quickly, "because he told his henchman here to do the erasing. In fact, Chief Walsh telling him to erase the tape is *on* the tape."

"How intriguing," Malcolm said with barely suppressed glee, rubbing his triple chin. "Let's have a look at this tape, chief, shall we?"

The chief pointed an angry finger at Young Crewcut. "You twit, the next time you buzz someone in the front door, don't just sit on your ass and let him waltz right by you!"

"He's so fat, I didn't think he could run that fast—"

"Get out!" the chief exploded, and Young Crewcut zipped out as fast as he could. Then the chief shoved a finger at Foxwell. "You, too." The lieutenant gave him a hurt look, then eased out with as much dignity as he could muster.

Finally, with just the three of us in the room, Chief Walsh turned to Malcolm. "What do you want?"

"My client's freedom."

The chief snorted. "Can't do that and you know it. I suspect him of committing his second murder in six days. What if he grabs a machine gun tomorrow and shoots up City Hall, for Christ's sake?"

"What evidence do you have to suspect him of this second murder?"

"Don't be absurd. I can't tell you that."

"He's just bluffing—" I began, but Malcolm said, "Shut up," and I did.

"I have plenty of evidence, believe me," the chief declared.

"That's a lie—" I began, and Malcolm said "Shut up" again, but this time I didn't. "All he has is the fact I live next door. That's it."

I was looking hard at the chief's face while I said this, trying to determine if I was really right or if he *did* have more. He stared me down for a few moments, but at last he looked away and I knew I had him. Malcolm knew it, too.

If I were Malcolm, I'd have messed with the chief's mind now. But Malcolm surprised me; he picked this moment to soften up. Settling his oversized frame into one of the chief's comfortable chairs, he said gently, "Chief Walsh, I sympathize with how difficult this situation is for you. But if you book him now with insufficient evidence it won't do you any good, since I'll be able to spring him right away. And besides," he shrugged casually, "if you decide *not* to book him, I'll be glad to forget whatever . . . *indiscretions* . . . are on your videotape."

The chief scowled, probably thinking the same thing I was: That videotape contained my allegations of police corruption, and he had no desire for them to be made public. Especially since at least some of them were true.

Finally he waved his hand magnanimously. "All right, Malcolm," he said, "take your boy out of here."

My lawyer got up out of his chair. "Thank you, Chief. And I want you to know, Jacob and I sincerely hope that you find the killer, or killers, as quickly as possible, and if there's anything we can do to assist you—"

"I appreciate that," the chief cut in, "but don't worry, we already have the killer. We've got all the evidence we need on the first murder, and we'll get it on the second one too, I guarantee."

Then his eyes narrowed into slits and his voice went cold. Eyeing me up and down like he was looking for the right spot to insert a pitchfork, he said deliberately, "It's just a matter of time."

"Let's go," Malcolm said. I stood rooted to the spot, hypnotized by the venom in the chief's voice. Malcolm took my arm. "Jake, let's go."

We went.

16

"It's just a matter of time."

He was right.

My weak link was Dave. When the chief and his minions got around to questioning him—which they would, if only because Dave was a neighbor and they'd be questioning all the neighbors—he would feel duty bound to give me up.

And when he told the chief about my knife-wielding, I'd be tossed in the hoosegow pronto, lawyer or no lawyer.

But maybe if I got to Dave first, and explained the whole situation . . .

"Give it up," Malcolm ordered me as we headed for his Volvo.

"Give what up?" I asked innocently.

"What happened between you and that Waldo guy."

"*Nothing* happened between me and—"

"Sure, and Deep Blue is really a little green man from Mars."

"Malcolm, I didn't kill the man."

"No, but you did *something*." We got in the car. Malcolm had to jiggle and squirm to fit behind the wheel. "Correct me if I'm wrong," he said as we pulled away from the police station with a cop car right on our tail, which I doubted was coincidence, "but are you doing some investigating on your own?"

I didn't answer. I guess I should have had faith in my lawyer and told him everything, but lately I was so used to not trusting anyone that it had become a habit. Malcolm banged the steering wheel in frustration. "Damn you, Jake, I'm hiring *professional* investigators this week. Please, let *them* do it. I know you got lucky and solved a murder once, but lightning doesn't strike twice. If it does, chances are you're the one who's gonna get fried."

"Relax, I won't do anything stupid. I just want to go home and get some z's."

So he drove me home. I lay in bed with my exhausted, frantic wife and rubbed her back until she finally succumbed to a troubled sleep. But I didn't fall asleep myself. Instead I slipped out of bed, careful not to wake her. It was still only 4:30 a.m., and I'd slept a total of maybe twelve hours in five nights, but no matter. It was time for Macho Man to get moving.

Dave's car still wasn't in his garage, and when I called him there was no answer. So where was he?

I didn't know much about Dave's love life. A few months back I'd tried setting him up with my friend Madeline, who owned Madeline's Espresso Bar in town. I felt something of a personal obligation to get Madeline hooked up, since in a roundabout way I'd been responsible for her last relationship falling apart. But unfortunately, Dave and Madeline didn't seem to light each other's fires.

The first person I tried was Dave's ex-wife, who still lived in Saratoga. They'd been divorced for five years now, but hey, cops in TV shows are always sleeping with their ex-wives, so maybe Dave was, too. I remembered her name, because who could forget a name like Polly Esther Fiber? Even worse than Waldo. In the phone book, she just listed herself as P. Fiber. I couldn't say I blamed her.

Her phone rang six times, then finally a sleepy, irritated voice answered, presumably P. herself. "Hello," she snarled.

"Hi, I'm sorry to bother you at this hour, but it's an emergency. I'm looking for Dave Mackerel—"

Slam.

Ah, well.

There was one other obvious possibility: Dave's mom, who was the only black woman in the town of Hadley, he'd told me once. Hadley was just half an hour north; maybe he was spending the night there for some reason. Doing his laundry. Mrs. Mackerel answered her phone in the middle of the second ring. "Hello?" she breathed, her voice quavering—with fear, I realized. Must be hard being a cop's mom.

"Mrs. Mackerel, I'm sorry to bother you in the middle of the night, but it's an emergency." She sucked her breath in sharply. "No, don't worry, Dave's fine," I said quickly, "it's something else. My name's Jacob Burns—"

"Jacob Burns? The writer?"

Grateful that she hadn't said "The murderer?", I answered, "Yes, that's me—"

"Davy and I talk about you all the time. I tell him and I tell him, *you* didn't kill anyone, of *course* not."

Hurray, someone who actually believed in my innocence! "Thank you very much, Mrs. Mackerel. I just hope Dave agrees with you."

There was a silence on the phone that I wasn't too

wild about. Finally she responded as tactfully as she could, "Well, I'm working on him, Mr. Burns."

"Call me Jacob. Actually, I need a little help from Dave right now. Do you know where I could find him?"

"Certainly. He was here until pretty late helping me with my weather stripping, then he went to go see his girlfriend."

A girlfriend? This was news. No wonder he hadn't been interested in Madeline. "Do you know her name?"

"Sure. It's Madeline."

"Who?"

"You know, the girl that owns that fancy coffee shop."

What a riot! So they were playing games with me, huh?

I thanked Mrs. Mackerel, then called Madeline. Her machine picked up, her voice said the usual boring stuff, and then the thing beeped at me. "Madeline," I said, "could you put Dave on the phone? Hey, the jig's up, kid. I know he's there . . ."

Oh God, what if he's not? What if he's with some other girlfriend? "Dave, could you pick up the phone, please . . . Dave . . ." This is the pits, I thought. What if Madeline figures out from my phone call that Dave's not at home, and he's out screwing around? Had I just busted up another one of her relationships?

Well, but if he's cheating on her, it's best that she find out now, I tried to reassure myself. I shouldn't feel so bad . . . "Okay, well, uh, sorry to bother you, Madeline—"

I heard a click. "How'd you find me?" Dave's pissed-off voice came over the phone. *Hallelujah.*

"I'm an ace private eye, you should know that by

now. So what's the deal with you and Madeline playing it so close to the vest?"

"Look, what do you want?"

"Man, I'm hurt. I introduced you, you should've told me."

"Are you in trouble again?"

"Who, me?"

"Jake—"

"Don't move, I'll be right there," I said, and hung up. I was at the door to Madeline's apartment, upstairs from her espresso bar, about three minutes later. She opened the door before I even knocked. Dave stood right behind her, with a hand on her shoulder.

Weird. I was the guy who set them up in the first place, but as I saw them standing together in their night clothes, I have to confess I was taken aback. It hit me in a flash why they hadn't told me or any of their other friends (so far as I knew) about their relationship. Black men and white women get so much grief when they couple up, Dave and Madeline probably wanted to make sure it was the real deal before they went public.

"What's up?" Dave asked.

"Listen, I just want you guys to know, I won't tell anyone."

Madeline and Dave both nodded. Their heads were synchronized, I noted—always a good sign for a relationship. "Come in," Madeline said.

"Dave, something happened tonight," I began, but he held up his hand.

"I have a bad feeling," he grumbled. "A bad feeling you're about to tell me something I shouldn't be hearing."

"But if you listen to me anyway, I'll be your lawn care slave for life."

Dave put his hand on the shoulder of Madeline's nightgown. It was virginal white with pink flowers, but that still didn't keep me from getting lascivious thoughts. "Honey," he told her gently, "maybe you should go back to the bedroom."

She didn't like it, but she went. "So, okay," Dave asked me when we were alone, "who'd you kill this time?"

I gave a start. "Funny you should put it that way," I said. "Remember that guy I pulled a knife on? There's this theory going around that I killed him. Totally false, I hasten to add."

Dave groaned and rubbed his hand through his hair. "Zapper is *dead*?"

"That's what usually happens when most of your face is shot off."

"Why don't you shut up and start from the beginning."

I didn't shut up, but I did start from the beginning. I told him the whole story, complete with a visual aid: my tape of the payoff, which I stuck in Madeline's VCR. Since my microcassette recorder was busted, I narrated the part where Zapper and Cole were discussing the bribe.

Dave and I sat on the sofa, watching the tape. On the tape, Zapper had a face. Now he didn't.

If I hadn't made this tape, would Zapper still be alive?

Beside me, Dave whistled through his teeth. "So Cole is taking over Pop's accounts."

I translated silently to myself. *Accounts*, that meant bribes. "Dave," I asked, "are all Saratoga Springs cops this crooked?"

"*I'm* not."

"Is that unusual?"

He pushed the pause button on the remote, just as

Cole was in the middle of stuffing the hundred bucks in his pocket. "Look, I really don't know how many Saratoga cops are crooked. There's forty of us, and for all I know, it's just these two—Pop and Cole."

"You're forgetting Chief Walsh. I'll bet you a dollar to a doughnut he knew what Pop was up to, but he didn't do a blasted thing to stop it."

"Maybe he couldn't. Or maybe he just didn't think it was worth the trouble. That doesn't make him *crooked*."

"Sure, it does."

"Look at it from his perspective." Dave stood up from the sofa and paced the room. "There's always gonna be a certain amount of dealing in Saratoga—we're the biggest city in the county. People come here all the way from Galway and South Corinth to score their drugs. Pop worked it so the dealing is confined to just three houses. Everything's relatively quiet, no turf wars or shootouts. And instead of wasting our time on penny-ante bullshit, busting dealers on one block and having new ones spring up on the next, the police are free to spend our time on more important things."

"More important things? Like what?"

"Like robbery, like rape—"

"Cut the crap. The reason the police department doesn't bother to bust these dealers is because they're on the West Side. Nobody in city government gives a squashed turd about anything that happens in our part of town unless somebody forces them into it."

"Get off the soapbox. The question is, who killed Zapper and Pop if it wasn't you?"

"You know damn well who killed Zapper," I said.

He waited.

"It was Manny Cole." Dave raised his thick eyebrows. I kept going. "Zapper called him last night, and told him about me putting the squeeze on him. Cole got scared Zapper would crack and spill his guts to the D.A. So he solved the problem by killing him."

Dave frowned. "I don't buy it."

"Why not?"

"The thing is, killing Zapper still wouldn't solve Cole's problem. It wouldn't get rid of that incriminating videotape. So why bother killing him?"

I'd had plenty of time to think this through. "Because Cole had another teensy little problem he was worried about. A case of homicide that Zapper happened to witness."

Dave scratched his neck thoughtfully, then looked over at the TV set, which was still showing Cole stuffing money in his pocket. He turned the TV off. "Only one flaw in your theory."

"What's that?" I said belligerently. I hate skeptics.

Dave threw up his hands. "Okay, let's say you're right and Zapper got smoked because he witnessed Pop's murder. Sounds good, I'll buy it. But that still doesn't mean it was *Cole* who smoked Pop and then Zapper. Could have been anyone. Could even have been you.

"In fact," he went on, "I'm not saying I necessarily believe this, but if I were Chief Walsh, I'd say you made that tape to *blackmail* Zapper so he wouldn't testify against you at your murder trial. And then when he refused to let himself be blackmailed, you killed him."

I slumped back against the sofa. Madeline came out of her room. "How you guys doing?"

"Peachy," I told her. "Just peachy."

17

Dave was right, hypothetically it could have been anyone. But Cole was definitely the guy with the motive. To quote that famous old 70s proverb, *Follow the money*. Who benefited the most from that bullet hole in Pop's neck?

Manny Cole.

The way Dave and I estimated it, tallying up figures on a page from Madeline's phone message pad, Pop was clearing at least five hundred bucks a week from his various West Side hustles: a hundred from Zapper and Dale; a hundred apiece from his other two drug dealer tenants; a hundred from his prostitutes; and a hundred from his tenants that sold stolen goods or whatever it was they did. Add to this any cash Pop was scamming from Arcturus, plus other sleazy deals we might not be aware of, and who knows? The weekly take could easily go as high as a grand.

Which worked out to between twenty-six and fifty-two grand a year. Not bad. Since it was tax free, even the low end would just about double a Saratoga cop's regular salary.

Was it enough to kill for? I'd have to study up on

Cole's finances, see if he was having trouble paying off a mortgage or something.

One thing I did know: The timing fit perfectly. One and a half months ago, according to Dave, Cole was assigned to weekend foot patrols on the West Side. And he was probably asked, either subtly or in so many words, to look the other way from Pop's tenants' activities.

So what did Cole do? No doubt he did what any red-blooded American would do: He asked for a piece.

But let's say Pop refused. Cole is outraged—hey, this is no way for one cop to treat another. So he comes at Pop again, this time *demanding* a piece. Pop again refuses, and now the tempers and testosterone get really out of hand. The two men argue, they come to blows, Pop executes one of his North Korean torture maneuvers . . .

And in the heat and hormones of the moment, Cole shoots Pop with his own gun.

Having experienced both cops' violent streaks at first hand, this scenario was easy for me to believe.

Unfortunately, believing in Cole's guilt and proving it were two very different things. I could leave this whole mass of confusion to whatever private investigator Malcolm hired, but to quote another old chestnut: If you want something done right, you better do it yourself.

Dave and I agreed that for my next move, I should get evidence that Cole took over Pop's "accounts" after Pop was killed. That would establish a murder motive for Cole.

With motive in hand, Malcolm and I could go to the chief and demand that he widen the murder investigation to include Cole as a suspect. If the chief said no, we'd threaten to air out his department's dirty linen with good old Judy at the newspaper. (Which reminded me: I better talk to her and make sure she didn't open that envelope I'd FedExed her until I gave her the okay.)

Even if the chief refused to budge, and I was put on trial, it sure would be nice to have an alternative murder theory to present to the jury. Especially if they were "poisoned."

But I'd have to do all my requisite evidence-gathering without any help from Dave. Not surprisingly, he showed zilch enthusiasm for helping me bust a fellow cop. "Come on, bro," I pleaded. "Here I set you up with Madeline, the second most beautiful woman in the world, and you still won't help me?"

"Bet your ass. I've helped you way too much already."

So I set off on my mission alone. First, though, I touched base at home. It was getting to be a routine: check in with my traumatized family to let them know Daddy is still alive and at large.

This time I'd conscientiously left Andrea a note that I was going out for a couple of hours and I'd be back before breakfast. But that still hadn't been enough to assuage my boys' fears. As I came up the stairs to our bedroom, I heard Raphael saying, "Mommy, maybe we should send out a church party"—*church party?*—and Leonardo was fretting, "Did they revoke him back to jail?"

I walked through the door calling out "Hey, guys!", and they immediately jumped all over me like starved puppies.

After we spent a half hour wrestling and tickling each other, and another half hour chowing down on the homemade waffles that they ordered me to prepare for them, Andrea and the kids piled into the minivan and headed for their various Tuesday morning destinations. Meanwhile I went to the shed in our backyard to get my bicycle, so I could head over to the *Daily Saratogian* to see Judy.

Biking to the *Daily Saratogian* turned out to be something of an adventure. Zapper's murder had brought the TV vans back in full force this morning. It must have been a slow weekend for news, because the reporters were in a surly mood. They were stubbornly insistent on getting a comment from me, holding their cameras and microphones so close they bumped into my nose. I tried to get up a head of steam on my bike so I could escape them. But they were crowding me so much that I couldn't get my wheels clear.

Finally I tried the oldest trick in the book. "Ladies and gentlemen," I announced, "if you'll all give me some room, I have a statement to make." So they all backed up a few yards to give me room—and I jammed my feet down hard on the pedals and took off. By the time they got back into their vans and started following me, I was gone.

The *Daily Saratogian* building is a block off Broadway, across the street from the police station entrance at City Hall. I practically broke out in hives as I pedaled past the entrance, but I made it by there without any cops dragging me inside and attacking me.

I quickly locked my bike and scooted inside the newspaper office, eager to get out of sight of the police station. I slipped past a couple of receptionists who were busy selecting doughnut holes from a Dunkin Donuts box, and came to Judy's corner office.

Through her plate glass window I saw Judy sitting at her desk, biting her nails as she stared fretfully at a familiar large brown envelope. She was eyeing my handwriting on the cover—TO BE OPENED IN THE EVENT

OF MY DEATH—and trying to decide whether to go ahead and open it anyway.

Finally her jittery fingers reached for the envelope clasp and pried it open. Then she closed it, then opened it again. She was desperate to look inside, but knew she'd feel like a sleaze if she did. It was fun to watch, like seeing Eve and the Apple, take two. Pandora redux.

Then at last Judy made a decision. She opened her desk drawer, flung the envelope inside, and slammed the drawer shut with an air of finality.

So Judy had actually managed to resist temptation. Eve and Pandora would have been impressed—

But then Judy opened the drawer back up and took the envelope out again. She fiddled with the clasp and chewed at her bottom lip so hard I was afraid it would bleed, as she went through her agonized mental convolutions all over again. I took pity on her and opened the door quietly. "Hi, there," I said.

"*Aauuh!*" she screamed, jumping startled out of her chair. "Jesus H.," she said reproachfully as she caught her breath, "don't give me a heart attack."

"Just wanted to let you know I'm not dead," I said, gesturing at the envelope.

"Jake, how could you *do* this to me? I'm a newspaperman, for God's sake—"

"You mean newspaper*woman*."

"You can't expect me to just sit on something like this and not even *read* it."

I sat down. "Actually, if I were you, I'd stick that envelope in my bottom drawer and not mention it to anyone. Two people have been killed already."

She gulped and hid the envelope away. "Thanks for the tip."

"Jude, I'm sorry to get you involved, but I really need you to do some things for me."

She eyed me dubiously. "Like what?"

Ignoring her lack of zeal, I plowed on. "There's a nine-year-old kid I know who might need an emergency place to stay. He's a good kid. You think you could play hostess, just for a little while?"

I was counting that Judy's soft spot for needy kids, which I knew about from her work with the Literacy Volunteers, would cause her to say yes. And I was right. "I guess so," she said grudgingly. "Who's the kid?"

"I'd rather not say right now. But I'll let you know. The second thing is, I'm looking for photographs of Pop Doyle and a cop named Manny Cole."

"Yeah, I know Cole. What's he got to do with this?"

"I'll tell you when I'm ready. And while you're at it, I need a list of addresses for all the properties Pop owned on the West Side. I'd go to City Hall for the info myself, but I break into a cold sweat whenever I go near the place."

"Jake, what are you up to *now*? Does Andrea know?"

I stood up. "Enough questions, okay? Look, I know you think I'm a killer, but how about helping me anyway, just for old times' sake."

Judy stood up too, gazing at me steadily. "I'm not sure you're a killer, but you're definitely a damn fool. Stay here," she told me, and went out. Half an hour later she came back with the photographs, along with addresses for the seven slummy houses that Pop owned. She also had addresses for three other West Side buildings that Pop owned a piece of: the Grand Hotel and two light industrial buildings.

"And here's a whole bunch of other stuff too, like partnership and incorporation papers," Judy said, handing them over to me. "I was talking to the lady in the city clerk's office, and somehow she figured out you were the person I was getting stuff for, and she got real helpful all of a sudden. She said to say hi."

That must be the gray-haired lady who'd gotten me the records for 107 Elm on the day of the zoning hearing. Between her and Dave's mom, I seemed to have a way with older women. I should mention that to Malcolm when it came time to pick a jury.

I shuffled randomly through the various papers, not expecting to find anything useful, when something caught my eye: the list of partners for the purchase of the Grand Hotel building. I did a serious double take.

The partners included Paul "Pop" Doyle; John Walsh, the chief; William Foxwell, the lieutenant; Douglas Beach, a.k.a. Young Crewcut; a couple of names I didn't recognize—

And *Dave Mackerel.*

My friendly neighborhood cop.

What the hell was going on here? I thought Dave hated these guys, especially Pop.

"Is something wrong?" Judy asked me, registering the bafflement on my face.

I didn't answer. My mind was racing. Dave had told me about Pop's real estate holdings, but he never mentioned the Grand Hotel. And he certainly never mentioned that he and Pop were partners. Why had he hidden that?

And what else was he hiding? I thought back to when Pop was still alive and I asked Dave to help me fight him, but he refused. Was it because Dave, as the only cop who lived on the West Side, was getting a piece of Pop's action himself?

I must have looked pale or something, because Judy asked me, "Jake, do you need to sit down?"

I shook my head and stared unseeing at the partnership papers, trying to get a grip. What exactly was I suspecting Dave of? After all, he had been *helping* me this whole time . . . hadn't he?

Actually, no, he hadn't. He was the guy who busted me in the first place. And come to think of it, when Pop got shot in the backyard of 107 at one A.M., Dave suddenly appeared out of nowhere—even though he'd told me once that he slept in the rear of his house and never heard noises from 107.

An icy feeling spread through me. I had to face it. I was suspecting Dave of murder.

But what would be his motive? Did Pop rip him off somehow in their dealings? Or had Dave killed Pop in a moment of blinding fury because Pop was beating the crap out of him?

But then why had he played along with me all this time, instead of just feeding me to the wolves? Maybe his good buddy routine was just a camouflage. Had he just been *acting* helpful, to keep me from suspecting him of murder?

Judy interrupted my frenzied thoughts. "Listen, I do need to get back to work soon. I have a meeting . . ."

I came back to myself. "Sure, Judy, thanks. Appreciate your help." I walked out of her office, still dazed.

As I headed down the steps of the *Daily Saratogian* and started to unlock my bike, two cops came out of the police station laughing. I tried to put on my bike helmet before they recognized me, but they glanced over just in time, and their laughter died. They gave me hard stares, and then one of them took out his nightstick and started tapping his hand with it, trying to unnerve me.

He succeeded. My hands shook so badly I couldn't

unlock my Master lock. I did the combination three times, but I must have been getting the numbers wrong somehow, because it wouldn't open no matter how hard I yanked at it.

The cops watched me struggling helplessly with my lock and began laughing again. The one with the nightstick jeered, "Need some help, pal?" and the other one slapped his thigh and screeched like a hyena, as if it was the most hilarious thing he'd ever heard.

Terrific. Mister Macho Man, trying to take on the entire Saratoga Springs Police Department, and I couldn't even get my damn bike lock open.

18

After my embarrassment with the bike lock, I needed some java to steady my nerves. So I headed over to Starbucks, which I normally avoid like the plague. But how could I go to Madeline's and casually ask her for a cup of coffee, please, while suspecting her boyfriend of murder?

Not that I was so sure Dave had done it. For one thing, I couldn't let Manny Cole off the hook. It was odd that he wasn't partnered up on the Grand Hotel deal with all of his cop buddies. Was there some hidden animosity there . . . and was he jealous of Pop's wealth?

If only there were some way to get behind that blue wall, I thought, as I paid for my coffee with a handful of lint-covered change. I had to find out what was really going on between these cops, but without a good connection—

As if in answer to my prayer, I suddenly spotted Hal Starette sitting over in the back corner with Lia Kalmus. True, Hal wasn't a cop, but he'd negotiated with them, and that was something.

I swallowed my pride and walked over. They saw me coming and threw each other panicky looks. Well, I've crashed parties before. "Guys, let's play pretend," I said as I joined them. "Let's pretend I'm not the man who killed Pop."

The way they screwed up their faces and moved their chairs as far away from me as they could, you'd have thought I was a dangerous foreign terrorist with a bad case of halitosis.

"Look, all I want to know is this. When you were buying that building, Hal, did you see any tension between the cops themselves?"

They just looked at each other, hoping I'd magically disappear. Hal's nose started getting shiny right before my eyes. Lia's bad eye blinked furiously.

"Lia, we've known each other for a long time," I said, calling in every chit I might have earned over the years as an S.O.S. volunteer. "Have you heard of any fighting between Pop and Dave Mackerel, or between Pop and Manny Cole?"

Finally she spoke. "I haven't heard of anything like that."

"Me, neither," Hal added.

"You sure? Did anyone ever complain about getting ripped off in any way?"

"No," Hal said. Lia didn't bother to answer. She excused herself and went off to the bathroom. Meanwhile Hal gave me an apologetic half-smile.

I mumbled a useless "Okay, well, let me know if you hear anything," and shuffled off. When you're an accused murderer, good help is hard to find. I gulped down my coffee and got the hell out of there.

Fortunately, I didn't need Hal or Lia or anyone else to help me with my research into Pop's and Cole's payoff scams. That I could do by myself. The first stop on my itinerary was scenic 46 Beekman Street, home to another one of Pop's drug dealer tenants.

I knocked on the rotten, splintery door, still unsure

what approach to take. How about: "Good morning, I'm conducting a research survey for the Saratoga Chamber of Commerce. We were wondering, have you bribed any policemen lately?"

I waited, then knocked again, then waited some more. I was about to leave when the door finally opened. Standing behind it was a shrimpy little white guy who was naked except for a pair of torn and dirty white underwear—actually, grayish-yellow underwear. He was five feet tall and looked about as tough as my four-year-old. He had an odd face: His mouth was wide, his skull was flat, and his eyes were sunken in. He looked familiar, but I couldn't quite place him.

I gave him my warmest smile. "Hi, my name is Jacob Burns—"

"Oh, God!" Mr. Dirty Underwear jumped back in fear. *"Oh God, oh God, oh God!"*

Yet another bad entrance.

"What's wrong?" I asked, smiling even harder, but that just seemed to unnerve Dirty Underwear all the more. He was so rattled he forgot to close the door on me, and when he retreated he tripped and fell to the floor. Maybe he was on some mood-altering substance. If he was, I hoped he wasn't selling much; it was bad stuff.

He scrambled to his feet, then backed up against a wall that was covered by torn and dirty grayish-yellow wallpaper. It blended in well with his underwear. "Y-y-you're the guy whacked Zapper!"

I started to say no, but then stopped. Instead I put on my fiercest prison scowl and swaggered up to him. I felt a little guilty terrorizing a guy this small and this wasted, but hey, a man's life was at stake. Mine. "Yo, muthafucka," I growled at him, "you paying money to Cole?"

Dirty Underwear blinked. "Cole?"

"Yeah, prick lips, Cole. This man," I said, and showed him a photograph.

Dirty Underwear looked distraught. "Sure, I'm paying him just like he said. I don't want no trouble. He send you here?"

"You paying him the same amount you paid Pop?"

"Yeah."

"How much?"

"A hundred dollars." A dim light of intelligence flared up in his bleary eyes. Interestingly, the whites of his eyes were grayish-yellow, too. "Hey, if Cole sent you, then how come you don't know how much I pay him?"

His eyebrows beetled together as he tried to puzzle it out, and I suddenly knew where I recognized him from. He looked exactly like a picture I'd seen in the newspaper recently of what fetal alcohol syndrome does to a person's face.

All that booze he drank in the womb seemed to have done a number on his brain, too. How did he manage to make a living at a difficult entrepreneurial business like street-level drug dealing? Maybe his secret was that he looked so wimpy and stupid, everyone trusted him.

I must have been staring hard at him, because he gave me an anxious smile and put his hands up. "Yo, I didn't mean nothing by it, dude. I'm sorry."

He looked so pathetic I didn't have the heart to give him any more shit. I just walked out.

The truth was, most of the criminals I'd met during the past week at the city and county jails weren't arrogant jerks like Zapper. Most of them, I reflected as I walked up to the house where Pop's prostitute tenants lived, were the most miserable, sorry-ass people you ever saw.

That certainly was true of the greasy-haired, pallid-faced, forty-something woman who opened the door at the prostitutes' house wearing a shapeless nightgown with what looked like moth holes. She yawned in my face. "Kind of early, ain't it?"

"Yeah," I said uncertainly, feeling my way.

"I don't usually work mornings."

"I don't blame you," I said, trying to be agreeable.

"It'll cost you double," she said, lazily scratching her crotch as she sized me up. Maybe that was supposed to be sexy, I don't know. "Fifty for a jiffy lube." *Jiffy lube?* "Hundred for a new muffler." *New muffler?*

"Forty's all I got." I reached in my wallet and handed it over. Credit card debt, here I come.

She stuck out her hand and felt my crotch. "Come on in, big boy," she said.

Jiffy lube? New muffler?

"Actually, I was wondering if you recognize this man," I said, showing her the photograph of Cole. She looked down at it and up at me. Then she took her hand off my crotch, swiftly stepped back, and started to shut the door in my face.

I threw my foot in the way. "Whoa. You don't have to answer, but give me back the forty."

She brought out the money. I reached out to take it, but then she stuffed it right back in her pocket. "Get your ass in here," she said.

So I did. Meanwhile she went out on her porch, looked both ways to make sure no one was watching, and came back in and closed the door.

I looked around me. This was no high-class New Orleans–style bordello. The most romantic thing in the place was a box of rubbers sitting next to some

Band-Aids on top of a grimy old bureau. I wondered what the Band-Aids were for, then quickly realized I didn't want to know.

The prostitute faced me with her hands on her hips. "Why you want to know about Cole?" she asked. Her lips were big and pouting and her eyes were open wide. She still had a good body, and in this dark hallway, where I couldn't see the pallor in her face or the grease in her hair, she actually looked attractive. I was so surprised, I stood there with my mouth open.

"What you staring at?" she said angrily.

I couldn't think of any answers that would be better than the truth. "I'm sorry, it's just I hadn't noticed it before, but you're very pretty."

She stared at me incredulously, then burst out laughing, a surprisingly hearty sound rising from deep inside her. "Man's sweet-talking me," she gasped between guffaws, "sweet-talking the old neighborhood whore. *Shit,* now there's a gentleman for you. Sit down. What you want?"

I told her, and she gave it to me. She explained that Pop used to take his payoff in trade, not money. He'd come to the whorehouse twice a week.

Then, two days after he died, Cole showed up. Since then, he'd been coming over every night at the end of his shift. "He hurts too," she said, wincing. "I ain't saying he's big, 'cause he ain't, but he just jams into you, know what I'm saying? I told him, and the other girls did too, but he just thought that was funny. Started doing it even harder." She shook her head. "Man's fucked up. You figure out some way to get him out of our short hairs, we'd sure as hell appreciate it, but you better not let him know I ratted on him."

"I won't," I promised. "By the way, what was Pop like? He seemed like a pretty sadistic guy, too."

The prostitute laughed again, but harshly this time. "Pop wasn't a problem. All you had to do was piss on him, and he'd be happy."

I shook my head, amazed. "Gee, I wish I'd known. I'd have been glad to piss on him myself, free of charge."

She wagged a finger at me. "Hey, don't be cutting in on our business now."

On my way out the door, I asked her, "By the way, I'm dying to know. What *is* a jiffy lube, anyway?"

She winked. "Pay me another forty and find out."

After spending most of my adult life at a computer, wrestling with words and feelings, it felt good to explore the Sam Spade in me. Acting like a hard-ass, I was learning, was fun. No wonder so many guys do it.

And not only was it fun, it was productive. I now had evidence that Cole had strong economic incentive to kill Pop. Come to think of it, he had strong sexual incentive, too. I mean, unlimited access to free jiffy lubes—what a deal!

There was only one problem with all of this. It didn't prove that Cole was the killer. The killer could conceivably be any one of the many drug dealers, prostitutes, and thieves that Pop was extorting money from.

It could even be Dennis.

As I headed up Beekman toward Arcturus, I tried to picture Dennis getting into a crazed, one a.m. fight with Pop and killing him. Once again, I found myself almost rooting for a friend of mine to be unmasked as a murderer. I opened the door to Arcturus and walked in.

The place smelled of incense, candle wax, and all the other ingredients of a teen arts center and hang-out spot. "Hi, Dennis!" I called out cheerfully, like I was his best buddy.

"Hi, Mr. Burns!" Tony called back as he ran in from the other room. His T-shirt was covered with splotches of paint. I was glad to see that he didn't look like he had suffered any under Dennis's care.

I hugged him, being careful not to get any paint on me. "How you doing, Tony? Everything okay?"

"Yeah," he said solemnly. "I heard about Zapper. Do you know who did it?"

"No, I'm trying to find out."

"You need some help? I went by your house this morning but you weren't there."

I didn't want Tony to be any more involved in all of the recent carnage than he already was, so I changed the subject. "Wait a minute. It's Tuesday. How come you're not in school?"

"Mr. O'Keefe said I don't have to go to school if I don't want."

"He said *what*?"

"Mr. O'Keefe is so *cool*." I felt a sharp twinge of . . . what was it exactly? *Jealousy*, that's what, jealousy that another man was replacing me in Tony's affections. As he talked about Dennis, his face filled with adoration. "He says school is just a propaganda tool of the imperialist ruling classes."

I closed my eyes. "Oh, no."

"He says school is a ridiculous waste, and I should use my time more wisely—"

"Look, let me tell you something. You can't take everything Dennis says seriously. He's a great guy and everything, but he's stuck in time to about 1967, and—"

"Hey, but I'm right, aren't I?" Dennis broke in. He

was standing in the doorway, filling it with his belly. Today's T-shirt carried my favorite slogan from the 60s, ESCHEW OBFUSCATION. It struck me that if his beard and long hair suddenly turned white, he'd look exactly like a radical left-wing Santa Claus. "Name one thing you learned in elementary school that you couldn't have learned a lot easier somewhere else. All school really teaches you is how to raise your hand and wait in line."

"And a few other minor details, like how to read and write."

"School didn't teach those things to Tony, did it?" Dennis was standing close to me, and he peered into my eyes. There was an edginess to him today; he was talking even faster than usual. "So what happened last night with Zapper? You have anything to do with it?"

Since I had the uneasy feeling that the videotape I made *did* have something to do with it, I didn't answer his question. "Look, if Tony doesn't go to school, they'll sic Social Services on him by the end of the week. He'll have to go back to his mother, or some weird foster care situation. If you open your home to kids that need help, you have to take responsibility."

"I *am* taking responsibility. Come here. Wait 'til you see this." He headed off to the back room, and I had no choice but to follow.

As soon as I entered the room, the smell of paint overpowered my nose, and a medley of colors overpowered my eyes. The whole floor was covered by a huge square of brightly painted cardboard. When I say "painted," I'm using the term in its most liberal sense. Some of the colors looked like they had been thrown on, and still others had been dripped on, or fingerpainted on, or mixed with mashed potatoes and then *splotched* on.

Ordinarily this kind of stuff is not my cup of tea, but the hodgepodge of colors and techniques somehow "worked," as they say in the art world. Even more impressive, the painted cardboard had been carved into a giant jigsaw puzzle with about fifty pieces, and each piece had its own fullness of color and proportions, its own artistic integrity.

"Who made this?" I asked, not trying to hide my amazement. Dennis pointed at Tony, who was beaming like a thousand-watt bulb. "You're kidding," I said to Tony. "This is *yours*?"

He was too overcome with pride to say anything, so he just nodded. Dennis spoke up for him, that slightly manic edge still there in his voice. "I asked Tony what he was into, and he said jigsaw puzzles. So I gave him some old cardboard and leftover paint and other junk, and he's been in here working ever since yesterday morning. Not bad, huh?"

"*Not bad?* It's fabulous!" I slapped the kid five. "From now on I'll have to call you Picasso."

"Picasso? Who's that?" Tony asked.

Dennis cut in quickly. "So tell me, you think Tony would be doing anything remotely this exciting if he was in school? *Hah.* He could go to school twelve years straight without a single one of his teachers ever giving him stuff to make a puzzle with. They'd never even know he was into jigsaw puzzles in the first place."

I felt bad that I hadn't known about Tony's love of jigsaw puzzles myself. Dennis's idealism was making me feel like an old fogy, as I often felt when I was with him. Time to put an end to this line of conversation. "Dennis, I need to talk to you."

"So, *nu*?" An Irishman who spoke Yiddish—it was hard to dislike the guy. "Go ahead, talk."

"Privately."

We both looked over at Tony, who squirmed and said, "Okay, see you later—"

"No, stay right here," Dennis interrupted, frowning at me. "Children deserve for us to be up front with them, not whisper behind their backs." For a guy who'd never had any children, Dennis sure had a lot of opinions about them. If he ever got around to having pipsqueaks of his own, I'd root for them to be especially wild kids who drove him crazy. "If you have anything to say about Tony—"

"I don't. It's about me and you." I was surprised by the tough-guy timbre of my voice. Without even meaning to, I'd switched into Sam Spade interrogation mode. It was becoming second nature.

Dennis was startled into silence—no small achievement. Tony said, "I'm going skateboarding," and started out.

I expected Dennis to warn him to be careful and stay on the sidewalk. But he offered no such admonitions; maybe they didn't fit in with his ultra-laid-back childrearing philosophy. So that made it my job to play the cautious parent, a role I hate. "Watch out for cars," I told Tony.

"Yeah, yeah," he called back, in a bored voice.

"Jake, I got to be honest," Dennis told me as soon as Tony was gone. "I'm not too comfortable being alone with you."

"Why not?"

"Because as far as I can figure it, you killed two people."

Hmm. That would explain the manic edge I'd noticed. But on the other hand, maybe he had other reasons for feeling uncomfortable, reasons he wasn't telling me. I cut to the chase. "Dennis, why were you paying extortion money to Pop?"

His eyes widened in surprise. "What in God's name are you talking about?"

He looked utterly sincere. But Zapper had been positive that Pop was getting money from Dennis. I acted like I was positive, too. "Don't fuck with me."

"Have you gone off the deep end?"

"Hey, I thought lying was supposed to be bad for your sobriety."

"Jake, I realize you're under a lot of pressure, but—"

"And now you're paying off Manny Cole, aren't you?"

He shook his head in bewilderment. "Are you kidding? Why would I pay *him* off?"

Had Zapper been wrong about Dennis? Was he actually clean?

I felt like crawling underneath Tony's jigsaw puzzle, but instead I forged full-speed ahead. "Here's the deal. Pop extorted money from you and about five other people. Cole found out and demanded that Pop share the profits. When Pop said no, Cole killed him and took over the business for himself. Now you can either help me prove it, in which case I do my best to keep you out of it; or you stonewall me, I go straight to the cops with everything I know about you, and your ass is theirs. Your choice, buddy."

He just stood there looking stunned, but not afraid. *Damn,* he was calling my bluff. My Sam Spade act had failed miserably. I better get out of there before I broke down and started crying. I threw him a fierce glare, snapped, "Suit yourself," and walked around the jigsaw puzzle to the door.

But then he stopped me. "Hey, you think those cops will even give you the time of day? They're all a bunch of asshole buddies, from the chief on down. Even if Pop and Cole *were* extorting money, Walsh would hush it up."

My heart pounded. Was this an oblique admission? Had Zapper been right about Dennis after all?

"Let me straighten you out: *nothing* is getting hushed up around here," I said, keeping my hand on the doorknob like I was threatening to leave at any moment. "This is a murder investigation. I've got Dave Mackerel on my side. You don't help me out, then Dave will be all over you, and so will Bobby Hawthorne, the Assistant D.A." I was throwing names around like crazy. If Dave found out what I was saying about him, he'd shoot me.

"I still don't see what all this has to do with Pop being murdered," Dennis whined.

Yes, *whined.* I *had* him.

"Well, too fucking bad. You either eschew the obfuscation—right now—or I tell Dave to come in here and throw the book at you." I was so full of shit my ears should have turned brown. I turned the doorknob, praying silently for Dennis to stop me—

And he did. "For God's sake, *all right*!" he said, putting his hand to his forehead like he had a headache. "If I really thought this had anything to do with the murder, I'd have told you a long time ago." He glowered at me. "I still think you did it. You're just looking for some stupid alibi."

"Spare me the legal commentary and tell me what happened."

He gave an exasperated wave of his arm. Then he sank down defeatedly on the floor next to Tony's puzzle and told me his sordid tale.

It all started back in January, when Pop cited Arcturus for littering the sidewalk out front. Cost to Arcturus: $100.

Then in February, Pop gave Dennis and several Arcturus volunteers numerous nitpicky parking tickets. Total cost: $200.

In March, Pop cited Arcturus for a grab-bag assortment of traffic, littering, and noise violations. Total cost: $400.

In April, Pop cited Arcturus for improving the rear exterior of their building without getting prior approval from the Zoning Board. Arcturus had to hire a lawyer to deal with it. The lawyer gave them a bargain-basement price, but even so . . . Total cost: $600.

In May, Pop came to Dennis one evening when he was in the building alone. He showed Dennis a citation he'd written up against Arcturus for operating a skateboard store in a residential neighborhood without a proper license. Total projected cost, if Arcturus fought it: who knows? At least four figures, maybe even five.

And if Arcturus fought and lost, they'd be forced to find another building. "Only we have a cash flow problem right now, until our Youth Services and CDBG grants come in. So by the time we sold this building and found another place that's cheap enough, we'd be bankrupt," Dennis said bitterly. "*Sayonara,* Arcturus. I'm out of a job, and more important, all the kids who depend on Arcturus, kids who are growing up without decent parenting or food or love, except what they find here—"

I cut him off. "So what happened?"

Dennis made a fist, either wanting to punch Pop or punch me, I'm not sure. "I paid him to go away."

"How much?"

Dennis rubbed his forehead with his fist. His headache was getting worse. "Two hundred bucks a month."

I whistled through my teeth. "Two hundred a month? You mean, like, *forever*?"

"That was the arrangement. And then we'd operate free from police interference. If the neighbors bitched about skateboarding or noise or whatever, he'd take care of it."

"So this payoff thing started in May?"

"Yeah."

"And kept going all the way until he died?"

Dennis nodded ruefully. "First of every month. Regular as the phone company."

"But with Arcturus dead broke, that must have been a huge hardship."

"You're telling me. August and September, it came right out of my own paycheck."

My heart was pounding again. I tried to keep cool. "So when Pop died, you figured that would be the end of it."

"Hell, I won't lie, I was ecstatic when he died. But then that asshole Cole came along, and now I have to pay *him*."

I gave Dennis a friendly nod. "Fucking pigs, huh?"

He nodded back, grateful that I was being so agreeable. "Yeah, fucking pigs. I don't blame you for killing the guy."

"Only one thing."

"What?"

"I didn't kill him. You did."

Dennis's head snapped back, and he tried to laugh. "That's crazy!"

"Where were you that night?"

"How the hell should I know?"

"Because you do." I stepped around the puzzle, giving him my best Clint Eastwood look. He backed up, almost knocking over a paint can. "Here's what happened that night. You were driving home from the Thursday night coffeehouse at Arcturus. You saw Pop's car parked in front of 107 Elm. It was the first of the month. You were broke. You decided to confront him about lowering the payoff amount. But he just laughed at you. So you got on your usual high horse. He lost his temper and popped you a couple. You got mad and grabbed his gun—"

"I don't believe this. You're trying to frame me!"

"And you killed Zapper too, didn't you?"

"Why would I do that?!"

"Because he saw you kill Pop, and *he* started blackmailing you, too!"

Dennis's big, hammy hands opened wide, like they were eager to squeeze my neck. "You get out before I . . ."

"Before you what? Kill me?"

"Get the fuck out!" he roared.

No problem. I'd gotten what I came for. I opened the door.

Little Tony was standing right there, with a skateboard under his arm and paralyzed fear on his face.

"Tony—" Dennis and I both said at the same time.

But Tony threw his skateboard at us and ran away. By the time I made it outside he was gone from sight.

Dennis was right behind me. "Now look what you've done. He was just starting to trust me."

"Good thing he stopped," I said.

But I wasn't sure I meant it. Was Saratoga's left-wing Santa Claus really the killer?

I jumped on my bike and headed down the street, looking for Tony so I could try to comfort him. I didn't know what I'd say to the kid, but maybe I'd come up with something.

I rode all around Saratoga for the next hour, but never found a trace of him.

19

The wind picked up and the temperature dropped another five degrees. I wasn't wearing my jacket and I was chilled to the bone.

I rode my bike up Elm Street toward home. Maybe a PB and J sandwich for lunch would cure all of my physical and spiritual ills. It often does.

The TV vans were gone, but there was a cop car parked in front of my house. Well, hell, I hadn't done anything wrong . . . had I? Fighting an impulse to turn my bike around and have lunch in town somewhere, or maybe get started on that trip to Mexico, I pedaled resolutely onward.

As I rode closer, I noticed the cop car was empty. A sudden thought hit me: *What if there's some cop lying on the backseat in a pool of blood?* Breaking into an instant sweat, I squealed my brakes. Why was all this shit happening to me? Now I really did turn my bike around and zoom off.

But then I turned my head for one last look and saw a cop: Manny Cole. He wasn't lying in a pool of blood, he was walking stealthily underneath my grape arbor. And he was looking all around, to make sure no one was watching him.

I veered my bike hard to the right, hiding myself

behind the same bedraggled bushes that I'd thrown Zapper's knife into. Safe from Cole's sight, I studied him. He was sneaking off toward the backyard of 107. Why was he acting so furtive? And why did that jacket he was carrying under his arm look so familiar?

Because it was *my* jacket!

I got off the bike and stashed it in the bushes. Then I stashed myself in there too and waited.

A minute passed, maybe two. It felt like hours. From my hiding place I could see Cole's car, but not Cole himself. Was he in Zapper's backyard, or mine? And what the heck was he doing with my jacket?

I poked my head out from behind the junipers, then quickly poked it back in again. Cole was walking down my driveway toward his car.

But he wasn't acting furtive anymore, he was strutting proudly.

And he was minus my jacket.

After he drove away, I jumped out of the bushes, deposited my bike on the driveway, and ran to Zapper's backyard. The jacket wasn't there. I ran to my own backyard; still no jacket.

I didn't get it. Had Cole planted my jacket inside Zapper's apartment, to incriminate me? But that didn't make sense; no doubt the cops had already gone through the apartment for clues last night, after the murder.

But Cole had *something* up his sleeve, that was for sure, and I better have something up mine. Screw it, maybe I should just break into Zapper's apartment and find out what Cole had done. Had he stuffed my jacket behind the sofa or under the bed, so the other cops would believe they must have missed it when they went through the apartment the first time?

I was an old hand at breaking and entering; when I was busy solving that other murder, I did it three times. All I needed now was the hammer from my kitchen tool box, so I could smash open a window. Eager to get the B and E job done before any cops came back, I stepped quickly to my side porch, opened the screen door—

And right there, hanging on its customary hook, was my jacket.

How bizarre. Why did Cole take my jacket only to put it right back?

I picked it up. There didn't seem anything different about it. I checked my pockets and found the usual crumpled chocolate bar wrappers, nothing else. There were the customary faded areas on the elbows; some muddy spots here and there, most of which came from my trip to the cemetery; a couple of dark reddish stains near the right wrist, which must have come from . . .

From what?

Grape juice? No, not purple enough. I brought my nose close and sniffed. It smelled a little like iron, and something else I couldn't identify—

Oh, my God. I sniffed again. Horrified, I threw the jacket away from me to the ground.

It was *dried blood.*

Cole had rubbed some of Zapper's blood into my jacket! Some time soon—today, I'd bet—the cops would come roaring up to my house with a search warrant.

And I'd be stone busted.

Gut-wrenching panic took over my body. I grabbed the jacket from the ground, jumped into my old Toyota Camry, and backed up. I heard a *thunk;* it was my bike, getting crunched beneath my wheels. My trusty old Raleigh that had been with me for fifteen years, since before I had the money to buy a car.

But I had no time to mourn. In the rearview mirror I spied a cop car coming up Elm toward my house—and toward me. Was the big search about to begin? Would their warrant cover my car, too? Next to me, that incriminating bloody jacket was burning a hole in my car seat. I could just imagine Cole's evil grin as he picked up my jacket and pretended to spot the blood for the first time.

Slamming my foot on the accelerator, I tore off as fast as my antique Camry could carry me.

Behind me the cop car sped up, honking its horn. No, wait, not just one cop car—there were two of them.

Praying to the god of Japanese cars, I zigged right on Hyde Street and zagged left on West Circular, trying to shake the cops. But they closed in on me. Their sirens started screaming, and so did I. A recycling truck lumbered along ahead of me, forcing me to slow down. *Damn.* The cops raced toward me, lights flashing.

Only one thing to do. I sped around the truck—and came face to face with a television van bearing down on me from the other direction. I caught a quick glimpse of Max Muldoon's thick mustache and terrified face in the driver's seat as I swerved back to the right just in time, almost crashing into a parked minibus. I heard the agonized squealing of the TV van's brakes as we missed each other by inches. I raced on.

Behind me the sirens blared. But the cop cars were temporarily stuck. Muldoon, petrified by his near accident, had stopped his van cold in the middle of the street. That left the recycling truck and the cops immobilized behind the parked minibus. I turned left on Washington and put my pedal to the metal, feeling more like Bruce Willis than I ever expected to feel in this life.

But then the sound of the sirens changed, and I could tell the cops had broken free of their tormentors. If they turned right on Washington, I had a shot. If they turned left, I was one dead action hero.

I looked in the mirror. They turned left.

But I was a block ahead of them, and there were about four cars between us. Maybe if I slipped off of Washington Street right now, while they were still busy straightening their wheels, they wouldn't see me. No time to think about it; I swerved sharply into the Grand Hotel parking lot and raced to the other side of the building. *Oh, shit—the exit on the other side was blocked!* Because of the renovation work that had just begun, there were two huge Dumpsters barring my way.

If the cops had seen me, I was trapped. I ducked my head down under the wheel, as if that might somehow protect me from danger. The sirens screamed closer and closer, and a vision of those cages at the Saratoga City Jail came unbidden into my head.

But then the sirens screamed off down the road.

I got my Toyota in gear, backed up, and tore off down Washington in the opposite direction from the cops. I turned left on Broadway and realized too late that my route was taking me right past the police station. There were two more cop cars idling out front. I slowed way down to something approaching the speed limit, gritted my teeth . . . and drove past them without incident. Then I sped up and kept on going.

I needed to get rid of that goddamn jacket—fast.

* * *

Taking back roads, I drove out to Price Chopper, near the mall. I scrounged up four dollars in nickels and pennies from the ashtray, went into the store, and bought a pair of scissors. Then I went back to the car and hacked my jacket into three different pieces. I didn't want some lucky garbageman finding the jacket and wearing it, then learning from the local TV news that it was an important piece of evidence in a homicide case.

I threw two pieces of my jacket in the Price Chopper Dumpster. The third piece, a small section of sleeve containing the bogus bloodstains, I stuffed in an empty shoe box. I shoved the box deep into a garbage can outside The Perfect Fit, a clothing store next door to Price Chopper.

Breathing a sigh of relief, I got back in my car and started it up. Then I froze. What would I tell the cops when they asked me where my jacket was? I needed to buy a replica. It was a pretty standard denim jacket, from The Gap. But I was scared to go to The Gap in Saratoga Mall—what if the cops questioned The Gap salesmen?

So I went back into Price Chopper and got some money out of the cash machine. Then I drove half an hour north to Aviation Mall in Glens Falls. I left the radio off, afraid I might find out the cops had an all points bulletin out on me.

I fished a well-worn Adirondack Lumberjacks baseball cap out of the trunk and pulled it down low over my eyes, trying to look as commonplace and unmemorable as possible. Hopefully Pop's murder hadn't made such a big splash up in Glens Falls, and I wouldn't be recognized. Keeping my head down, I went into The Gap, picked out a denim jacket quickly before any salespeople came over to help me, and paid in cash.

Of course, I couldn't face the cops with a jacket that looked brand new. So on my way home I turned off of Route 9 onto a cornfield, got out of the car, and rolled the jacket around in the mud.

Now I was ready.

And so were the cops, as I discovered when I got home.

There were cop cars and TV vans galore out front. Before I could get into the house, I had to pass a gauntlet of TV cameras. I expected Muldoon to ask me why I'd raced around him before, but he didn't. I guess I'd driven by him too fast for him to see my face.

Inside my house, Cole and five other cops were having the time of their lives turning the place upside down. Andrea was begging them to take it easy, but they paid her no attention. They could barely contain their vicious delight as they threw our books, blankets, clothes, and the rest of our worldly possessions into big piles in the middle of all the rooms. Thank God Leonardo and Raphael were off at a friend's house.

The cops claimed they were looking for the gun I'd shot Zapper with. But I knew what they were *really* looking for—or at least, what *Cole* was really looking for. I wondered, did Lieutenant Foxwell, Young Crewcut, and the other cops who were ransacking my house know about Cole's evidence-planting scam?

When I walked into our upstairs bedroom, Cole and Young Crewcut were rummaging through Andrea's underwear drawer. I eyed them silently from the doorway. Then Cole turned, his large hands full of my wife's panties, and saw me.

His eyes immediately went to the denim jacket I was wearing. He dropped the underwear on the floor and got an excited gleam in his eyes, which he tried to hide by acting angry. "How come you ran away from us?" he growled.

"Ran away? What are you talking about?" I asked innocently.

"Talking about you hauling ass in your gray Toyota like some kind of wacko. I should bust you for reckless driving."

"Must have been some other gray Toyota."

"No way, you dumb fuck. I got your license plate."

I took a chance. "Oh, yeah? Then tell me, what *is* my license plate?"

His nostrils flared angrily. I'd caught him. But he recovered quickly. "What clothes were you wearing last night?"

"Why?"

"Because we got a warrant for your clothes, too."

I dropped my jaw and let my mouth hang open, doing my best imitation of a frightened fish. "M-m-my clothes?"

Cole gave a big sneering grin. "Yes. We'll start with your jacket."

"No! You can't have it!" I shouted in a panicky voice.

"We'll see about that." He advanced on me, with Young Crewcut at his side.

I let them back me up until I hit the bedroom wall. "All right!" I screamed. "I'll give it!"

With shaking hands, I took off my jacket and turned it over to Cole. He flashed me a triumphant look and began examining the jacket, trying not to be too obvious about knowing there were bloodstains near the wrist. So first he checked the neck, then the back, then he worked his way down the arm to the sleeve . . .

And suddenly his eyes filled with alarm. *Where was the blood?!*

Frantic, he turned the sleeve over. *Still no blood!* Then he tried the other sleeve, wildly turning it every which way. *Nothing!*

Bewildered, he stared at me.

I couldn't resist. I stuck out my tongue.

20

But it's a lot easier to stick out your tongue at a cop than it is to prove he committed two murders and is now trying to frame you for them.

Fortunately I didn't have a chance to sink into the slough of despond, because Leonardo and Raphael needed me to be strong for them. After the cops left, Andrea and I ran around cleaning up as much as we could before the boys came home from their friend's house. We didn't want them to know that the cops had torn our house apart.

When our Ninja Turtles did come home, and there were still huge piles of stuff everywhere, we told them we were just rearranging a few things. They believed us. It's amazing how gullible kids are.

So we tried to act normal during dinner and fake the kids into thinking everything was okay. But acting normal was hard. I kept getting visions of Cole sitting in his cop car, smoking his evil-smelling cigars and contemplating new ways to do me dirt.

Needing a break from all this *sturm und drang,* I decided to go to chess club. Aside from having sex and doing B and E's, playing chess is the one activity that gets me to totally immerse myself and forget all my cares.

The kids weren't enthusiastic about my leaving, but I took the sting away by practicing karate moves with them before I left. Andrea wasn't too enthused either, since it meant she'd have to finish cleaning up from the cops all by herself, but she eventually went along with it. I told her a little white lie about needing to meet Malcolm at the club, so we could consult on legal strategy.

As it turned out, though, Malcolm wasn't even there that night; he was playing in a chess league match down in Albany. So I spent the night playing with Dima, a Russian Jewish immigrant who must be at least a hundred years old but still kicks my ass routinely at chess. Not only is he one heck of a player, but he has a very distracting habit of picking his nose when he plays. He has the biggest nostrils I've ever seen. That night I tried a new defense against him, an aggressive variation of the Sicilian called the Accelerated Dragon, and he whupped me with ease. Maybe I should just stick with the Hedgehog.

Despite my ignominious loss, which was followed by two other even more ignominious losses, chess club was intensely relaxing, just like always. Even Hal Starette's presence didn't bother me; we just stayed at opposite ends of the room and ignored each other.

The great thing about chess club is, no one ever talks about anything besides chess. I'd been going there for years now, seeing the exact same men week after week and month after month; but I still knew basically nothing about them, like what their jobs were or how many kids they had or how much money they made. All I knew about them was which openings they preferred, and if they liked to castle queenside, and how they handled rook and pawn endgames.

I really believe that, in some strange way, this very lack of knowledge about the facts of each other's lives is what made us all feel so close to each other. Our relationships were totally existential.

Whenever I try to explain this to my wife, she just shakes her head and says it's further proof men are from Mars.

That night, even though all the men there undoubtedly knew I was a murder suspect, no one bothered me about it. The closest anyone came to even mentioning it was the moment I came in. A manic depressive guy in his twenties named Billy, who plays very well when his medicine is properly adjusted, looked up from his game and mumbled, "Good luck."

I nodded, then looked over at his board. "Queenside majority. Tough endgame."

"Yeah," he said, moving a pawn, and that was that.

Okay, maybe we *are* sort of Martian.

I played Dima until midnight, then realized I was so tired the bishops were starting to look like pawns. So I bade everyone good-night and headed for the parking lot.

"Jacob," I heard someone call.

I turned. It was Hal; he'd followed me outside. Now I caught a quick sour whiff of him as he stepped toward me and said, "I've got something for you."

I blinked. "What?"

Hal registered my surprise. "Look, maybe you're guilty, maybe you're not. But I can't just show up at chess club with you every Tuesday night without telling you what I know. I play lousy when I'm distracted by stuff like that."

"Sorry," I said.

He nodded. "So here it is. One chess player to another, right? You know Manny Cole?"

My skin prickled. "Sure as hell do."

"Okay. Sal, the bartender at the harness track, says Cole was in there Sunday night waving hundred-dollar bills around, making huge bets and buying drinks for everybody."

"How intriguing," I said, and it was. Further proof of Cole's newfound wealth since Pop's murder.

"Cole wasn't one of the cops who owned the Grand Hotel building," Hal went on, "so whatever he did, it had nothing to do with me."

Wait a minute. I looked at Hal's shirt. It was *drenched* with sweat.

Why was Hal busy implicating Manny Cole? Was he really just helping out a fellow chess player—or was he trying to divert my attention from something?

And what would that something be?

"Okay, Jacob, now I've told you everything. Take care," he said, and walked off toward his car.

I watched him go. His smell went with him. Had *Hal* killed Pop?

I shook my head, feeling dizzy. Dennis, Dave, Hal . . .

Next thing I knew, I'd be suspecting Max Muldoon. I better go home and get some serious shuteye.

By the time I got home it was already 12:30. There were no bothersome cop or media vehicles parked out front, and 107 was dark—Dave's house was dark too, I noted. So I looked forward to a quiet night of sleeping and letting my subconscious do its best to piece this whole thing together. I unlocked the side door, walked in—

And heard a noise in my study. Someone knocking against something. "Andrea?" I said.

No answer.

It must be Leonardo, I thought. The kid has a tendency to sleepwalk when under stress, and God knows he was under plenty of stress lately. "Hey, Leonardo," I said, turning the corner into the study.

It wasn't Leonardo.

Whoever he was, he was way too big to be Leonardo. He snarled at me, "Where's your fucking money?"

In the darkness, I couldn't make out his face. I could see his eyes, though, and unless it was my imagination they held a wild gleam. There was no question about the other gleam in the room; it belonged to a long curved knife the guy was waving at me. It looked exactly like Zapper's. Could this be Zapper's ghost?

"Where's your fucking money?" the ghost repeated, coming closer with the knife.

I backed away. "What? What money?"

"Don't play with me, asshole! I know all about it! The kid told me!"

It finally clicked: This must be Dale, Zapper's partner. And that's why his knife looked just like Zapper's—the two of them must have bought their knives together. How sweet.

Dale took a swipe at me with the knife. Not so sweet. I jumped backward, but not before the blade caught a piece of my jacket and ripped it. "You killed Zapper! You *shot* him!" Dale screamed shrilly. "We were gonna buy a shitload of dope together and go to Schenectady and get rich!"

He came at me again. Calm him down, I thought.

"Listen, Dale, that's a beautiful dream, and I'm sorry it didn't work out, but—"

"But you smoked him! You owe me, motherfucker! Where's your money?"

"Look, I don't have any money—"

Suddenly Dale swooshed down with his knife. This time he caught more than just my jacket. The blade ripped into my right shoulder, maybe an inch deep.

Intense, jagged pain flew through me. I could feel the blood flowing out. I started to scream, then forced my mouth shut. The last thing I needed was for Andrea or the kids to come downstairs and get stabbed by this drug-addled madman.

My strangled scream, or maybe the smell of my blood, got Dale excited. He made a gurgling animal noise in his throat and lunged forward.

I leapt sideways. Dale brought his knife around and attacked again. "I'll give you the money!" I said quickly. Dale's knife stopped just short of me.

My arm was killing me, but the truth was I was lucky he'd brought his knife instead of his gun; otherwise I'd be dead by now. Maybe he was using the knife as a sort of tribute to Zapper. I backed up and walked out of the room, with no particular plan in mind, and he followed close behind. I felt his blade against my back. "Don't try anything, asshole."

"Okay, man, okay." I led him into the kitchen. I didn't turn on the light, because I didn't want to look at my blood. I've never been good at that. My eyes searched around the dark room frantically for a bread knife or some other kind of weapon—but just my luck, when Andrea cleaned up from the cops, she put away everything I might be able to use in the cabinets.

Unless . . .

There was a big metal pot on the front burner of the stove, with the handle sticking out. Once someone had knocked me senseless with a pressure cooker. Maybe now I could do the same thing, if I could somehow just get hold of that handle.

"Where's the goddamn safe? Come on, where? Where?" Dale's voice was fast and high-pitched, like a record album playing at the wrong speed.

"It's down there." I pointed to the cabinet just to the right of the oven. "Back of the bottom shelf."

I was hoping he'd bend down to open it, giving me a chance to grab the pot handle. But he was too smart for that. His knife tickled my ribs. "Get down and open it. *Open it!*"

Shit, now what? "I need the key. It's under the pot here." I lifted up the pot, but then hesitated. I could feel his blade at my side. By the time I brought the pot back far enough so I could get leverage for a good solid swing at him, he'd figure out what I was doing, and his knife would be through my ribs in half a second. I felt horribly miscast, like Woody Allen trying to play a role meant for Arnold Schwarzenegger.

"Fuck are you doing?"

"Take it easy, will you? The key is inside the stove here, under the burner. See, the burner doesn't work." Keeping one hand on the pot handle, I used my other hand to remove the iron ring from the top of the burner. Moving as slowly as possible, I set it aside.

"Hurry up!" Dale barked, prodding me with the flat of his knife.

"I'm going as fast as I can, man, you busted my arm!" I did some exaggerated wincing to convince him of how pained and helpless I was. Meanwhile I removed the inner metal ring from the burner, moving at a snail's pace. Then I bent down toward the burner and peered around, as if searching for the key.

Whatever drugs Dale had ingested were clamoring for his attention, making him desperate to see that damn safe already. He opened the cabinet and stooped down, looking for it—

And I brought that big pot down as hard as I could on top of his head.

But his head was moving downward and to the right, so the pot glanced off him without doing much damage. He stood up and roared. I couldn't think what to say to him. "Sorry, just kidding" didn't seem to cut it. Then he charged at me knife-first.

Instinctively, I lifted up the pot to shield myself. The knife hit with a clang and bounced off.

But the collision between knife and pot sent a jolt of pain through my wounded right shoulder, and I dropped the pot. Now Dale had his knife ready again. He was about to attack me.

My left hand closed around the iron ring from the burner. As he rushed at me, I lifted the ring and flung it desperately in the general direction of his head.

Bull's eye!

The guy went down like he'd been karate chopped by Splinter himself. Then he just lay there, breathing peacefully.

I grabbed his knife and a telephone, planning to call the police. But then I stopped.

Would the cops believe me about what had happened? Or would they pin this on me somehow and revoke my bail?

Based on my recent experiences with the cops, maybe I better take care of this situation by myself.

So when Dale came back to life about thirty seconds later, I had his knife and was standing over him. He looked up at me and gave a confused groan. I held the knife where he could see it better. His eyes widened with fear.

"That's right, sucker," I told him. "I got the knife now. So why don't you just go on home and make yourself a nice hot cup of tea."

He nodded nervously and started to get up. But then I kicked him hard in the head and he went back down. I wish I could say I kicked him just to scare him some more, so he wouldn't get any ideas. That wouldn't be totally honest, though. I kicked him because it felt good. *Real* good. I reared back my foot to do it again.

But then it hit me that with my luck, the bastard would probably up and die on me. So I let him go without committing any further acts of violence. I did, however, give him a parting word as he stumbled out the door.

"Oh, and one more thing," I told him. "Forget Schenectady. It's a beat town."

Then I closed the door, latched it, and turned on the kitchen light. Jesus—the upper arm of my blue denim jacket was soaked with blood. More blood was spattered around on the kitchen floor. Looking at it made me almost faint, and it occurred to me, not for the first time, that a sensitive artist type like me should be doing other things with his life besides getting into car chases and beating up drug dealers.

I didn't call Andrea yet, because I didn't want to get her all upset. So I took off my jacket, trying not to look at the part of my flesh that was flopping around loose. Fighting the angry sparks of pain that were somersaulting up and down my arm, I grabbed some towels from the countertop and rags from under the sink and bound the arm as best I could.

I wanted to call an ambulance, or else attempt to drive to the emergency room myself. But I was still wary of the cops, and I was trying to decide if going to the hospital with this injury might get me into trouble, when the doorbell rang.

Was deranged Dale coming back for more?

I grabbed the knife with my good arm and headed for the door. But then I looked out my front window and saw red lights flashing. *The cops*. What the hell did *they* want?

The doorbell rang again. Maybe I should ditch the bloody knife. I quickly hid it behind the TV set, then came back to the front hall. But by the time I got there, my wife and kids were there, too.

"What's going on?" Andrea asked fearfully, as the kids watched me with wide eyes.

"Nothing. Go back upstairs," I replied.

She stared at all the rags and towels covering my arm, and her face went white. "What happened to you?"

"Really, it's nothing," I said inanely, "it's okay."

She pointed at some redness that had seeped out from under one of the rags. "Is that *blood*?" she asked, horrified.

The doorbell rang a third time. Andrea looked out the window. "It's the police. They can take you to the hospital."

"No, we're gonna shoot them!" Leonardo called out.

"Shoot them dead!" Raphael agreed.

"Shush!" Andrea said, and opened the door. Manny Cole and Young Crewcut stood on our doorstep with their hands near their guns, poised for action. Their faces looked dead serious, but their eyes were sparkling with excitement. Behind them another cop car pulled up.

Andrea was saying, "My husband's been injured. He needs to be taken to the hospital immediately."

"I'll be glad to help, ma'am," drawled Cole, enjoying himself immensely. "Let's go, Mr. Burns."

"Wait," I said. "What are you doing here? How'd you know I needed help?"

"We can talk about that on the way to the hospital, Mr. Burns. No need for your wife and kids to know all the details, wouldn't you agree?" He gave me a nasty wink.

"You talked to Dale, didn't you? What did he tell you?"

Young Crewcut chipped in. "*Everything,* Mr. Burns. How you came to his house, trying to bribe him into lying about the murders. And when he said no, you attacked him with a knife."

Andrea gasped. Raphael gazed up at me and asked, "Did you really attack him with a knife, Daddy?"

He looked impressed. Andrea, however, looked alarmed. She looked like she was wondering if Dale's story was true.

Framed again.

The world was closing in on me. The pain in my arm was searing. It reminded me of the fateful little pinch that had started it all. I was so sick and tired. I wanted to give up. Just lay down and cry. Let them pick me up and carry me off to the hospital or the jail or wherever they felt like taking me. I'd confess. I'd confess to anything, if they'd just leave me alone.

I turned to Cole. "Let me get my jacket."

He nodded. I went to the kitchen, where I slipped and fell on a bloody patch of the floor. Then I got up, picked up my blood-soaked jacket—

And ran like hell out the back door.

21

I had a seven-second head start at best. I was still in my own backyard when Cole and Young Crewcut exploded through the back door shouting, *"Freeze! Stop right where you are!"*

And I was still vaulting over the back fence when I heard the first gunshot.

What the hell—? Was Cole just shooting in the air?

I landed on the other side of the fence, then kept on running. My arm was throbbing but it didn't slow me down.

The back fence did slow *them* down, though. I gained about four seconds while they climbed over it.

And every second counted. The next two gunshots came as I ran into Western Alley. After the first shot I felt a sharp pain in my neck and I was sure I'd been hit; then I realized the pain was radiating up from my stab wound.

The second shot hit the alley right behind me. Then it ricocheted and rattled a garbage can just to my left. No, Cole was definitely not shooting at the air.

He was shooting at *me.*

Maybe he figured if he killed me while escaping arrest, it would put him in the clear for capping Pop and Zapper. With me dead, the chief would go ahead and close those cases, and no one would care enough to investigate any further.

I hit Ash Street and veered right. I could hear the cops racing up Western Alley behind me. What should I do? If I kept running down Ash, they'd have a clear shot at me as soon as they came out of the alley. So at the second house on the right, I did a quick dive behind some juniper bushes.

Lately my whole life seemed to depend on successful dives behind juniper bushes.

I couldn't see the cops through the greenery, but I heard them come to a stop at the top of the alley. "I see you, Burns!" shouted Cole. "Come out *now* or I'll shoot!"

Then there was silence. At one a.m. on a Wednesday morning, the neighborhood was quiet. Deathly quiet. No one around to witness it if the cops shot me. They were fifty feet away, with just one house between us. I tried to slow my ragged breathing.

"I don't think he got away. He's probably hiding behind some bushes somewhere," said Young Crewcut.

"Yeah. Fucker's dead meat," Cole answered. Then his voice changed; he must be speaking into his radio. "Suspect is hiding out on Ash, near Western. Request immediate assistance."

"Ash near Western, here we come," was the radio reply.

"Remember, he's armed and dangerous," said Cole. "He's got a knife, probably a gun, too."

Great, Cole was laying the groundwork for justifiable homicide. He was about to get away with his third murder; a couple more and he'd qualify as a bona fide serial killer. I wondered if he was carrying an extra gun to plant on me.

From my spot behind the junipers, I saw two

flashlight beams coming on. Cole was telling Young Crewcut, "We'll start on this side. I doubt he crossed the street. You go left, I'll go right."

Oh, shit—*I* was on the right. As soon as Cole finished checking out the exterior of the first house, he'd come to mine. And he'd find me, no sweat. I watched, paralyzed, as Cole's flashlight played over the front porch of the first house. Then his body loomed into view. He stepped onto the porch and looked around the railing to see if I was hiding behind it. His gun was out in front of him, cocked and ready.

Then he started back down the porch. Another three seconds and he'd be coming my way.

I moved my feet, about to make a desperate dash—and the movement made a crunching sound, because I was standing on a bunch of small pebbles. Some kind of fancy landscaping job. The noise terrified me, but then I got an idea. I quickly reached down and grabbed a handful of pebbles. I reared back my left, uninjured arm and threw those pebbles over the bushes, hoping they'd make it across the street.

Two seconds later, they hit. From the sound of it, they hit someone's porch. And Cole heard it, too. "He's across the street!" he yelled.

Then he ran over there, and so did Young Crewcut. Just at that moment the backup cop car raced up, without a siren but with its red light flashing. Two cops jumped out and raced across the street to join the others.

One of the cops was Dave. I thought about yelling to him for help. At least then I'd be guaranteed they would take me to jail instead of killing me.

But with a sudden start, I remembered: Having Dave there was no guarantee. He might be the murderer. Hell, for all I knew, all four of these cops were in on the murders together. And even if they weren't, they didn't exactly strike me as crusading Serpico types who would rat on one of their own for a minor infraction like shooting and killing an unarmed civilian.

The fearsome foursome were charging around the house across the street. In the midst of all their noise and commotion, I left my trusty juniper behind and dashed into the backyard. Then I crossed through another yard and found myself back in Western Alley, running toward home. I'm not sure what I was thinking; maybe I was hoping to get my Camry.

But there was another cop car guarding the front of my house. So I took off through some more yards and found myself on somebody's driveway back on Ash, a block and a half away from Cole, Dave, and the others. They were splitting up, with two of them heading my way.

Meanwhile yet *another* cop car rounded the corner and came at me from the other direction.

If I was counting right, there were at least six of them and one of me. Somehow that didn't seem sporting.

But I did have one thing going for me: I was on my home turf. This was the West Side, and by God, I was a West Sider.

I quickly scurried off the driveway and stuck to the hedges and backyards until I came to the rear of the Orian Cillárnian Sons of Ireland building. At this hour the place was deserted: a perfect hideout. Unfortunately the cops would realize that, too. They'd probably check it to see if anyone had broken in. So I couldn't just bash a window open, I'd have to pray one of them was unlocked.

I darted around the building, trying the doors and

windows. But my prayers weren't answered; everything was locked. I'd have to resort to Plan B.

Only one problem. I didn't *have* a Plan B.

Three cops were approaching, going house to house, just one block away now. They all had flashlights. I better haul ass, plan or no plan. I backed away from the Orian Cillárnian and tripped over a tree root. As I scrambled back to my feet, I happened to glance upward.

Right above me on the second floor, there was a window that was open two inches. It was about a yard away from the relatively thick branch of a tree.

If I could just:

a) climb the back fence;

b) hop onto the tree;

c) climb to the end of that branch;

d) while hanging on to the branch with two feet and one arm, reach out with my other arm and open the window; and

e) dive out of the tree and land inside . . .

No, it was impossible. Even if I had two good arms, it would still be impossible.

I started to run away, but then cop car number five or six—I was losing count—raced toward me. It screeched to a halt four houses away on Ash, meaning I now had cops less than a block from me in both directions. Two cops poured out of the car and came toward me. They hadn't seen me yet, but—oh, God, it was Chief Walsh himself, accompanied by Lieutenant Foxwell. Were they coming to help capture me, or help kill me?

Was the chief somehow involved in the murders, too? That would sure explain his eagerness to pin them on me, regardless of any guilt on my part.

Walsh and Foxwell didn't have tiny little flashlights like the other cops. They had powerful search beams they were throwing all over the neighborhood. Meanwhile, lights were turning on in a lot of the Ash Street houses, and I knew that pretty soon the residents would be coming out onto the sidewalks to join in the fun. Already a couple of civilians in pajamas and nightgowns were standing on their front porches, looking all around. I was surrounded. There was no place to go—

But up.

So I went up.

Doing (a) and (b)—climbing the fence and hopping onto the tree—was surprisingly easy. And I even managed to do (c)—crawling out to the end of the branch—without having a heart attack, despite the chief's search beam swooping past me about five feet away.

But doing (d) and (e)—reaching out to that barely open window and forcing it upward—was another story entirely.

First I tried reaching out with my good arm. But the strain of holding on to the branch with my bad arm was too much. I almost fell out of the tree.

So I tried it the other way around, holding on to the branch with my good arm and opening the window with my bad one. But that was equally useless. The window was heavy enough, or stuck enough, that when I tried to lift it the pain in my stabbed shoulder made my head spin. Again I almost fell out of the tree.

Any moment now one of those search beams would find me. Or else some well-meaning civilian in pajamas would notice an oversized monkey hanging off of a tree behind the Orian Cillárnian.

What an undignified way to get arrested.

I grabbed hold of the branch with both arms and

desperately tried to contort my body so my foot would reach the window. If only I did yoga.

If only I were Tarzan.

If only I were sitting in some quiet café somewhere, sipping cappuccino.

But I wasn't. I stretched my thigh muscles more than they'd been stretched in years, and finally managed to reach the windowsill with my foot.

I paused for breath, then pushed up at the window with my toes, straining with all my might. But the window was stuck. I lifted it a quarter of an inch at most. Then my foot fell back to the windowsill, exhausted.

I heard voices on the street, close by. I shoved upward with my foot again. My leg was in agony, with all kinds of muscles and tendons popping and tearing. This time the window went up maybe half an inch before my leg couldn't take it anymore and dropped back down.

Somebody's searchlight flashed along the back fence and wiggled up and down. I froze. Had they heard me? The voices were talking quietly, and I couldn't tell what they were saying. Then the searchlight swept across my tree trunk. Shit, they *had* heard me.

I felt like a raccoon treed by a pack of especially bloodthirsty dogs. I might as well just drop out of the tree and give myself up. But then, amazingly, the light veered off and aimed for a porch across the street. The voices moved away, too.

I didn't take time to contemplate the miracle. Instead I frantically walloped the bottom of the window with my foot, and lo and behold, I hit the jackpot at last! The window went up a full twenty inches.

One more kick like that and the window would be

far enough open that I'd be able to dive right in. With a surge of strength, I kicked again.

But nothing happened.

I kicked yet again. Still nothing. I kicked and kicked, harder and harder, faster and faster, until my thigh muscles felt like they were on fire. But it didn't do any good. This time the window was totally stuck. The opening was still way too narrow for me to dive through.

Then a cop car drove up and stopped right in front of the Orian Cillárnian. Cole got out. He looked toward the back of the building, where I was.

God, now what? I couldn't just stay on this branch and wait to get shot. I looked down at the ground. I could jump, but it was pretty far, thirty feet at least. My arm and leg would be totally destroyed, and besides I'd make a lot of noise. I'd be handing myself to Cole on a silver platter.

He was talking to another cop and pointing in my direction. They were about to come my way.

There was only one thing to do.

I put both feet on the shivering branch and tried without success to steady myself.

Then I dove for the window.

My arms made it through the narrow opening and grabbed onto the windowsill from the inside. But my head banged hard into the window sash, hurting like hell and almost jarring me loose from the sill. My feet were dangling, unable to find purchase. I hung on to the side of the building by my arms—by one arm, really, because the other arm was fading fast. I could feel myself falling down to the cold hard ground, and from there to Cole's arms and jail—or death.

If only I could get my damn elbows onto the windowsill, then maybe I'd have a fighting chance to squeeze myself through the window. I closed my eyes and fought with all my might to pull myself up. Straining with my one good arm and struggling to find any infinitesimal toeholds between the bricks, I jerked my body slowly, painfully up the wall. My elbows crawled upward one tiny lurch at a time: half an inch higher . . . one inch . . . one and a half inches . . .

The pain was so great that I started drifting out of my body, like it belonged to someone else. But after what felt like hours, my elbows finally hit the edge of that windowsill. I gave a desperate lurch and was able to plant my elbows on top of the sill. Then with one last rush of adrenaline I wriggled my body under the stuck window sash until, more dead than alive, I found myself plopping into the building headfirst.

From way down below I heard Cole saying, ". . . neighbor thought he heard a noise back here." As quietly as I could, I closed the window.

Then I collapsed to the floor and passed out.

If they wanted me, they could have me.

22

I woke up several hours later with an aching head, a torn-up leg, and an arm that felt like it should be amputated. Dawn was breaking, and so was I.

With my adrenaline long gone, I was shaking from the cold. Looking around me, I saw I was in the Orian Cillárnian bar. The bar was separated from the back room by a curtain; I tore it down and wrapped it around my body. Some tablecloths were stacked on a table in the back room, next to a pile of S.O.S. flyers, and I wrapped them around me, too. If anyone invited me to a toga party, I was ready.

But I was still shaking. Maybe it wasn't the cold; maybe it was fear.

Or hunger. I suddenly realized I was famished. I wildly searched the cabinets behind the bar for beer nuts, pretzels, Sweet and Low packets, *anything*. But I found nothing except glasses of every shape and size. There was one locked closet and a locked refrigerator; no doubt they contained all the food, but in my exhausted state, I couldn't figure out how to bust them open. I was sorely tempted to just go outside and turn myself in; then at least maybe I'd get something to eat.

Why did I keep having this urge to surrender? It

was morbid. I'll bet Cary Grant never felt that way in *North by Northwest.*

And speaking of Cary Grant, why did I keep comparing myself to movie characters?

Fortunately, any thought of surrendering was instantly forgotten when I noticed a mini-refrigerator right in front of my nose. I opened it and was greeted by the most beautiful sight my eyes had ever seen: a half-eaten liverwurst sandwich and a half-full bottle of Mountain Dew.

It took me all of about ten seconds to suck down both the sandwich and the Dew. My mind defogged; I could feel my IQ rising with each calorie. Even my arm felt better. When I found a half-sour pickle in the back of the mini-refrigerator, I knew today must be my lucky day.

There was a pay phone at one end of the bar. I felt in my pocket and was astonished to discover three quarters there. Further proof that my luck had turned. First I called Andrea. She picked up in the middle of the first ring.

"Hello?!" she gasped.

"I'm okay, honey," I said. My voice startled me; it rattled hollowly, like it was coming from deep inside a cave.

Andrea started crying. "Jacob, where are you?"

"I'd rather not say. But I'm really okay, and I'll see you soon."

She spoke quickly, to keep me on the phone. "Honey, they found the knife behind the TV, and it was all full of blood. Maybe you should just give yourself up. Jacob, I want you to know, I love you," she gulped, "no matter what you've done."

No matter what you've done. Thanks for the vote of confidence. "Look, they may be tracing this call. I love you, too." Then I hung up.

After that I called Malcolm, or tried to. But his home and beeper numbers weren't listed in the ancient phone book hanging from the phone; and when I spent my second quarter dialing Directory Assistance, the weary-sounding woman who answered my call didn't have Malcolm's numbers either. I thought about trying him at his office, but he almost certainly wouldn't be there yet. I only had one more quarter, and I better not waste it on an answering machine.

On the other hand, who was there left for me to call? Dave? Dennis? There was no one. I was all alone.

No, I wasn't.

Footsteps. Someone was inside the building.

They were coming toward the bar.

I ducked into the alcove behind the pay phone.

Lia Kalmus loomed into view. She started past me toward the back room, no doubt to pick up those S.O.S. flyers.

But then she saw me. She screamed.

She was too petrified to move. I lifted my hands carefully to show I didn't have a weapon. "It's okay, Lia, don't be afraid. I won't hurt you."

I must have looked pretty strange, covered with curtains and tablecloths. She backed away from me slowly. I thought about rushing her and trying to tackle her before she could make it to the front door. Great idea—throw in an aggravated assault along with all of my other crimes.

"Lia, *please,*" I begged, "I need your help. You've got to believe me, I didn't kill anybody, I didn't do anything, I'm being framed!"

She was still backing away. Any moment now she would bolt. "I'm a political prisoner, Lia!" I pleaded.

"Just like your Dad! They're gonna destroy me, same way they destroyed your family!"

She stood at the far end of the room, giving me that horrified stare I'd noticed once before, so panicked her droopy eye almost stopped drooping. She was poised to dash madly for the great outdoors.

But at least she wasn't dashing madly yet. If I could somehow get Lia on my side, with all of her connections and power, maybe I could get things to finally turn around. We could force the police to do a *real* murder investigation.

Maybe I could even turn myself in without getting shot at by some rogue cop.

But first I had to convince this woman. "Lia, it's like this," I said rapidly and nervously, like one of those late-night TV hucksters. "Pop Doyle ran a whorehouse, and some drug dealing operations, and an extortion business . . ."

I laid out the whole fantastic story. The way I described it, our quaint small town was almost as corrupt as post-Soviet Russia.

I may have exaggerated a bit.

But thank God, it seemed to do the trick. No doubt Lia already had some inkling that the Saratoga cops weren't totally kosher. Now, as she listened, her expression toward me slowly softened.

Then her jaw and her good eye hardened into a determined look—a look I recognized from all those S.O.S. meetings I'd attended over the years. She broke in and interrupted me. "Look, here's what we need to do," she said crisply. "We'll go see the mayor. Right now. He'll make that idiot police chief do his job like he's supposed to. And then I'll take you to the station myself. If any of those hoodlums do anything to you, I'll crack them over the head."

I was so overcome I couldn't speak. An ally at last!

I could never have gone to the mayor by myself—it's a long story, but during my previous murder investigation I'd left him writhing in pain on the ground. With Lia behind me, though, the mayor would do the right thing. If he wanted to get re-elected, he'd have to. "Thank you, Lia," I breathed fervently. "*Thank* you."

She brusquely waved me off. "No big deal. My father was innocent—and so are you. Take those tablecloths off you, and let's get out of here."

But that turned out to be easier said than done.

When Lia opened the front door, there was a cop car idling right across the street, and one glimpse told me it was Dave. I ducked quickly back inside the building, so quickly that I wrenched something at the back of my knee and tore up my leg even more.

Ignoring the pain, I started to run out the back door of the building, certain that Dave was about to come racing in after me. But Lia shushed me and motioned for me to stay where I was. She held the door open a tiny crack and watched until Dave finally drove off. Thank God for Estonians, I thought to myself.

With the coast finally clear (or at least it looked that way), we hurried out to Lia's car. I jumped in the backseat and lay down low. I was so revved up I forgot all about my busted body parts, but when they hit the floor of the car, I remembered in a hurry.

Lia started the engine. "We're okay now, Jacob, but stay down just in case. So let's work this out. What exactly do we tell the mayor?"

As we zigzagged toward the mayor's house—carefully avoiding Broadway and other main streets, it looked to me from where I lay—I described again for her, in greater detail, all the evidence I had against Cole. I even told her about the videotape I made, figuring that would be the nail in Cole's coffin.

I couldn't see Lia's face, but somewhere in the middle of my rendition I got the vibe she wasn't as impressed as I wanted her to be. She confirmed it by saying, "The problem is, you still don't have any real proof that Cole killed Pop."

"I have plenty to start with, though. And if we keep shaking the trees long enough, something is bound to fall out."

From my prone position, I was relieved to see the back of Lia's head bobbing up and down in agreement. "You're right, maybe something will. Okay, what the hell, let's go for it." She stopped the car and got out.

"We're at the mayor's house already?" I asked as I sat up.

Wait, this couldn't be right; we were parked outside the cemetery.

Lia opened the back door, pointing a gun at my face.

23

"Get out of the car," Lia said.

"W-what?" I stuttered.

"Get out."

"Get out?"

"GET OUT OF THE GODDAMN CAR!"

I got out.

I looked around for cops. Where are they when you really need them?

She motioned with her gun for me to go through the gate into the cemetery. "Move."

"Jesus, Lia, *why*?"

She aimed her gun. *"Move!"*

I moved.

It was a cold, gray dawn. She followed me into the cemetery. "Up that hill," she ordered, pointing to the hill a hundred feet ahead of us where Gideon Putnam's family was buried.

I walked toward there as slowly as I could, desperate to think up a way out. What the hell was going on here? "I don't get it, Lia. *You* didn't kill them, did you?"

"That bastard stiffed me out of twenty thousand dollars—and then he tried to rape me."

Was I dreaming? "Who are you talking about—Pop?"

"Yeah, *Pop*," she spit out, her damaged face twisting with rage. "Lousy creep was gonna make a fortune from selling the Grand Hotel to the SERC. So he promised me twenty grand if I got their plan approved." The way Lia's burn scar moved when she talked, it was almost like a living thing. "If I let you shake the trees, you'd have found out about the twenty grand, because that idiot Pop couldn't keep his mouth shut. Told Hal Starette and three or four other people all about it." She bared her teeth. "You'd've found out other stuff, too. Keep moving," she snapped. "Don't turn around."

I did what she told me. The hill was just forty or fifty feet away now. Was she planning to kill me when we got there?

I tried to think of some way to get her talking again, to distract her so I could go for the gun. But she didn't need any prompting. Her words flooded out like she'd been damming them up forever. "I did what I was supposed to do, goddamn it. Got all those brainless sheep on the West Side to vote yes. But I go to Pop's house that night after the vote to get my twenty thousand, and he just laughs in my face. Says I should've known better, gotten my money up front. Then he gets in his car and just drives away, the fat jerk. So I follow him. He stops at that house next to you, so I do, too. I go after him to the backyard. I'm thinking maybe I'll settle for *ten* thousand."

I was still walking ahead of Lia, looking back at her from the corner of my eye, watching for the right moment to strike. But even though she was wrapped up in her story, she kept her gun pointed steadily right at the back of my head.

"So we're arguing about it, and then he *hits* me,"

she went on, her voice filled with hurt and fury. "He hits me real hard, in my breasts, so hard I'm screaming, and then he hits me *again*. He's standing over me, laughing, squeezing my breasts, and he's going, 'Hey, you got a nice body, for an ugly bitch. Bet you're a virgin, aren't you?' And then he reaches for my pants. He was gonna rape me!"

She took a deep breath. "So I grabbed his gun and shot him."

We were at the foot of the hill. Above us was Gideon Putnam's family burial plot. I stopped and turned around to Lia. *"Move!"* she yelled, gun outstretched. *"Up the hill!"*

So I went up the hill. But I kept my face turned toward her and whistled through my teeth, trying to sound sympathetic. "Well, God, Lia, that's just self-defense. No one would blame you for that."

An angry growl rumbled from her throat. "And then that drug dealer calls me up. Says he saw me kill Pop, and if I don't pay him off he'll tell the cops. Says this Jacob Burns guy is getting on his nerves, and he wants money to get out of town." She gave a short mirthless chuckle. "Screw that. I had to kill him, too. Stand up against the gate."

Stand up against the gate.

Was it as simple as that?

No fanfare, no drum roll? Was this the big good-bye?

My throat went tight. "Don't do this to me," I pleaded, my voice raspy and barely audible, "I've got a wife and two kids—"

"You should've thought of that before. Now stand up against the goddamn gate."

I did.

"Lia," I said, sounding disturbingly whiny, "I just don't get it. I thought you were such a wonderful person."

She snorted derisively. "I'll tell you who was wonderful. My father. It got him *killed,* and it got me *this.*" She pointed at her ruined face. "To hell with being *wonderful.*"

"But you did so much good for the West Side."

"Yeah, I know, I made you feel good about being an American," she said, sneering sarcastically. "You know how many landlords have slipped me money over the years to go easy on them? Believe me, it adds up. If Pop had just come through with that twenty grand like he promised, I'd have enough money to buy a nice big farmhouse in Greenfield."

On second thought, Lia Kalmus was no longer my favorite all-time public statesman. "Greenfield?" That's a rural town about five miles from Saratoga. "Two people are dead because you wanted a farmhouse in *Greenfield*?"

"Make that *three* people," she said, raising her gun at my head. "Hey, you saw my house, it's tiny. I've got stuff filling up the basement. I need a bigger house."

"You're kidding me," I said, incredulous. "This whole thing started because you want a bigger house to put your *stuff*?"

"No, it started because I'm sick to death of all you people on the goddamn West Side!" Something seemed to snap in Lia. Her face contorted and her gun arm waved around crazily. "*I* do all the work for *everybody* around here! *I'm* the whole reason this neighborhood is turning into a decent place to live again! But does it matter? *No!* I know what you people all think of me! I'm the ugly Estonian with the weird face!"

"I never thought of you as the ugly Estonian—"

"Like hell you didn't, you pathetic liar. Now shut up and close your eyes. Make it easier for both of us."

Her gun arm had stopped waving around, and for

better or worse she had herself back under control. "Lia—"

"Shut up—now!"

And finally, I ran out of words. I stared transfixed at Lia's horrible scar. It seemed to be dancing in the cold morning light.

"Don't worry," she said, and my fear must have been making me hallucinate, because somehow her bad eye looked like it was dancing too. "If you cooperate I'll do it painlessly. Up close, so it looks like suicide. One shot and you'll be dead so fast you won't even know it. Now stand up straight and close your eyes."

I didn't close them. "Don't kill me," I whispered.

She shrugged. "You want to die with your eyes open? Suit yourself."

She was standing about twelve feet away, but then she started moving closer to me, slowly and carefully, gun hand extended. It was clear what she was doing: She was getting as close as she safely could before she shot me, to make it look as much like suicide as possible.

I had to admit, it was a good plan. If the cops bought that it was suicide, then they'd close the book on all three deaths. Lia would get off scot-free.

I was in shock, staring into that black gun barrel. But at last, somewhere in the dark animal regions of my brain, a plan formed. My good arm tensed at my side. If this madwoman came close enough, I'd duck my head and simultaneously swing out sharply at the gun, using the "side block" that my Ninja Turtle sons had taught me.

She was getting closer. Nine feet . . . eight . . .

As we stared into each other's eyes, I suddenly realized she knew exactly what I was planning. This was the most terrifying game of chicken I'd ever played. She was trying to figure out exactly how close she could risk coming before shooting. What if she decided the feigned suicide idea was just too tricky to pull off? Then she'd go ahead and shoot me right from where she stood.

And it would be too late for any fancy Ninja Turtle moves to save me.

Maybe I should just forget the whole Turtle thing and lunge at her right now.

Seven feet . . . six . . .

I couldn't take it anymore. Trying to keep any sign of my violent intentions out of my eyes, I got ready to lunge, bending my knees ever so slightly so she wouldn't notice.

But she did. Her drooping eye twitched. Her finger squeezed the trigger tighter. In less than a second she would shoot me. In less than five seconds I'd be dead. I started my desperate, off-balance lunge—

And then a lot of things happened at once.

Lia looked up above my head, and her face instantly changed from vicious to startled. She swung her gun upward and shot wildly.

And suddenly . . .

Suddenly a runty, snot-nosed, nine-year old kid named Tony Martinelli fell down from the sky and landed on Lia's head.

He knocked her down to the ground, and she dropped the gun. I dove. When she got back up, the gun was in my hand and pointed straight at her.

She charged at me. But I didn't pull the trigger, I just couldn't do it. So she threw me down. Then she jumped on top of me. She grabbed for the gun.

This time I did pull the trigger.

Lia died in my arms.

24

"You had to do it, sweetheart," Andrea said as we sat on the swing underneath our grape arbor, a week later. "She was trying to kill you."

"I know." I shook my head in bewilderment. "Jeez, I had so much respect for Lia. When she gave that speech about the Grand Hotel, it renewed my faith in the whole human race."

"Hey, if you want your faith renewed, just look in your backyard."

I did. Tony was out there blowing soap bubbles to Leonardo and Raphael, who were popping them with fierce karate kicks and punches.

My sons were so beautiful, so perfect, so strong. By God, they'd be able to handle whatever knuckleballs and knuckleheads life threw their way. And Tony . . .

Good old Tony.

Ever since he saved my life, he somehow didn't look half as runty as he used to. He must be standing straighter now or something.

And even more amazing: For the first time since I'd known him, his nose wasn't pouring forth snot.

He'd been having a great week, recounting his heroism to newspaper and television reporters, radio talk show hosts, and even someone from the *National Enquirer*. (Though on a special request from me, he'd refused to give any quotes to Max Muldoon.)

As Tony explained to them all, on the night when Lia hijacked me, he was sleeping in the Gideon Putnam burial plot, hiding out from all the crazy grown-ups. Then, when Lia woke him up shouting about how she was going to kill me, he waited for just the right moment to sneak to the top of the wall and jump down at her. HE LEAPT FROM THE HEAVENS, was how one adoring headline put it.

For now, Tony was back living at Dennis's house. The two of them had had a reconciliation, and were growing more attached to each other with every passing day. Which was a darn good thing, because Tony's mom continued to be basically missing in action. Andrea and I went over there several times to talk to her about rehabs, but she was too drugged up for conversation. We'd keep trying. In the meantime, Malcolm was helping Dennis jump through all the necessary hoops to get temporary custody. To impress the judge, Dennis was even making Tony go to school now. I wondered if the responsibility of having a child of his own, even temporarily, would turn Dennis into yuppie scum.

After all, it happens to the best of us.

And speaking of yuppie scum, I was a free man at last. After shooting Lia, I did have to spend two nights in the county jail, but the cops eventually figured out that Tony and I were telling the truth, so they let me go. They had no choice, really. Malcolm's P.I. and Judy Demarest were doing some tree-shaking, and they found strong corroborating evidence for Tony's and my story.

For instance, Pop's neighbor across the street heard Pop and Lia arguing heatedly outside his house the night he was murdered. And the gun that killed Lia—and Zapper too—had been tentatively traced back to a "West Side Turn In Your Guns Night" that Lia and S.O.S. had sponsored the previous year. Evidently Lia had kept one of the guns for herself.

Now why couldn't the police have found that out on their own?

Also, Hal Starette admitted that Lia was telling the truth about the twenty grand, though he claimed he thought the payoff was legal, a "consulting fee." I can imagine how he must have sweated while he tried to explain that one.

Chief Walsh might have kept me in jail longer just for fun, but I guess he was hoping to buy my goodwill—and my silence—by letting me out quickly. Didn't work, though. I told Judy about the corruption I'd uncovered and the shoddy investigation the chief had run, and she did a big story on it just three days ago. Now the dung was hitting the fan. The same media that was lionizing Tony was dogging the chief, and the D.A. was getting involved, too. Even if Walsh managed not to get fired or arrested, his credibility and any chance of career advancement were down the toilet, where they belonged. I saw him being interviewed by Muldoon yesterday, and his distinguished silver hair actually looked messy.

As for Muldoon, I was amazed to see that he'd shaved his 'stache. Maybe my words of advice had gotten through to him.

Meanwhile, Manny Cole had already lost his job, and was probably about to lose his freedom. Couldn't happen to a nicer guy. I saw him on the street yesterday and gave a big friendly wave. For some reason, he didn't wave back.

My friend Dave, I had decided, wasn't really guilty of anything. He had bought into the Grand Hotel building along with the other cops, in a vain attempt to be "one of the guys" instead of feeling like an outcast. But he hadn't been a party to the $20,000 bribe offer, or any of Pop's other illegal schemes.

At least I didn't think so.

There were a couple of other things I wasn't quite sure about, either. For instance I still didn't know what would become of the house next door. Right now it was empty, because Dale had disappeared—probably gone to Schenectady, the land of his dreams. Would the house be going up for sale soon? And would the new owner fill the place with a new motley crew of despicable tenants?

Not if the new owner was me. I mean, hey, I'd just gotten back my three hundred grand from the state of New York. The stock market was acting funky these days and I needed to diversify. I was seriously considering buying 107 Elm myself.

Although the very idea made me laugh. If you'd told me fifteen or twenty years ago, when I scorned all things material and believed only in *art*, that I would one day become a yuppie landlord . . .

Well, to quote Shakespeare or Yogi Berra or somebody like that, life is funny. Would I go back to writing? Would I sell *"West Side Gory"* for a couple of million bucks?

My musings were interrupted by the whir of an electric hedge trimmer; Dave was making good on his promise to trim my hedges for a year if I turned out to be innocent. There's nothing more fun than having someone else do your work for you. I smiled contentedly, and lazily reached up for a bunch of grapes.

"What are you thinking about, Jacob?" Andrea asked.

Like any well-trained modern husband, I knew the

correct answer. "How beautiful you are, and how lucky I am to be with you."

"No, really. What are you thinking?"

I looked at her. Then finally I said quietly, "Andrea, you kind of figured I did it, didn't you? For a while there, you really thought I killed Pop."

She gave me earnest, wide-open eyes. "No, I didn't think that. Of course not. Not really."

I raised a skeptical eyebrow.

Her mouth tightened. She looked away for a moment, then turned back. "Well, maybe I did—just a little," she whispered nervously. Her lips were quivering with fear that I'd get really upset. "Jacob, will you ever forgive me?"

I thought about it. "Sure," I said, "but only if you peel me some grapes."

So I sat there rocking gently on the swing, with my neighbor trimming my hedges, my wife peeling my grapes, and my kids popping bubbles in the backyard.

Hey, talk about heaven.